"It's good to see you."

When Poppy made no response, he lifted an eyebrow. "Don't remember me?"

She opened her mouth to tell him of course she didn't because she'd never seen him before in her life, when his smirk clued her in. While a man might add six inches to his height, put on thirty pounds of muscle and grow a beard, his mannerisms didn't change.

Beck Lefebvre.

And just like that, her spark of attraction turned to anger. "No." She lied, enjoying the surprise on his face.

Of course, she'd expected him to be here. He was Jamie's cousin. It would have been weird if he didn't show up. She just hadn't thought he'd have the nerve to approach her. Or worse, to act like they were long-lost friends having a reunion.

But he merely smiled in the face of her rudeness and stepped closer. "I'm disappointed, Red."

Poppy bristled. Her hair was auburn with definite shades of brown, *not* red. She tossed it at him as she walked away.

Dear Reader,

I've always loved the idea of old flames reconnecting. There's something so compelling about people who go their separate ways but somehow find themselves back together. And is there a more romantic setting for them to be reunited than at a wedding?

Picture then, two people catching a glimpse of each other across a crowded room and everything else going quiet as they fall back into each other's arms with nothing to stand in their way. Now scratch it. Because reality? Never that simple.

Poppy Sullivan is *not* happy to see her old beau, even if he seems to think she should be. But she needs his help, and the more time she spends with Beck Lefebvre, the more she realizes she might need him, too.

Not Another Wedding was a blast to write. And if you're wondering what music I played and who I imagined in the roles of the characters while writing, visit my website, www.jennifermckenzie.com.

Happy reading,

Jennifer McKenzie

Not Another Wedding

Jennifer McKenzie

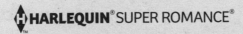

HARLEQUIN® SUPER ROMANCE®

Recycling programs
for this product may
not exist in your area.

ISBN-13: 978-0-373-60806-5

NOT ANOTHER WEDDING

Printed in U.S.A.

www.Harlequin.com

ABOUT THE AUTHOR

Jennifer McKenzie lives in Vancouver, Canada, where she enjoys being able to ski and surf in the same day—not that she ever does either of those things. After years of working as a communications professional and spending her days writing for everyone else, she traded in the world of watercoolers, cubicles and high heels to write for herself and wear pajamas all day. When she's not writing, she's reading, eating chocolate, trying to talk herself into working off said chocolate on the treadmill or spending time with her husband.

Books by Jennifer McKenzie

HARLEQUIN SUPERROMANCE

1827—THAT WEEKEND...

Other titles by this author available in ebook format.

For my parents, Ron and Colleen, who have been married many long and happy years.
May we all be so lucky.

CHAPTER ONE

Poppy Sullivan still couldn't believe Jamie, one of her oldest and dearest friends, was getting married in a week. She glanced at the pink-striped wedding invitation sitting on the passenger seat of her car and swallowed the concern souring on her tongue.

Mr. and Mrs. Clive Burnham
request the pleasure of your company
at the marriage of their daughter
Emmy Bianca
to
Mr. James Cartwright
son of Georgia Cartwright
on Saturday 29th June
at five o'clock
Goldfinch Estate Winery
Naramata, BC

The information had been emblazoned on her brain for six weeks. From the moment she'd received the invitation and the sparkling hearts inside the envelope had spilled across her beautiful walnut floors, clashing with her cream decor.

Poppy still hadn't found them all. One had been grinning at her, as much as an inanimate and juvenile cutout could grin, just this morning when she stumbled toward the kitchen for her first cup of coffee. She knew more lurked, hidden and waiting for the right breeze to waft in and blow them out. She wasn't about to let them haunt her. Just as she wasn't about to let a mistake haunt Jamie for the rest of his life.

She pressed the gas pedal harder and watched her speed climb. She didn't get to drive often in Vancouver, living close enough to her office to walk, so she enjoyed every opportunity she got to take her little blue convertible out. But today she didn't appreciate it quite so much. Wind funneled through the open window, making her russet hair pop and snap like an angry bonfire.

Jamie and his fiancée, Emmy, had only known each other two months. Hardly long enough to make parental introductions, and who in their right mind decided to get married after eight weeks? It was ludicrous. And Poppy should know. She'd only dated her last boyfriend for a month before they decided to move in together. And look how that turned out.

Not that Poppy'd been able to talk to Jamie about her concerns over his rushing into marriage. No, because whenever she called Jamie, Emmy was with him whispering in the background or giggling and telling Poppy how she couldn't wait to meet in person. And Poppy refused to tell him through email.

This was a serious matter and deserved a face-to-face conversation.

Her fingers tightened on the wheel. Time was officially running out. She had only eight days left to find a way to stop the madness.

IT TOOK HER longer than anticipated to get to Naramata, BC, the small town where she'd grown up and her parents and older sister still called home. Poppy blamed the out-of-towners who flooded the community during the summer months, tripling the population between June and September. They clogged up the roads driving either too slow—fearful of the twisty, mountainous route—or too fast, flying into the curves indifferent to the oncoming traffic and thousand-foot drop-offs.

She'd left Vancouver before noon, refraining from stopping by the offices of her event planning business and limiting herself to checking email only. But by the time she pulled into her parents' driveway, she had less than an hour before they were due at a welcome barbecue being held at Jamie's boutique winery. All wedding guests had been invited, which was pretty much everyone who had ever called Naramata home.

"Poppy, sweetheart." Rose Sullivan came barreling out of the house, her arms wide, and practically knocked Poppy back into the driver's seat when she reached her. "What took you so long? We expected you an hour ago."

"I know." Poppy had planned her route down to the last detail. Almost. "I forgot how bad vacation traffic is on a Friday." Apparently, half of Vancouver had headed for the area to spend the weekend lounging by the lake or touring the many wineries in the region.

Her dad, Bob, stood stoically behind, waiting until her mom finished fussing before giving her one of his famous bear hugs that squeezed out any breath left in her lungs, but Poppy didn't mind. She inhaled deeply, enjoying the pleasure of being back with her family even if just for a week.

"Can I get you a drink?" Rose put an arm around her as she ushered her inside. "You look warm."

Poppy was warm. The interior of the province ran much hotter and drier than the coast. "No, I need to grab my bags and a quick shower though." She hugged her mom again. They didn't see each other enough living so far apart. They kept in touch through regular phone calls and emails, but neither took the place of in-person contact.

"Your dad will get the bags," her mom said. Poppy glanced behind and found her father already dragging her golf clubs and the three full-size suitcases from the trunk. "Let's sit down for a minute and catch up."

Poppy would love to put her feet up and hash over everything in their lives, but she refused to show up at the barbecue with hair that looked as if she had been through a hurricane and mascara that had become a smeary mess on her cheeks. Unless the only thing she wanted to convince Jamie of was that she had turned feral.

She managed to extricate herself after another long hug. "Tomorrow morning, okay?"

"All right. I guess I should get ready for the barbecue, too." Her mother embraced her again. "It's so good to have you home."

It was good to be back.

Poppy's old bedroom was on the second level and hadn't changed much in the twelve years since she'd graduated high school and left for university in Vancouver. The walls were still a pale green and the prints were the same black-and-white botanicals she'd picked out when she turned thirteen. She wished she could flop down on her old double bed and rest for a moment. It might not be as comfy as her king-size bed with its four-hundred-thread-count linens in the city, but she'd appreciate the respite. Plus, the room seemed deliciously cool thanks to the air-conditioning.

But duty called.

She didn't have time to wash and blow-dry her hair, so she twisted it into a heavy knot on top of her head to keep it from getting wet and stepped in the shower. She stayed under the spray long enough to strip the tension from her muscles from the drive and then a few minutes more. By the time she flicked off the water, she felt much improved.

She decided to leave her hair down, letting it

frame her face with its natural waves. Poppy had learned a long time ago not to fight her hair. It was too thick and bouncy to fall into one of those sleek, stylish cuts. And when she'd tried coloring it in her youth—once blond and once a disastrous black that had left little patches of dark all along her hairline— she'd looked like death. So she worked with what she had. Though there were still days she wished she'd inherited her father's straight brown hair, she'd come to appreciate that not everyone had hair like hers.

She returned to her bedroom, discovered the suitcases on the bed and rooted through until she found the one holding her outfit for tonight. The dress was a tight, cap-sleeve, bandage style in dark blue that made her feel sexy and just a little naughty, even though the hem came almost to her knee and the neckline only hinted at the faux boobs her amazing underwire bra created. Wynn had whistled when she'd shown him. And as her best friend, business partner and gay man about town, he would know if it was worthy of a whistle or two.

A quick glance at the clock told her she had five minutes before her mother started making noises that the bus was leaving. No time to bother with much makeup. But since it would be hot outside until the sun dipped behind the mountains about three hours from now, and Poppy had zero interest in running to the bathroom every two seconds to make sure her face hadn't melted off, she didn't mind. She only put on concealer to hide the circles under her eyes from the late nights at work this week, a touch of blush and a couple coats of mascara.

Satisfied she no longer looked as if she'd been living in the forest subsisting on nuts and berries for the last year, she tucked her lip balm and face powder inside a gold clutch, grabbed a pair of matching gold sandals and headed downstairs.

There was a wedding to call off and no time to waste.

BECK LEFEBVRE STOOD at the edge of Jamie's lawn, which was covered in a blanket of pink flower petals, and frowned. He did not want to be at this wedding barbecue welcome or whatever Jamie called it. There were things to do at the office. Important things, like the delicate deal he was in the midst of finalizing, and now had to manage by phone and email. The Lefebvre Group owned five hotels and would be adding their sixth next month under Beck's guidance. Not that his mother had cared when he'd explained it to her.

Instead of realizing Beck couldn't just up and leave Seattle to come to Naramata for a week of wedding celebration for his cousin Jamie, she'd told him as best man he was expected to be in attendance and had laid down one hell of a guilt trip.

As if he needed another reason to avoid family entanglements.

Besides the flowers scattered across the yard, bunches of some filmy white material lay draped over everything that was stationary, including the rows of grapes surrounding the back lawn. A small wooden floor covered the pool and a band in the corner played a mixture of seventies rock and classical music. They wore matching tuxes and had a sash strung over the drum kit proclaiming congratulations to the happy couple. The whole thing was sickeningly sweet. Like Barbie's Dream Wedding, which Emmy would probably consider a compliment.

Though scarcely past six, the party was in full swing. Jamie told him things started early here, where people farmed for a living and rose with the sun. Beck recognized no one, but that didn't come as much of a surprise, considering he hadn't been back for more than ten years.

He was working on finishing his first Laphroaig when his mother hunted him down. He should have seen her coming or heard the sound of her heels, but he'd been entertaining himself by calculating how many parquet squares were on the dance floor and wondering how long he had to stay before he could leave Jamie's winery located on the bluff and return to the family compound by the lake.

"Beck, darling. What are you doing over here?" Victoria Antonia Lefebvre Jackman Hastings smiled at her only child and reached up to lay a hand on his arm.

"Having a drink." Beck showed off his scotch, which offered the bonus effect of knocking her hand loose.

Hurt flashed in her blue eyes, but her voice remained friendly. "I meant, why are you standing over here like a lump instead of mingling?"

"It's not my party." Beck refused to feel bad. Just because she wanted to pretend they were one big happy family didn't mean he had to play along.

"You're the best man."

"I'm here, aren't I?" He turned from her, pretending interest in the scene before them. He spotted Jamie in a white suit, the counterpoint to his own charcoal one, just as Jamie was blond and kind and all things sugar and light, while he was dark and not so kind—all the better not to get run over in business. Beck doubted anyone ever referred to him as sweet.

"A wedding is a big moment in a person's life. Jamie needs you."

"Jamie is doing just fine." Shouldn't it be enough that he'd shown up a week before the main event?

"Beck."

"He's fine." Beck double-checked to make sure. Jamie stood with his arm around Emmy, who wore a light pink dress and shoes with matching pink polka dots. He knew because she'd pointed them out to him at the start of the night. "He doesn't need me."

Victoria tilted her head to meet his eyes. Beck stared back.

"All right." She sighed, her perfect blond bob swinging. "I've arranged for us to have brunch on

Sunday with Emmy and her family. You're expected at eleven."

"Joyous." Beck couldn't wait to spend even more time with his twice-divorced parents, aunt, cousin and his soon-to-be in-laws.

"It's Jamie's wedding, Beck. You have duties."

"Yes, and I've already planned the bachelor party." A tame one, with no strippers, as requested by the groom. This Wednesday, there'd be golfing followed by dinner and drinks. As far as Beck was concerned, the only other thing he had to do was show up to the wedding on time and in his tux.

"Well, consider this brunch another duty. This is our way of welcoming Emmy into our family. Grace will be there."

Beck kept his face bland. Grace was Emmy's younger sister, and for some reason his mother had decided they'd make a good match. As if he needed a blonder, sillier version of his cousin's fiancée in his life. "I'm sure she'll appreciate your company."

The hopeful light in Victoria's eyes dimmed. "Beck." She laid a hand on his arm again. "I expect you to arrive on time and be polite."

This time he waited before shrugging it off, then swallowed some of the melted ice from his glass to wash away the bitterness on his tongue. "Aren't I always on time and polite?"

"No." Her hand hovered, before she let it fall to her side without touching him. "But I have faith that one day things will change."

Beck couldn't return her smile. He didn't think he could manage the pretense of the friendly, functional relationship she pretended they had.

"Has your father mentioned the potential build he's considering up here?"

Beck frowned. "Since when do you and Dad talk?" They'd divorced for the second time just after Beck's eighteenth birthday. As far as he knew, that had been the last of their contact.

She didn't reply immediately. He started to get a bad feeling. One that increased when a telltale blush colored her cheeks.

"Oh, Christ." He should have realized something was going on when she'd insisted he stay at the family property this week. Where all three of them were staying. At least he was in the guesthouse and not trapped under the same roof as them. "Are you two getting back together again?"

He did not want to be roped into another wedding.

Victoria maintained her silence, accepting a glass of champagne from a passing waiter and sipping. To the outside eye, she appeared cool and elegant. Simply a woman enjoying a refreshing beverage at her nephew's engagement party.

Beck knew better. His stomach turned at the thought of yet another parental reunion. Did they think marriage was a game? To be played like baseball where it took three strikes to be out? His skin began to itch under the expensive suit and he looked for an exit strategy. Something to say, somewhere to go so he didn't have to hear about the latest chapter of Victoria and Harrison Lefebvre's love story.

"I didn't mean to upset you."

"I'm not upset," he fibbed, hoping to encourage her to move along.

"You're pale." She raised a hand to his cheek.

He brushed away her fingers. "I'm fine." Or he would be as soon as he downed another scotch... or twelve.

"Are you sure?"

"Yes." He forced a smile.

She smiled back and smoothed her palm along his face. "Last time I saw you, you were clean shaven." Beck had been sporting a beard for the last nine months. "How long are you planning to keep it?"

"Until someone convinces me to shave." It was actually more work keeping the beard neat and trimmed, but Beck liked it. Plus, he didn't have a shadow to deal with come five o'clock.

She studied him for another moment before nodding. "Try to enjoy yourself tonight. Don't forget about brunch." Like he could be so lucky. She'd probably hunt him down in an hour to reconfirm and maintain the pretense of the perfect family.

"I'll be there."

He watched her move off, crossing the lawn to join a small group at the edge of the dance floor that included his father. His dad's face brightened the moment he became aware of her, and that awful scratching under Beck's suit started up again. He'd bet good money wedding number three would happen before the year was out. Great.

He supposed he should be thankful he had insisted on staying in the smaller guesthouse instead of taking his old bedroom in the large family home. The guesthouse was still big, close to twenty-five-hundred square feet, but was dwarfed by the main house. Beck didn't care about the size. He cared that he'd have his own space, away from his parents loving it up inside.

Deciding to skip the mingling, Beck slid over to the bar and let the party swirl around him. The sun still beat down on them, but the heat didn't seem to keep anyone from enjoying themselves. The crowd continued to increase in size and volume. Their frivolity was giving Beck a headache.

He wished it was dark already so he could slip away under cover of night, but he knew the chance of sneaking past his mother was slim. Still, he was seriously considering the ramifications of what his mother might do even if he did leave early—ground him, tell him he wouldn't be getting any dinner, send him to his room—when something else grabbed his attention.

Or *someone* else. A low, pleased thrum echoed in his blood.

Poppy Sullivan. Winding her way through the crowd, hair glowing like a beacon and poured into a dress that begged a man to wonder what was underneath. Beck's lips curved in the first legitimate

version of a smile since he'd arrived this morning.
Well, well, well.

And she was coming straight for him.

CHAPTER TWO

POPPY SCANNED THE crowd, taking note of the "happy couple" as she headed toward the bar. She wasn't particularly thirsty but the bar offered the best vantage point to keep Jamie in view. She just needed to wait until the horde around him thinned, then she'd capture his attention and drag him away for a private moment.

Having this conversation at a wedding event wouldn't be her first choice, but Poppy didn't see another alternative. Time was tight. Though, if Emmy and Jamie remained attached at the hip, the lip and every other body part, it wouldn't matter if Poppy had a century at her disposal. Even now Emmy put her hand on the back of Jamie's neck to pull him in for a kiss. The group around them clucked appreciatively. Poppy remained unmoved.

She had no doubt Jamie thought this was true love. The man had the instincts of a puppy. Everyone and everything were wonderful and a new adventure to be experienced. And Poppy understood dating exclusively, even moving in together after only knowing each other a short time—been there, done that—but getting married was a completely different animal. If things ended badly, there would be settlements and splitting of assets, and Jamie was a wealthy man.

Poppy didn't assume Emmy was a gold digger, but Emmy wouldn't be the first one to get a glimpse at Jamie's handsome face and fat bank account and decide theirs was a love not to be denied. Seeing as he seemed incapable of taking care of himself, Poppy would do it for him. Friends kept an eye out for each other, and she and Jamie had been friends since kindergarten.

She'd just ordered a glass of wine when she noticed the tall, dark man watching her from across the patio. His eyes glittered with hunger and naked appreciation, and her breath caught. She didn't recognize him. Poppy was friendly with almost everyone in town, but judging from the cut of his suit, he wasn't from the area. Most residents of Naramata didn't have occasions to wear designer clothes worth thousands of dollars.

She quashed the desire rising in her belly and turned away from the stranger. His black hair was a little too long anyway, the ends curling over his collar, and he had a beard. Though facial hair on men didn't generally appeal to her, she thought it suited him. He looked like a Wall Street banker gone rogue—one who had been in a brawl or two, judging from the bend in his nose.

Even though Poppy wasn't here to flirt, she risked another peek but wished she hadn't when she discovered his eyes still on her. His lips twisted in a half smile, and her face grew hot. She glanced in the opposite direction, willing her cheeks to cool and reminding herself to focus on Jamie and her reason for being here.

Although who knew if she would ever get a chance to speak to him. The crowd around Jamie showed no signs of leaving and neither did Emmy. Poppy sighed. She wanted to do this as soon as possible, but if no one was going to cooperate…

"Poppy Sullivan."

She turned. Of course, Mr. Tall, Dark and Dangerous had sidled over to her side of the patio. She ignored the ripple of interest cresting through her and put on her best politely disinterested face. "Excuse me?"

"It's good to see you." When she made no response, he lifted an eyebrow. "Don't remember me?"

She opened her mouth to tell him of course she didn't because she'd never seen him before in her life, when his smirk clued her in. While a man might add six inches to his height, put on thirty pounds of muscle and grow a beard, his mannerisms didn't change.

Beck Lefebvre.

And just like that, her spark of attraction turned to anger. "No," she lied, enjoying the surprise on his face.

Of course, she'd expected him to be here. He was Jamie's cousin. It would have been weird if he didn't show up. She just hadn't thought he'd have the nerve to approach her. Worse, to act as if they were long-lost friends.

But he merely smiled in the face of her rudeness and stepped closer. "I'm disappointed, Red."

Poppy bristled. Her hair was auburn with definite shades of brown, not red. She tossed it at him as she turned away. The crowd of well-wishers still surrounded Jamie.

Beck laughed, and her nerves clashed. He was laughing at her now? She sniffed. Clearly, he hadn't developed any charm in the preceding decade. "And here I thought I'd made an impression." His words whispered against her ear.

She jerked away from him. "Do you mind?"

"Not at all." He smiled. "Nice night for a party."

She shrugged, took a step back. He moved with her. Not touching, but close enough that the heat rolling off his body warmed her skin. Silently, they watched the scene playing before them.

Poppy focused on the details of the party instead of the man behind her. Occupational hazard. She couldn't attend any event without thinking about how she would have done things differently, and taking notes of what she might use in future.

Emmy and Jamie had made smart choices, getting all the key points right. Plenty of light, good flow and loads of food and drink. The other bits were simply details adjusted to suit the client's personal preference. Poppy wouldn't have tossed tulle over everything *or* matched the table runners and flowers to Emmy's shoes. Obviously, Emmy had chosen the colors with her outfit in mind and Poppy doubted any well-reasoned logic would have convinced her it wasn't a wonderful idea.

Brides were notorious for being temperamental, insisting on one thing and then sobbing when they changed their minds, as though one minuscule detail meant the difference between a long, happy marriage and one filled with strife. Poppy had stopped planning weddings a couple of years ago for those exact reasons, choosing to focus on business events and functions. Less indecision *and* no one had ever cried all over her because the napkins at their holiday party were ruby instead of crimson.

"So?" Beck's voice drew her attention, caused her to turn before she thought better of it. "Aren't you going to ask how we know each other?"

Oh, he'd like that, wouldn't he? Though she might not have seen him for years, she knew his type. He prided himself on being unforgettable to women. Well, it was time he learned a lesson.

"No." But she couldn't help noting how good he looked. Really good. Though she'd give up chocolate before admitting it.

She turned on her heel, intending to return to the party and find someone—anyone else—to talk to, but his hand caught her bare arm above her wrist. His fingers were warm. She shivered.

"I guess I've changed. You're as gorgeous as ever, Red." His blatant appraisal of her body should have pissed her off—she was not his to behold. But the attraction sizzling through her was impossible to deny.

Poppy shook the thought off. She did not want him looking at her. Not even a little. He'd lost that privilege years ago, and a bit of sexy banter and warm hands didn't change anything.

"If you'll excuse me." She pulled her arm free and hurried away before he could stop her again. As Poppy made her way through the partygoers, she did her best to ignore the sudden knocking of her heart. But when she sneaked a glance back, Beck was still watching. He even had the audacity to raise his glass toward her as though to toast her running away.

Fabulous.

She got less than halfway across the yard before she found herself smushed into a very large, very pregnant tummy. "Finally. I've been looking for you forever."

"Cami." She leaned back to get a better look at her older sister, pleased by the hug as much as by the opportunity to shove Beck out of her mind.

Cami looked as she always did, except for her belly, which was nearing the nine-month mark. Her hair, the same color as Poppy's, was cut in a short pixie style and her gray eyes sparkled. "I'm so happy you're here."

"Me, too." Poppy left her arm around her sister's shoulders. It was a point of pride that she stood exactly one-eighth of an inch taller. "We don't spend enough time together."

They spoke often, sometimes daily, and emailed regularly, but living hundreds of miles apart and leading completely different lives could make staying close tricky. Like their mother, Cami had married her high school sweetheart, settled in her hometown and started a family. Though her mom and sister had never been anything but supportive, Poppy recognized they sometimes wondered why she'd chosen Vancouver to be her permanent home.

"Oh, stop. I'm going to get all sniffly. It's the pregnancy hormones. They make me emotional." Cami swiped at her eyes, beautiful even with her nose turning rosy. "When's Wynn getting in?"

"Not until Monday." Wynn had remained in Vancouver to manage an event for two hundred happening tomorrow night. Normally, Poppy would have stayed, too, but she and Wynn agreed the Jamie situation was an emergency and couldn't be put off. Plus, he had the rest of their four-person team to help. "Have you heard about his new boyfriend?"

"What? No, I have not." Cami clutched Poppy's hands. "Are they serious?"

"I think so. He hasn't introduced me yet."

"Really? I can't believe he didn't tell me." Wynn's parents had died when he was a teenager and his only sibling, an older brother, worked in the Yukon as a blaster for a mining company. Since the brothers spoke rarely and saw each other less, Wynn had been pseudo-adopted into the Sullivan family. Poppy sometimes teased that he was the brother she never wanted. "We'll have to grill him when he arrives."

"Absolutely." Wynn wouldn't be able to resist Cami's pleas for details. Not once she brought out the swollen-feet and aching-back cards.

"What about you?" Cami asked.

"What about me?"

"Any men in your life?"

"Not right now." Beck flashed through her mind before she shut the thought down. She didn't know why he'd even approached her. Had he honestly expected open arms and a friendly greeting after what he'd done? "But," she said before Cami could start lecturing, "I'm going to work on that. Wynn thinks I should sign up for one of those dating services."

"You should." Cami was resolute. "It's way past time you got back out there."

"It hasn't been that long."

"It's been more than a year since you and Evan split."

"No." Poppy paused and then sighed. "Okay, it's been a while." Ten months. Which was not a year. "I needed some time. But I'm ready now."

And she would handle things her way, which according to her mother and sister was wrong. But they didn't understand. They had lived the fantasy of marrying a first love with a white picket fence and kids. She was more practical. And as soon as this wedding was over, she was going to put *her way* into action and become a dating machine. Or, at least, a dating widget.

"Auntie Pop-pop." Holly, Cami's two-year-old daughter, interrupted with a bright giggle. She ran over and held up her arms for a kiss and hug, which Poppy was happy to oblige.

"Hi, Holly Hobbie." She juggled her niece and the wine she still carried. "I like your shoes."

Last time she and Cami had talked, her sister had mentioned Holly's obsession with a pair of hard-soled Mary Janes. The constant tapping was driving her to the brink of insanity. According to Cami, Holly wouldn't even take them off for bed. So Poppy had gone on a toddler-size shopping spree and sent up three pairs of sparkly shoes, all soft-soled, as well as two dresses, some striped leggings and a matching hat-and-scarf set for winter.

Holly proudly displayed the silver pair of shoes for Poppy to appreciate. Sparkly shoes might not be practical for an active toddler who spent more time digging in the dirt than playing dress-up, but Poppy hadn't been able to resist. What was the point of being an aunt if she didn't spoil her niece?

"Beautiful," she told Holly. "They match mine." She showed Holly her own glittery heels. Holly oohed and, when Poppy set her back down, petted them.

"You're creating a monster," Cami said as she smiled at her daughter.

"Probably, but she'll be a nontapping monster.

Doesn't that count for something?" Poppy handed Cami her glass when Holly tugged on her dress and demanded to be lifted up for another hug. "Do you like the shoes?"

"Yes." She wrapped her tiny arms around Poppy's neck with surprising strength.

"I like them, too." Cami inhaled the scent of the wine. "And I like this. I want some."

"Soon." Poppy untangled herself from Holly's little monkey arms before they strangled her. "Only a few more weeks, right?"

"I hope not." Cami sighed and pouted at the glass. "I feel like I'm about to explode."

"Well, don't explode here." Poppy had a sudden vision of her sister's water breaking all over her expensive gold shoes and having to hustle her off to the hospital.

"As if I would be so tacky." Cami rubbed her swollen stomach. "Holly, don't play with Auntie Poppy's earrings."

Poppy captured the toddler's busy hands before she could get a good grasp and pull. "Where's Mom?"

"She's talking to the band." Cami gestured at the foursome. Poppy didn't spot her mother's strikingly colored hair nearby, but that didn't mean she wasn't around. "She wants to hear 'Old Time Rock and Roll.'"

Poppy snorted and glanced back at her sister. "Please tell me you're joking."

"Oh, it gets better." Cami took another sniff of wine. "She's already made Dad promise to dance with her."

"Which, of course, he will."

"Of course." Cami grinned and rested the glass on her belly. "Don't worry, I've scoped out a corner where we can hide."

"Will there be room for both of us?"

Cami laughed and pinched her. "That's for calling me fat."

"Down, down, Auntie Pop-pop," Holly demanded and spun in a circle when her feet touched the grass. "I go play," she announced and darted off into the party.

Poppy watched her run. She was a cute little thing, with her happy laugh and zest for life and shoes. Poppy adored her.

"Who's the babe?" Cami wanted to know.

"What?" Poppy turned back and found her sister studying her with a knowing eye. "What are you talking about?"

"The babe." Cami gestured to her left with a cocked eyebrow.

Poppy's eyes followed the gesture and found Beck staring right at her. Why was he still watching her? Didn't he have something better to do? Some other unsuspecting woman to stalk?

She made a noncommittal sound and turned away, pretending she had no idea who Cami was referring to even though they'd both gawked at him.

"Don't play coy." Cami took a step closer. Her swollen belly bumped Poppy's hip. "He's hot."

"No, he's not." She refused to look back at him. Bad enough she still felt his gaze on her.

"Oh?" Cami's eyes lit up. "I thought you didn't know who we were talking about."

"I don't." Poppy brushed at her spotless dress. She sensed Cami still ogling Beck as if her life depended on it. She stopped brushing and frowned at her sister. "Quit looking at him. He's going to think he has an invitation to come over."

"Good." Cami upped her bald appraisal.

"Cami."

"Mmm?"

"Need I remind you you're happily married with 1.8 children?"

"I'm well aware of that." A wistful sigh. "Who is he?"

"I have no idea." Poppy stuck to her lie.

"Right," Cami scoffed. "I saw you talking earlier and I refuse to believe you didn't even get his name."

"Believe it." If she refused to waver, she hoped Cami might.

No such luck.

"Then I think we should introduce ourselves. He probably doesn't know anyone. It's the right thing to do."

"Cami, no." Poppy stepped sideways to block her path. She'd rather give up chocolate. And coffee. Forever.

"But look at him standing there all alone. He needs a friend."

Poppy was immune to Cami's wheedling tone. "I'm not going anywhere." Cami's belly knocked into her, but Poppy held her ground. "And neither are you."

"Why not?"

"Because." Poppy studied her sister's face and realized resistance was futile. Cami would keep hammering and pushing until she got an answer. "His name is Beck."

She banked on the fact that giving in would satisfy her sister so they could shift to a new topic, preferably one that didn't send her blood pressure skyrocketing.

Cami had other plans. "Beck. Jamie's cousin Beck?"

Poppy startled. She hadn't expected Cami to remember his name. She'd been out of high school for more than a year by then and had spent that summer hanging out with her boyfriend and now husband. "Uh, yes."

"The one you…you know." Cami wiggled her eyebrows, implying exactly what "you know" she was referring to.

Poppy felt her entire body blush. "How did you…"

"You told me. Back when you were young and foolish."

"Right. Of course I did." She eyeballed her sister. "Poppy, you tell me everything." She put her hands on her hips. "Wasn't there some swooning about the scent of sawdust?"

Poppy closed her eyes. She'd forgotten that part. Beck's family had been building a guesthouse, which he'd taken over for the night, setting out candles and flowers and romancing her out of her pants. Not that it had required much effort on his part. She'd been more than half in love with him even before he told her he was falling for her. She opened her eyes and disregarded the sudden ache in her chest.

"He never did call," Cami remembered.

Of course, her sister would recall that particularly humiliating part of the story. Poppy snatched her wine back and took a large sip. "It's in the past. I'm over it, though I'm not thrilled he's here, so if you can prevent your hormones from introducing themselves, I'd be grateful."

Cami glanced over Poppy's shoulder and sighed. "He sure grew up nice."

"Cami." Poppy's voice carried more than a warning note. More like a red alert complete with flashing lights, bullhorn and threats of being surrounded.

"What?" Cami blinked, all innocence. "Maybe he regrets his former actions."

Poppy doubted that. "Let it go, okay?"

"I thought you said you wanted to get back to dating."

"I do."

"So why not start now? It's a wedding, romance is in the air."

Poppy stared at her sister. Had Cami forgotten how awful that time had been? How Poppy had cried herself to sleep for two weeks and spent her entire senior year single? The only reason she'd even gone to prom was because Jamie had dragged her. He'd been unaware of what had happened between her and Beck, and she'd been too embarrassed to tell him. "He's a jerk."

"A handsome jerk," Cami corrected.

Poppy didn't care. "Promise me you aren't going to try anything."

Cami continued to gawk at Beck. "I make no promises. Being pregnant makes a woman do crazy things."

"I don't think it's just the pregnancy."

Cami glared. "I heard that."

"You were supposed to."

Poppy noticed Jamie break away from his entourage and head toward the house. Her pulse jumped. This could be her chance.

"Where are you going?" Cami asked as Poppy started after him.

"I'll find you later, okay?"

She walked off without waiting for an answer.

CHAPTER THREE

BECK FOLLOWED POPPY as she slipped through the crowd. People were getting into the party spirit now, kicking up their heels in time with the band, having a blast. The party was a hit. Beck barely gave it a second thought.

He had other things on his mind. Like why Poppy Sullivan was pretending she didn't know him. Saucy minx. He knew he wasn't forgettable. At least, not according to the women he dated.

He watched as she sidled around a large group, nodding cheerfully to those who called out her name, but never wavering in her path toward the house. He trailed after her. She'd grown up nice. Very nice.

She'd always been attractive. He remembered those snapping blue eyes and her shiny fire-colored hair—he'd gotten up close and personal with them one memorable summer. And he wouldn't be averse to doing it again.

Assuming he could convince her to talk to him. And keep his mother from trying to shove Grace on him.

He'd spotted his mother chatting up Emmy's younger sister only minutes earlier. He didn't need o be psychic to know the next phase in her plan would be to drag the poor girl over to him and proceed to try to force them to have a connection.

She'd probably kick her plan into overdrive at the brunch on Sunday.

The thought made the scotch in his stomach burn. While Beck had only met Grace briefly this afternoon, it had been enough to know his mother's hopes of a love match were unfounded. Even if he did ever want to get married, Grace wasn't his type. Not even close. She was pretty enough and seemed pleasant, but he wasn't interested.

Beck watched Poppy's butt as she slipped through the large sliding doors that led from the patio into the house. Now, *there* was a woman he found interesting.

He followed behind her a minute later.

The sliding doors opened into a spacious great room with a state-of-the-art entertainment system. Beck knew because he'd personally picked out the equipment for Jamie last Christmas. He might not spend a lot of time with his family, but he never skimped on gifts. He was pleased to see Jamie using it.

The music and chatter from the backyard quieted as he closed the door and moved farther into the house. He knew the layout well since Jamie had grown up here and in the summer Beck had too.

They'd spent their days racing from the pool to the kitchen and back again, sliding across the tile floor and ignoring their mothers' warnings to be careful or they were going to crack their heads open.

When Jamie had decided to turn the acreage into a winery a few years ago, he'd bought his mother out and moved back in. She'd purchased a small cottage closer to town and her weekly quilting club, which Beck knew only because he'd been roped into helping his aunt move. His insistence that it would cost him less to hire professional movers had fallen on deaf ears, and he'd found himself spending the weekend moving boxes from one house to the other.

Until yesterday, that had been the last time he'd seen his aunt. He should probably make more of an effort. She'd always been good to him. But he didn't have a lot of free time, and his responsibilities kept him busy in Seattle. He shouldn't feel guilty because he didn't spend his weekends flying in to be with his extended family.

No sign of Poppy in the main room or the kitchen, which were attached in one long open space. He headed down the short hallway that led to the bedrooms and bathroom.

And there she was.

Standing in front of the closed bathroom door, her hands locked together in a tight grip. A thin strip of light shone from beneath the door. Obviously, she was waiting. Beck thought she needed some company.

"Hello again."

She whirled to face him and scowled. "Do you

hind?" She stepped back, bumping into the wall.
I'm busy here."

"Really?" He raised an eyebrow. She didn't look
busy.

"Yes, really." She scowled and rubbed the shoul-
er she'd banged. "Go bug someone else."

He placed his hand over hers. Her skin was soft
nd made him want to touch. "Are you okay?"

"I'm fine." She shifted to the side, out of his reach.
And do you mind not pawing me?"

In fact, he did mind. But he simply shrugged. He
adn't come here to antagonize her.

"What do you want anyway?"

Her. In his bed. Again. But he didn't think she'd
ike hearing that.

"I came in here for some peace and quiet." Not a
otal lie—he was avoiding another run-in with his
nother—just not the total truth. "You seem pretty
ngry with me for someone who claims not to re-
nember me."

The lines around her mouth deepened. "Fine, I
emember you."

"It's been a long time." He leancd back against the
vall opposite her. "Do I get a hello kiss?"

She snorted, but he caught the way her tongue
larted out to lick her bottom lip. "In your dreams."

"Come on, a couple of old friends reuniting for
he first time in a decade? I think a kiss is required."

She tossed her hair. "We were never friends."

True. They'd been much, much more. His blood

pounded at the memory. "Oh, I recall us getting pretty friendly one summer." He peeled himsel off the wall and ran his fingers through her fiery mass of hair. Still as silky as he remembered. "Very friendly."

"Beck—"

"Yes." He lowered his head. She smelled the same like lavender. He inhaled, his entire body recalling how her scent used to wrap around him when she laid her head on his chest.

"Get lost," she told him.

"Hey now. What's with the attitude?"

Her eyes pinned him, like a bug she'd like to crush beneath those pretty heels. "You seriously don't re member?"

"I remember a lot of things. Why don't you tel me which memory we're talking about?" His par ticular favorite had taken place in the now-finishec guesthouse where he was staying for the week. H wouldn't mind reliving that part of his youth.

"You never called me."

He frowned. "Pardon?"

"You never called me. After." She poked him in the chest. "You didn't even say goodbye. You jus left."

"I meant to, but my mother—" He stopped. Sh was right. He'd never called. "There were extenuat ing circumstances."

"I'm sure." Her lips puckered and not in the lean down-and-kiss-me-big-boy way he was hoping for

"Would it help if I apologized?"

"You have to ask?" She shook her head and her scent rolled over him. "Forget it. It happened a long time ago. I'm over it."

"I can see that."

She flicked her hair again. "I don't want to be friends, Beck."

"What if I do?"

"Why would you?" Her eyebrows drew together. "Are you trying to flatter me? Is this to show me you still find me appealing?"

"Yes," he admitted.

She laughed. "Obviously, you haven't changed. Why don't you run along, find some other woman to work your charms on?" She made a flicking motion with her fingers. "Maybe she'll enjoy your attention."

Maybe so, but Beck wasn't going anywhere. She'd challenged him. Him and his manhood, and he didn't intend to back down. "I don't want another woman." He placed a hand on the wall. "I want you."

"I'm not available."

"You married?" He didn't do married. Not in any way, shape or form.

There was a small pause, a smaller sigh. "No, but that doesn't mean I'm available."

He smiled, more sure of himself now, and edged closer to her. "A serious boyfriend?" When she didn't respond, he risked touching her hair again. "Not one of those either. You're single."

"I'm still not available."

"I can change that."

She opened her mouth, no doubt to say something snarky that would be an attempt to put him in his place but would only serve to heighten his interest, when the bathroom door opened.

"Hey, guys." Jamie stepped out.

Hell. Beck didn't think of himself as a violent man, but he could have happily punched his cousin for interrupting. He'd just been getting somewhere or, at least, close enough to touch more than her hair.

But now? Now she'd turned all her attention to his cousin, hugging him hello and jabbering about how much she'd missed him. Though Beck did appreciate the view of her dress riding up in the back, showing off her sleek legs.

The two spoke for a minute while Beck waited. He wasn't finished with Poppy yet, despite the sharp little frowns she kept shooting his way. They didn't bother him in the slightest. He leaned back against the wall and crossed his arms. He had nowhere else to be.

When Jamie finally excused himself to return to the party, Poppy shot Beck an irritated glare.

"What?" he asked.

"You're a pain in the butt." Then she stomped into the bathroom, shutting the door behind her with a hard click.

Beck continued leaning. He could wait all night.

POPPY STOOD OVER the sink, letting the cool water run over her hands, wondering how long before Beck got bored and wandered away. Why was he following her? Did he have nothing better to do?

And what right did he have to interrupt her attempt to have a private conversation with Jamie? She was trying to ensure Jamie wasn't making a mistake, but she couldn't talk about anything with Beck hovering.

She pressed her wet hands to the back of her neck. She hadn't thought about Beck in a long time. She'd heard the occasional update from Jamie when they'd been younger, but she never asked for them and eventually he stopped telling her. She knew Beck ran the family company, a string of hotels in the Pacific Northwest, but other than that, his life was a mystery. Fine with her.

Whatever he wanted, she wasn't interested.

She dried her hands, feeling calmer already. She would be fine. She'd go back out to the party, hunt Jamie down and, when she got a moment, ask if they might get together for coffee or lunch tomorrow.

She'd have to find a way not to include Emmy. Of course, her whole plan would fall apart if she couldn't shake Beck. Her hackles rose again and she forced herself to breathe out slowly. No, she'd sliced Beck out of her life more than a decade ago. Simply seeing him here looking all sexy and hungry wasn't enough to take her back to those days.

She checked her reflection in the mirror, made herself smile, adjusted her dress and unlocked the door. Her smile fell away instantaneously.

"Seriously?" She couldn't believe Beck still stood there. Surely the man had something to do besides wait for her? "What do you want?" she asked again.

"Anything you like." His gaze lowered. Rude man, looking at her faux boobs.

She realized she was letting him and started to move. She would not spend the little time she had hanging around a dim hallway with Beck. She had a friend to save.

He walked with her. "I should have called you. You're right."

She sent him her best withering stare and sniffed loudly. She didn't want his explanations. She wanted him to leave her alone.

"I'm sorry. I was young and stupid."

"You were an idiot."

"That, too." He smiled and she felt it all the way to her toes.

She frowned. A bone-melting smile and an apology a decade overdue weren't enough to earn her forgiveness. No, that would take some begging. "Fine, you've apologized. Now go find someone else to annoy."

"Poppy." He caught her hand and the sizzle went from her toes through her entire body. Not good. Not good at all. "How can I make it up to you?"

She opened her mouth to tell him he couldn't. She had things to do this week. Important, lifesaving things, and she didn't need Beck all up in her space making her forget why she was here. Bad enough she'd given him her virginity. "There's nothing to make up, Beck."

They weren't walking anymore. They'd stopped just shy of exiting the hallway. No one was around. No one could see them. He backed her into the wall, not letting go of her hand. "There must be something I can do."

The sizzle turned into a flame. Poppy tried to recall the last time her emotions and body had betrayed her like this. Not with Evan. Their relationship had been comfortable, like an old married couple. Not with her university boyfriend, Jason, either. No, there was only one time. One man. Beck. She closed her eyes.

"Tell me." His breath whispered across her neck, tickling the sensitive spot just below her ear. She loved that spot.

She swallowed, angled her head away from the delicious tickling and opened her eyes. "You want to make it up to me? Okay. You can get me some alone time with Jamie."

His brow furrowed. He didn't like that. Not one little bit. Poppy smiled. Good. It would build his character. "What do you want with Jamie?"

"I need to talk to him."

"About?" He leaned closer so their bodies almost touched.

Poppy reminded herself she'd gone more than ten

years without touching Beck. And she'd been perfectly happy. "I don't think that's any of your business."

"It is if you want my help." He had her there, and she didn't like it. "Is that why you were stalking my cousin to the bathroom?"

"I was not stalking him." Beck was the stalker. She was merely a concerned friend.

"Looked like you were stalking him." He eyed her thoughtfully. Poppy reminded her overheated brain she did not find him appealing. Not one little bit. "Or do you often follow men to the washroom?"

"Okay, no. That's gross, and why do you care what I want to talk to him about? Or have you and he suddenly become best buds?" Jamie didn't talk about it much, but she knew he and Beck weren't close as adults. According to Jamie, Beck had distanced himself from the rest of the family after his parents divorced.

"I care."

Poppy looked into his eyes, those dark eyes that hid all his secrets, and lifted her chin. "I don't believe you."

"Let me convince you."

She had an idea his convincing would lead to making out somewhere and divesting her of all her undergarments. Been there, done that. "Get me some alone time with Jamie. Private. Just the two of us."

"And what do I get out of it?" He'd shifted and his words tickled her ear again.

"The pride of knowing you did the right thing."

He laughed again. "Nice try, Red."

"My hair is not red as you well know." And if he thought otherwise, he obviously needed glasses. "Fine, if you won't help me out of the goodness of your heart or because you care about your cousin, then what do you want?"

"Brunch."

She blinked. "You want me to feed you?" She didn't do a lot of cooking, but she was confident she could throw together a breakfast. Especially if it got her what she wanted. "Done," she said quickly before he added a rider to the demand, like she had to serve him wearing a French maid's outfit. Or nothing at all.

"No, I want you to have brunch with me on Sunday. With the whole family." He placed a hand on the wall, preventing her from going anywhere.

"Why?" What game was he playing? And why was she considering joining in?

"You want to talk to Jamie, don't you? It's a family brunch. He'll be there."

She faltered, confused. "What does brunch have to do with any of this?"

He leaned down as though imparting a secret. He smelled like soap and leather. She tried not to inhale. "My mother has this insane idea of setting me up with Emmy's sister, Grace. You'd be running interference."

"At the brunch."

"Yes." He brushed the hair off her neck.

She should push him away, should give him a lecture about personal space and appropriate behavior when reuniting with an ex, but instead she enjoyed the moment. Shameful, but true.

Maybe there was something to the claims constantly championed by Wynn and Cami that she needed to get back into the dating scene. Surely, she wouldn't be having this reaction had she not been single for the past ten months.

"So you can act as a buffer—" she loved his voice, always had "—and I'll make sure you get a chance to speak with Jamie."

"Wait." Poppy swam through the fog corrupting her thought process. "If Emmy's sister is going to be at the brunch, won't Emmy be around too?"

"The whole family," Beck confirmed.

"And how exactly do you propose to get me a private conversation with Jamie?"

"I'll find a way." He played with the ends of her hair and Poppy had to grit her teeth to prevent the sweet shudder from overwhelming her. "Think of it as a business proposition."

"A business proposition." She stared at him.

"One that's advantageous for both of us."

"Advantageous for you, maybe. I come to this family brunch and you what? 'Find a way' to give Jamie and me a few minutes together? What's going to keep you to holding up your end of the bargain?"

"You don't trust me?"

"Why should I?" What had he ever done to earn her trust? Nothing, that's what. A big fat nothing. "No, Beck. I think I'll take my chances and handle this on my own." She started to walk away.

"It won't work," he called after her.

Her footsteps slowed. How was she going to invite Jamie out for lunch and tell him his fiancée wasn't invited without offending him? Quick answer? She wasn't.

She stopped, turned to face Beck, ignoring his smirk. "You promise to get us some alone time?"

He crossed the space between them. Even though she wore heels, high ones, he towered over her. "Cross my heart." He reached a hand toward her.

She swatted it away. "You're supposed to cross on your own heart." And tried to ignore the fact that hers now chugged like a freight train.

"So we have a deal?"

She swallowed and nodded. "Deal."

"Good."

Neither of them moved and for a minute, one long, steamy minute, Poppy felt certain he was going to kiss her and equally certain she was going to let him.

Everything slowed except her pulse. She remembered his kisses. How they used to make her head spin and her body ache for more. She wanted one now. Just one. Nothing would have to change. Her lips parted.

And Beck pushed away from her. "I'll pick you up at eleven."

CHAPTER FOUR

"YOU'RE BRINGING SOMEONE to brunch?" His mother's voice rose slightly. "A date?"

Beck shrugged and turned back to his laptop. His mother had love on the brain. As usual. A woman who'd been married four times, and twice to the same man—his father—clearly thought about love on a regular basis. Too bad she didn't put as much thought into who she decided to marry, seeing as she'd also been divorced four times.

He didn't bother to respond to her query. It was early Sunday morning, a few hours before everyone was due to arrive for brunch, and he'd been sitting at the kitchen table innocently doing some work when his mother barged in under the guise of bringing him some flowers. Like he cared about a bouquet of flowers.

"Beck? Is this a date?"

He shrugged again. It wasn't *not* a date. But he and Poppy hadn't gotten into specifics. If he'd pushed, he was pretty sure she would have changed her mind about attending and he needed her.

Just before he'd dropped his little guest bomb, his mother had made a sly comment about seating

Grace next to him at the table. Beck didn't mind if his mother got her own hopes up only to have them dashed—she'd be bringing that on herself. But he wasn't comfortable with her getting someone else's feelings involved.

Grace might be a bit sheltered, but she didn't deserve to have her head filled with nonsense about how Beck was waiting for the right woman to come along.

He wasn't waiting for anyone.

"Well." She clapped her hands together. Oh, yeah. She definitely had flowers, gowns and seating plans spinning through her mind. "I'm pleased to hear it."

He'd known his mother would behave like this, which was why he'd avoided telling her about his *guest*. That and the fact that he hadn't wanted to hunt her down at the big house where his parents were probably mooning over each other. So he'd barricaded himself in the guesthouse.

It wasn't as if he was hiding. Not exactly. He had a lot of work to do. Firing off emails to his lawyer and real estate agent, keeping in touch with the management at the five other properties the Lefebvre Group owned and drawing up a budget for the proposed renovation once the hotel purchase was completed.

This was the first project he'd be running single-handedly since this was the first hotel they'd acquired in a decade. Under his father's leadership, the company had maintained its status as purveyors of elegant boutique hotels for the luxury market, but Beck wanted more. To grow the Lefebvre brand into a global vision.

Assuming his mother let him get anything done.

She fussed with the flowers until she appeared satisfied with their appearance. Beck didn't know why she bothered; he'd forget about them when she left and they'd end up wilting into a sad mess until someone else removed them.

"So this date…" She let the words trail off casually. As though he didn't know she was already making plans for weddings and grandchildren. "Who is she?"

He said nothing, hoping she'd take the hint and go. Instead, she grabbed a coffee mug and poured herself a cup from the pot he'd made earlier.

"Is this the young woman I saw you with Friday night?" Victoria sat down in the chair across from him. Like they were a couple of old biddies settling in for a good chat. "The redhead?"

"Her hair is auburn," Beck found himself saying. The thought of Poppy's scowl whenever he claimed otherwise made some of the tension in his shoulders ease. "Poppy."

"Poppy? The Poppy from that summer?" Victoria's blond eyebrows shot straight up.

Beck's stomach knotted. "Yes." But he was surprised she remembered. She'd been caught up in her own life that particular summer. Before everything had crashed down on them.

"Poppy." She ran a finger around the rim of her cup. "You and she were pretty serious."

"Not that serious." He wasn't sure why he said that. He and Poppy had been serious. First loves, first lovers, first a lot of things. First heartbreak. He sipped from his own coffee, which had gone cold a while ago.

"No, I remember. You felt strongly about her."

Beck didn't reply. He'd felt strongly about a lot of things back then. But most teenagers did. His hormones had eventually calmed down.

A smile played around the edges of Victoria's lips. Clearly, she didn't have quite the same memories of that time in their lives. "You were upset when we had to leave. You wanted to call her."

"We didn't *have* to leave." Beck put a stop to her little walk down memory lane. "You decided we were leaving and told me I was coming with you. I didn't have a choice."

He recalled everything clearly, even if his mother didn't. Coming home after dropping off Poppy, plans for how he was going to spend the next two weeks with her by his side filling his head. The night had been cool and cloudless. He'd tried to convince Poppy to stay with him, to sleep under the stars and watch the sunrise in the morning, but she'd told him her parents would kill her and ban her from seeing him the rest of the summer.

They'd kissed for a long time before she'd finally climbed out of the car and skipped up the steps to her house. He'd waited until she'd gone inside and driven home slowly, everything about the night replaying in his head. Life had been good.

And then everything had turned to garbage.

The lights in the big house were all on, blazing a trail across the driveway. Beck had known before he parked that something was wrong. His parents didn't leave all the lights on unless they were having a party. Or fighting.

He'd thought about heading back down the side path that led to the unfinished guesthouse, grabbing the blankets and pillows, some candles, too, and sleeping on the dock. He could watch the stars and the sunrise on his own.

But he'd heard the raised voices, and he'd known he wasn't going anywhere.

"Victoria, I didn't."

"Don't lie to me. I heard the message. I heard her voice. You promised you'd never do that again. Never."

"I didn't, you have to believe me."

"I'm leaving."

"Victoria…"

Beck had slipped through the front door, but not quietly enough to avoid catching their attention.

"Beck—" his mother's eyes had been like ice "—pack your things, we're leaving."

"But—"

"No buts. Your father—" she'd paused long

enough to shoot him a look that probably froze the man's bits off "—has a *friend* coming to stay."

Beck had looked at his father as his heart sank. Again?

"No." Harrison had shaken his head. "That isn't true. You misunderstood the message, Victoria. Let me explain."

"Beck, let's go."

They'd left that night, headed back to Seattle, where she'd served his dad with divorce proceedings. It wasn't the first nor the last time they'd tried to drag him into their mess of a relationship. But it was the first time he'd understood he didn't have to let himself be dragged.

Rather than staying with his mother in Seattle, watching while she packed up his father's belongings and stuck them in the garage until he came and took them to his new house, Beck had moved in with a high school friend for the remainder of the summer and then bolted to his university dorm for the start of his freshman year.

Living on campus, away from the parental hubbub, made it easy to avoid phone calls and family dinners. He had essays and labs, finals to prepare for. He told them he wanted to get the full university experience, which wasn't possible if they called him home every other weekend.

His mother paused midsip and put the cup down untouched. "Beck, I—"

He cut her off. "Don't. Just don't." He didn't get

upset about the past. Not anymore. "It was a long time ago."

"You're still upset."

"I'm fine." He wasn't, but he didn't want to have a long, detailed discussion with her either.

"I'd like to talk about it."

"Another time." He gestured at his computer screen where his in-box sat empty. "I have to work."

"Right. Of course." Her smile, though friendly, didn't reach her eyes. She rose and carried her cup to the sink. "I'm looking forward to meeting Poppy."

Beck kept his eyes on the computer screen.

"I want you to be happy."

He raised his eyes and forced the smile she wanted. "I am happy." But he'd be a lot happier once this wedding was over and his life returned to normal.

"ARE YOU GOING to sleep with him?"

"Cami." Poppy's cheeks burned, no doubt returning to the red state they'd been in all last night. "It's just a brunch."

That's all it was: brunch. Just because he was still deliciously attractive, the kind of attractive that made a woman consider her stance on one-night stands, didn't mean Poppy would. He'd hurt her once. Badly. And though she'd moved on and he'd offered up an apology, she wasn't sure she was ready to forgive him.

Her sister, brother-in-law and niece had turned up

at the house about ten-thirty Sunday morning in a whirlwind of pregnant demands and laughter. Holly was currently running around the backyard, entertaining her father and grandparents with her imitation of an airplane, which left the sisters alone inside.

Poppy realized this was all part of Cami's plan to make sure she was around to check out Beck for herself.

Poppy had tried to figure out a way to avoid the brunch, but had come up with zero options. And when she'd texted to tell Beck she'd drive herself, he'd refused and told her he was picking her up whether she liked it or not. Which was why she found herself now with one ear on the conversation with Cami, and the other listening for signs of a car pulling up. If she was quick, she might be able to get him out of here before the third degree.

"I didn't mean during the meal." Cami grinned and settled into one of the chairs around the table in their parents' kitchen.

"Not any other time either," Poppy said, though she couldn't deny the lightning bolt of attraction that zipped through her when she thought of Beck. Whatever. She was an adult now and not interested.

She wore nude-colored heels and a simple green dress with white polka dots that was cinched at the waist with a skinny purple belt. Her hair was tied into a loose bun, showing off the dangling purple earrings that matched her belt. It was going to be another hot day, so she'd decided on a minimum of makeup again. Not that anyone could tell over her blazing cheeks.

"If you need privacy," Cami continued, a smirk spreading across her face, "I can get Mom and Dad to clear out for the afternoon. You can use your old bedroom."

Poppy shot her a dirty look. "Why are you here anyway? Don't you have your own house to eat breakfast in?"

"I do, but I'm too tired to cook, and Mom promised Holly pancakes. So? Should I tell them to make themselves scarce?"

"Of course not." Poppy brushed at the flirty skirt of her dress. It was immaculate, but she needed to do something with her hands before she strangled her sister.

"Why not? He's hot. You're single."

"We don't even live in the same country," she told her sister.

"Who said anything about that? I was just talking about the fling you could have, allowing me to live vicariously through you."

Poppy stared pointedly at Cami's stomach. "I don't think you need to live vicariously through any fling I might have."

"Who's having a fling?" Rose stepped into the kitchen, carrying a bouquet of fresh-cut peonies. She pulled a vase down from the cupboard and filled it with water before arranging the flowers inside.

"There's no fling," Poppy said.

"Poppy and Beck," Cami answered. "Don't you think they make a cute couple?"

"Adorable." Rose glanced up from the flowers with an interested expression. "Does this mean you're going to sleep with him?"

"No," Poppy said, trying not to shout. But really, talking to the two of them was like conversing with a brick wall. "It's just brunch and I'm not talking about this with *you*." Having the sex talk with her mother as a kid had been scarring enough. Wasn't it sufficient that she knew the basics of how to protect herself and her body? Did she have to share the details of who, when and where too? Even though there would be none of that with Beck.

"Well, if it's just brunch, there's no need for you to get so upset," Rose said, her voice mild as she carried the flowers over to the table, placing them in the center.

"Classic overcompensation," Cami agreed.

"What part of not wanting to talk about this did you two miss?" Poppy checked the front window, suddenly desperate for Beck to show up. She'd take his sexual baiting over this any day.

"I think you should." Rose stepped back from the table, admiring her display. "He's very attractive."

Poppy shut her eyes and counted to five. She wished Wynn were here already. He had a knack for charming her mother and sister on to other topics. Of course, knowing Wynn, he'd be as interested as them in her sex life. Maybe if she were lucky a giant hole would swallow her up. But when she reached the end of her countdown, her mother and sister both still watched her.

"You know, dear…" her mother started.

Poppy turned a beseeching look toward her sister. "Please, make her stop. You owe me. I found you soft-soled shoes."

Cami grinned. "Okay, Mom. Stop torturing your younger daughter."

"I'm not torturing her. I have plenty of knowledge and experience—"

"Ack!" Cami jerked back, causing the chair to squeak across the kitchen tiles.

Poppy clapped her hands over her ears, causing her earrings to slap against her neck. "Stop, I'm begging you!"

"—seeing as I've been happily married for thirty some odd years."

"No more. I give. Uncle. Whatever you want. I'll do it."

"You're going to make my water break all over your nice clean floor."

"Girls, I don't know why you're making such a fuss. Sex is—"

Poppy was so relieved when she heard a car pulling up outside, she practically ran for the door. Okay, no practically about it. She went into an all-out sprint.

"Where are you—" Rose started to ask as Poppy exited the kitchen.

"He's here." The chair squeaked again as Cami pushed herself up. "Go, Mom, go."

They reached the entryway before Beck had even gotten out of his car. They watched silently as he emerged, all dove gray suit and dark hair. Cami sighed first, followed by Rose. Poppy stared at both of them. "You're a pair of happily married women."

"That doesn't mean we're dead."

"We should invite him in for coffee. It would only be polite."

"No." Poppy clutched her purse to still the sudden shaking of her hands. He looked good. Too good. She reminded herself it didn't matter. He was an ex. One she had long since gotten over, and any relationship they had now was a means to an end. As soon as she had her conversation with Jamie and was satisfied he wasn't making a mistake, this back-and-forth with Beck would end. "His family is probably waiting for us."

When he knocked, she shooed the other two back before they bowled him over with their enthusiasm, then steeled herself to the inevitable small talk and opened the door.

He grinned down at her. "Good morning, Red."

"Stop calling me that." She scowled at him from the doorway and did her best to ignore her mother and sister snickering behind her. When the hyenas showed no sign of letting up, she shot a glare in their direction. "That nickname includes you two, as well, seeing as we all have the same hair."

They stopped laughing and regarded him with considerably cooler gazes. Poppy scored herself a mental point. See how wonderful they thought he was now.

But of course, he apologized and flattered them, accepted the cup of coffee her mother forced on him, and by the time they left, her mother and sister were practically begging to be his slaves.

"Smooth," Poppy told him as they pulled away from the house.

He lifted a questioning eyebrow at her.

"Winning over my family. I don't know why you bothered. This is only for today." She crossed her arms over her chest. "I'm only going with you so I can talk to Jamie."

"So it's like that, Red?"

Obviously he was trying to get a rise out of her. She *should* smile politely or ignore him entirely, but she couldn't help her reaction. "For the millionth time, my hair is auburn."

"Doesn't have the same ring." He snaked a glance her way. One that had a shiver trailing its way up her spine. "*'You look gorgeous enough to eat, Auburn.'* Doesn't work."

She ignored the banter—she was so above the banter—and curled her fingers around her purse. She didn't care if he thought she was gorgeous. "Then why don't you try using my name?" Her smile could have cut glass, which she knew because she caught a glimpse of herself in the side mirror.

"Not as much fun."

She tossed her hair. "You would say that."

"But I'm willing to cut a deal." His fingers played over the steering wheel. Poppy found herself watching them as they stroked the soft leather.

"What?" She yanked her eyes away. "You'll stop calling me that if I sleep with you?" The minute the words escaped her mouth, she wanted to stuff them back in. She blamed her mother and sister entirely. If they hadn't been harassing her all morning, she would be on her A-game and not thinking about sex with Beck.

"I'm definitely open to the offer."

"It's not an offer." Where was a corner to curl up into a ball and hide in when you needed it?

"It sounded like one."

She decided to change the subject. "How are you going to get me some time with Jamie?"

"I preferred the other line of discussion."

"I didn't." She forced herself to watch him and not notice the curve of his eyelashes. "Or would you prefer to handle your mother and Grace on your own?"

She saw the small shudder. "Definitely not."

"Right. So we have an agreement. You help me and I'll help you."

His eyes slid toward her. "We have *something*, Red."

Poppy thought about that as he turned down the road that ran the length of the lake. It was a gorgeous summer morning and people were already splashing around in the water. Brightly colored kayaks and swimmers dotted the flat surface. It had been a long time since she'd gone for a dip.

He was right. There was something left between them. She just wasn't sure what.

After about ten minutes, they turned up a winding road. The houses here overlooked the lake and had their own beachfront. They were spaced farther apart, too. Poppy hadn't spent much time up here. The homes were vacation properties for those who could afford them and, except for Beck, she hadn't known anyone who lived in them.

She recalled some of the rougher kids from high school used to come up here and drink on their lawns, leaving behind empty beer cans and chip bags as proof of their daring. She'd even come up once with them, shortly after the Beck fiasco when she'd been feeling used and sensitive and hoping to forget everything, but she hadn't liked it. Not the taste of the beer, the slithery sensation of her date's tongue or littering on a stranger's property.

"Here we are." Beck steered into a curving driveway, past trees and shrubbery, which opened onto a masterpiece.

Poppy had seen a lot of gorgeous homes in her years as an event planner. The glorious historic houses in Vancouver's Point Grey neighborhood, the elegant penthouse suites in downtown high-rises and the luxurious mansions in the British Properties. But this took her breath away.

All wood and glass, the house seemed to emerge from the trees in bits. Decks and windows and railings, with seats placed perfectly throughout for curling up and enjoying a book in.

"It's gorgeous." She itched to see the inside, already certain the interior would live up to the outside. The parties she could plan here. She pictured people spilling across the wide front lawn. Everyone in white, like a Gatsby party, with a jazz quartet playing on one of the lower decks, and champagne towers overflowing.

He pulled the car to a stop and loped over to her side to open her door.

"Thank you." She allowed him to help her out, stared at him when he didn't move or let go of her hand. "You're in my space."

"Yes." He leaned harder, pressing her into the side of the car. Their eyes locked. His filled with a gleam she couldn't identify. Teasing? Tingling? Terrifying? "My mother is probably watching. We need to make this look good."

"Make what look good? This is just brunch." But she didn't move. A bird warbled in the trees. Beck's head tilted, moved closer to hers. Desire and panic swirled through her. She placed a hand on his chest, surprised to feel the rapid beat of his heart.

He placed his hand over top hers. A pose she was sure appeared intimate from a distance. She should pull her fingers free, step to the side and suck in some fresh air to clear the mental haze from her head, but she stayed where she was, caught in the magnetism of Beck's eyes.

"If you think I'm kissing you—" she whispered.

He smirked. "I wouldn't ask."

Of course he wouldn't. She glared at him and dropped her hand. "I'm only here to act as a buffer." To make sure that his mother didn't try to sic Emmy's sister on him, though quite frankly, he deserved it.

Beck murmured his assent, but didn't move, his hips pinning her in place. She couldn't break their connection without making a big production. And she was willing to do it. Completely willing. As soon as her heart slowed down.

She watched Beck's head turn to the side. She turned, too, trying to spot whatever, or whoever, he was looking at, but the house remained a beautiful blank facade. Apparently that was enough for Beck.

He picked her hand back up and tugged her into motion. She almost stumbled. Would have had her fingers not been so tightly clasped in his. Or was that the reason she had stumbled in the first place?

She blinked to clear her head as they walked up the driveway to the tall, oversize front doors. But he surrounded her on every level. The sound of his shoes slapping against the pavement, the outline of his body pressed into hers, his soft scent of leather and soap and the sight of his smirk when he turned to look at her.

Maybe she should just focus on the house.

CHAPTER FIVE

THE HOUSE WAS as beautiful inside as out.

The entry showed off glorious vaulted ceilings, the wood beams exposed, awash with the morning sun pouring through the windows. The pine floors were buffed to a high gleam and a cozy armchair sat in the corner, offering a spot for visitors to sit and slip off their shoes in comfort. A wide staircase spiraled out of sight to the upper levels, while the rest of the house opened up its arms: a dining area and kitchen at the back, an office to the right and a sitting area on the left. Poppy stood and took the sight in.

The white Gatsby party took on a second life.

"Come on." Beck tugged her hand when she paused to study the space. "My mother will be waiting to meet you."

"Of course." Poppy pulled her hand free and brushed her skirt. That's why she was here. To assist Beck not to think about what kind of party she'd throw if she had access to this house.

"By the way—" his voice was casual, which should have been her first clue "—she thinks this is a date."

Poppy stopped cold in the middle of the entryway.

"Pardon?" She kept her voice pitched low, as every sound would carry to all rooms. She heard voices talking and laughing, the clink of glassware coming from the back of the house. "You told her this was a date."

A wicked grin crept across his face. "Does it matter?"

"Yes, it matters." She spun on him. "You didn't say anything about a date. This was supposed to be a business proposition." Wasn't it bad enough she'd brought up sex in the car? Now she had to act as if she was on a date?

"It is." He brushed her hair off her shoulders, exposing her neck. She had a sudden memory of him kissing it. "And this was the easiest way to explain your presence."

She swallowed. It did make sense. In a twisted I-don't-really-like-you-but-I'm-going-to-pretend-I-do sort of way. "Fine. Just don't try anything."

"Like what?" His fingertips stroked down her neck and back up.

"Like that." She jerked her head away and turned toward the sounds of the gathering. "Well? Are we going in?"

He studied her. She refused to drop his gaze. She might not know Beck, but she knew his type. He wouldn't intimidate her. Not with his hungry stares, his delicious touches or his fabulous party property.

"Right this way, Red."

The dining area and kitchen were as exquisite

as everything else Poppy had seen. But it was the soaring views that left her breathless. Another deck spilled off the back, floor-to-ceiling glass welcoming the outside in. There was a large pool, surrounded by comfortable loungers in blue. A cabana and scattered umbrellas offered protection from the sun on those few months of the year the pool would be in use.

"Poppy, hello."

She turned and spotted an attractive woman hurrying over to her. Her smile was a replica of Beck's, though hers didn't make Poppy squirm.

"Poppy, this is my mother, Victoria." Beck's voice was formal and more than a little stiff. She glanced at him before turning her attention to his mother.

"Victoria. Thank you for having me to your home."

"It's my pleasure." Victoria took Poppy's outstretched hand and pulled her into a hug. "Beck doesn't usually bring people home for us to meet."

"Oh." Poppy wanted to check how Beck reacted to the information drop, but couldn't without yanking away from Victoria's warm greeting.

"And this is my father, Harrison." Beck turned her toward a tall, dark, mustachioed man who welcomed her in an equally friendly manner. Then there were all the other guests to say hello to as well. Jamie and Emmy, Jamie's mom, Georgia, who Poppy hugged a long time before releasing—she'd always loved Mrs. Cartwright, the scent of cinnamon clung to her even when she wasn't baking—and Emmy's parents, Clive and Susan, and her younger sister, Grace.

Poppy studied Grace closely. She was as pretty as her sister. The light caught the highlights in their golden hair giving the impression of halos surrounding them. Beside the sisters, Poppy thought she probably looked as if she'd come from the fires of hell.

Grace was polite but uninterested, which was fine with Poppy. She wasn't looking to make a lifelong friend.

"Nice to meet you," Grace said before turning to ask her mother about a shopping trip they had planned for later in the week. She certainly didn't act like a woman plotting to trap Beck into marriage, but then, he hadn't said that. He'd told her his mother was the one doing the plotting.

Poppy glanced at Victoria and discovered she was the subject of an intensive stare. She forced herself not to fidget and begrudgingly hoped she met approval. And even when she reminded herself that it didn't matter if Beck's mother found her worthy or not, she couldn't shake the desire to be found suitable. When Victoria smiled, wide and clear of any concern, Poppy felt as though she'd passed a test.

There was a large living room off the dining area filled with soft couches and leather club chairs. A massive river-rock fireplace dominated one wall. They commenced to spend the next few minutes getting comfortable, drinking coffee and chatting while Victoria bustled about in the kitchen.

Poppy had hoped to get a seat beside Jamie—if she was lucky, they might be able to steal a few minutes before the meal was even served—but Emmy wasn't giving up her spot on the love seat and Poppy had to settle for taking the chair beside it.

Emmy smiled at her. "I'm sorry I missed you at the barbecue the other night, Poppy, but it's nice to finally meet you," she said. "I feel like I already know you from everything Jamie's told me."

Poppy wished she could say the same. "Yes, it's nice to finally get a chance to talk." She pasted on what she hoped was an open and interested smile. Although she couldn't ask Jamie what the rush was here and now, that didn't mean she couldn't suss out Emmy's intentions. "I love your ring."

It seemed an obvious place to start. If the woman was a gold digger, she probably wouldn't be able to contain herself from bragging about the number of carats. The stone was a round-cut pink diamond surrounded by a ring of smaller diamonds. Not Poppy's style, but it was pretty. Poppy admired it, noting it matched Emmy's dress.

"I have a thing for pink," Emmy admitted. No mention of the carats or any of the other Cs.

Poppy let go of Emmy's hand. "What do you do, Emmy?"

Although Poppy had run Emmy's name through a search engine when she'd first learned about the engagement, she'd found nothing. No Twitter account, no Facebook page, not a single hit. It was weird.

Everyone had an online presence these days. It was a rite of passage into adulthood.

"Oh, this and that." Emmy waved a vague hand in the air before letting it settle on Jamie's leg. "Lately I've been pretty busy organizing the wedding."

Poppy tried not to jump to conclusions. "So you don't work?"

"No, not right now." Emmy leaned into her soon-to-be husband.

"And before you met Jamie?" Maybe she was a freelancer and her most recent contract had ended and she'd decided not to take another one until the wedding was over. But Poppy didn't think so.

"Nothing as exciting as you. It must be wonderful to spend your days party planning."

Check and mate. She'd neatly avoided the question while turning the conversation back to Poppy. But Poppy had a little chess action on her side, too. "It is fun. You're lucky to be able to fully focus on your wedding." She let that hang in the air for a moment. "So once it's over, will you help Jamie with the winery?"

Emmy glanced up at Jamie. "I'm not sure."

"We haven't talked about that," Jamie interjected, laying his hand over his fiancée's. "But she's welcome to join me if she'd like."

The two of them proceeded to make goo-goo eyes at each other that left Poppy nauseated and the rest of the room cooing. Except for Beck, who sat across from her, watching. Why must he always watch her?

She fanned her face, grateful when Victoria called them into the dining room.

"Get the answer you wanted, Red?" Beck whispered in her ear as they walked.

She swatted his mouth away. Couldn't he see she was trying to work here? She didn't need him whispering sweet nothings or anything at all in her direction. "Not exactly."

She sat across from Beck at the long table, which easily sat their group of ten. Harrison was on her left at the foot of the table and Jamie was on her right. Poppy tried not to get excited. Asking him about his fiancée's financial status wasn't exactly polite conversation, but at least she'd get to talk to him,

Poppy unfolded the crisp white napkin and placed it in her lap. The silver place settings gleamed and the glassware sparkled. An elegant mix of red and pink roses decorated the center of the table. She was impressed by the balance. The red and pink were harmonious instead of conflicting.

The spread of food was incredible and Poppy helped herself to a little bit of everything. Platters of fresh-baked pastries that would have fit into any French patisserie. Plus, individual onion tarts, quiches, French toast with fresh berries and rashers of bacon.

Her excitement over the seating was short-lived. Although she attempted to engage Jamie in conversation, the table wouldn't allow it.

"Poppy," said Harrison Lefebvre. "So how do you know Beck?"

Clearly, dear old Dad wasn't in on the tangle of relationships at the table. "We met at the barbecue," she said.

"Remet," Beck said as his eyes bored into her. "That wasn't the first time, remember?"

"I remember," she said. Didn't he know she'd prefer not to, though? "But we hadn't seen each other for years. I'm amazed Beck even remembered who I was."

"There are some things you don't forget." Their gazes caught. Poppy had to force herself to blink.

"Good, good." Harrison did not pick up on the sparks flying between them. "Always nice to have another attractive woman around."

His eyes slid down the table to his ex-wife, and Poppy was pretty sure Victoria blushed, though it might have just been a trick of the light. Funny, she'd thought Beck's parents were divorced. She glanced at him, but he was studying his lap, frowning.

"Why did you lose touch?" Harrison's question opened up all those old abandonment wounds.

She glanced at Beck, but he didn't look up. So he had never called and disappeared without a word. It was a long time ago and unimportant. "Well, we were teenagers," she told Harrison with a smile. "And we didn't know each other that well."

"Not that well?" From Jamie followed by a chuckle. Seriously? Now he wanted to jump into a discussion with her? "It was only one summer," she told them. All of them.

"Beck and Poppy used to—"

"Jamie, would you mind passing me the sugar?" Victoria said before Jamie finished his thought.

Poppy sent her a grateful look, which Victoria received with a slight nod. Poppy decided she liked Victoria. A lot.

"I'd like to hear more about your work, Poppy. Do you own your own business?"

"I do." Poppy gave a short recap of how she and her best friend and business partner, Wynn, had started the company when they were struggling to find good jobs out of university and how a few years ago they'd been able to focus on it full-time.

"Do you plan many weddings?" Victoria asked.

Poppy noticed Beck's frown deepen. What was that about? "No," she answered Victoria. "I've done them in the past, but I generally run corporate events."

Victoria finished stirring the sugar into her coffee and took a sip. "I see. You should speak to Beck about working for the family company. The last holiday party was a disaster."

"How would you know?" Beck asked. His voice matched his face. Tight and tense.

"I was there," she said.

Surprise flashed across Beck's face, and Poppy wondered why he hadn't been aware of his mother's attendance. Were they that distant from one another?

"That's a lovely thought," Poppy thanked Victoria, wanting to dispel the sudden tension emanating from Beck. "But I don't work outside Vancouver."

"The company is expanding," Victoria said. She glanced at her son. "Didn't you mention you're buying a hotel in Vancouver?"

"The deal isn't finalized," Beck said. He turned to stare at Poppy and she felt that spark reignite. She didn't like that spark. "But perhaps we could discuss things once it is?"

Too much of an entrepreneur to let the moment slip away even if it had been forced by Beck's mother, Poppy smiled. "I'd like that."

He smiled back at her, which had the spark threatening to turn into a flame. She watched while he peeled an orange and slid a section between his lips, his eyes never leaving hers. She wondered if the heat cresting from her thighs to her face was a normal response.

When he pushed the tip of the orange outside his lips and then sucked it back in so smoothly that no one else saw, she decided the heat was completely normal for any red-blooded woman. But chose not to look at him again just in case.

BY THE TIME the brunch wound down, Poppy still hadn't spoken more than a few words to Jamie and those had been about her and Beck.

She'd already resigned herself to going back to her parents' place without having any private time with

Jamie, when he announced he wanted to go down to the lake. And Emmy didn't. Anticipation bubbled.

Poppy hurriedly placed the dishes on the counter. She'd offered to help wash the china and glassware that were too delicate for the dishwasher, but Victoria had declined. Now Poppy was glad.

She raised an eyebrow at Beck as she flew past him and out the door where Jamie had exited.

Jamie was halfway across the deck when Poppy realized she'd better step on it or risk being left behind with Beck. Beck and the perverted things he did to poor, innocent pieces of fruit. She reminded herself she did not want him to do those things to her. Ever again.

The sun was at its peak, throwing hot rays on everything in sight. Heat rose through her shoes as she hustled across the pool tiles after Jamie. He was really moving.

"Jamie," she called, trying to hurry but not wanting to twist an ankle either. Her shoes weren't made for hiking, unless it was along Robson Street.

He stopped and turned to face her. "Hey, Pop-Tart."

She grinned at his use of her old nickname. Jamie stopped at the edge of the stones, before the copse of trees that created a barrier and provided privacy from neighbors and anyone at the lake.

"Finally," she said when she reached him. She checked out the dirt path that led through the trees down to the lake and decided there was no point in keeping her shoes on. She'd only get a heel stuck and take a header. She slipped them off and hooked them on her fingers, linking her other arm through Jamie's. "It seems like we've barely had a second to say hello."

"Yeah. Emmy's been keeping me busy with wedding stuff."

Poppy tried to match his swoony smile, but she was pretty sure she failed. No matter. She wasn't here to compare expressions.

"How are you holding up?" she asked as they made their way down the path. Jamie slowed his natural pace so she could watch where she placed her feet. Fortunately, the path was well maintained and clear of all branches and other debris. No beer cans in sight.

"Good, really good."

"Good," she said, though she didn't think it was good at all. She glanced up at him, appreciating the sun that filtered through the trees and glinted on his hair. She used to tease him that he looked like an angel. An angel to Beck's devil. She shook the thought out of her head. There was no room here for anything except Jamie. "You feeling okay about the wedding?"

He nodded. "I guess it's true what they say about knowing it's right when it's the right person."

Poppy didn't believe that. And she wasn't about to let Jamie believe it either. But she didn't know how to bring up her concerns naturally.

The birds twittered around them and leaves rustled in the gentle wind as they made their way to the dock's steps. Jamie climbed up first, then held his hand out to help her. She smiled as his warm fingers clasped hers, and she didn't let go once they reached the top.

She needed to do this. Just jump in and ask.

"Jamie, I need to ask you—"

A loud crack stopped her short. She swiveled her head to look. *What the...?* And saw Beck crashing through the woods like a poorly trained elephant.

CHAPTER SIX

BECK GRINNED WHEN he saw Poppy glaring at him. She should be thanking him. The rest of the family was only seconds behind him. He heard them thundering down the path.

"Beck—" her voice was tight "—do you—"

"Emmy changed her mind about the dock," Beck said to Jamie, though he only had eyes for Poppy. "The whole group is coming down."

Understanding dawned on her face but didn't stop her from stepping away from him when he tried to sling an arm around her shoulders. Since that only made him want to get closer, he backed her up to the edge of the dock so she had nowhere to go, and wrapped his arm around her side.

"What do you think you're doing?" she whispered.

"Making it look good," he reminded her. And if he copped a feel of her lean body at the same time, well, he was only human.

She attempted to shrug off his arm, but Beck wasn't going anywhere. "They're almost here," he said to her. "So you might want to start looking a little appreciative."

She stiffened. "I was on the verge of success."

Beck doubted that. If she had been, she wouldn't be standing here with him scowling as Jamie hurried off the dock to greet Emmy as though the two had been separated by miles and months instead of minutes.

"I was," Poppy said when she caught sight of his skeptical stare. "We were about to share a moment and then you busted out of the trees and completely wrecked it." She tried shrugging off his arm again. "You're supposed to be helping me."

"I just did," he said, and settled his arm around her more firmly. "Or were you hoping to have your little talk with Jamie with an audience looking on?"

"You know I wasn't." She frowned at him as though this was all his fault.

In truth, he could have let the crowd descend on her while he stayed back at the house, but he hadn't. He'd tried to be the good guy here, which wasn't a role he played often.

"Couldn't you keep them away? You promised to get me some alone time with Jamie."

"And did you not get some?" By his estimate, they'd had at least five minutes to themselves.

"Well, yes, but—"

"No buts." Beck shook his head. "If you couldn't get the job done in the allotted time, that's your fault."

He saw her temper flare. "My fault?" She elbowed him in the ribs, smiled when he blanched. "If you hadn't horned in where you weren't wanted—"

"Oh, I think I was wanted." He cocked his head to indicate Jamie. "Did you get a look at his face, Red? He could barely wait to leap into the arms of his one true love."

"Do. Not. Call. Me. Red."

"Fine, Auburn." He noticed she didn't say anything about Jamie, just looked in his direction with a pinched expression on her face.

"Is it really so bad?" he asked. "They seem happy." Marriage might not be his thing, but it seemed to agree with Jamie. And Emmy was nice enough.

"Hello?" Poppy whispered. "She's a gold digger."

He frowned. "A what?"

It wasn't that he hadn't heard the term before. But Emmy? Emmy was the opposite of a gold digger. Her father owned the company that provided the Lefebvre Group with all their linens, from bedding to napkins. Neither Emmy nor Grace would have to work a day in their lives, but Beck didn't say anything. If he told Poppy now, she would end their business arrangement.

"A gold digger." She stared up at him with those bright eyes. "Don't tell me the thought didn't cross your mind. Didn't you run a background check on her or something?"

"No." But only because he hadn't needed to. "Look, Emmy's not a gold digger."

"How would you know?" She put her hands on her hips and did her best to stare him down. "You didn't even bother to look into her background."

"I just do."

"Well, I'm not so sure and I'm not about to let Jamie get tied down to someone who's only interested in his money."

"Maybe they really love each other?" Beck suggested.

"Right." Poppy snorted. Beck thought she looked adorable. All fired up and ready to protect her friend. "She just magically met Jamie and fell in love with him as soon as she found out he owned a winery."

"Not everyone who owns a winery is rich." He thought it was sweet that she was concerned on Jamie's behalf. He couldn't fault her for that, even if she was wrong about Emmy.

Poppy stopped trying to shrug his arm away and shook her head. "We both know that's not the case with Jamie."

It was true. Jamie's father had left behind the land where the winery now stood, and Jamie had turned the business into a profitable one in a few short years. But Emmy still had far more money to her name.

"Poppy, has she done anything to make you think she doesn't care about Jamie?" Beck hadn't observed anything, but he wasn't close to Jamie anymore. He ignored the twinge of guilt in his gut. Emmy might not be a gold digger, but people had reasons other than money to jump into marriage. Most of them bad ones.

"No, but she wouldn't be a successful gold digger if she did." Poppy turned to look down the dock.

Beck looked, too. Emmy's family had started back up the path. His own parents stood off to the side, talking quietly. While Beck watched, his father reached out and stroked his mother's cheek. He turned away.

"I need to talk to Jamie about it. Just to make sure." Poppy poked him in the side. "Everything would be fine if you hadn't intruded."

Her demand to get some private time with Jamie made sense now, but Beck shrugged off her complaint. If he hadn't intruded, the rest of the family would have come upon them like a swarm of locusts.

"Seriously," she continued, "you haven't held up your end of the bargain at all. You did nothing to get me this alone time. You just sat there molesting that orange while I did all the work."

"Liked that, did you?" He smirked.

She sniffed. "Not even a little." But he felt the way her body leaned into his for a moment and the desire of that long-ago summer flooded him.

She'd been so open and generous. Her laugh, her family, her life. And Beck hadn't been able to get enough of it. Enough of her. He should have called her from Seattle. Should have tried to explain what happened, but it had been easier to ignore. To pretend he was like every other student at university, starting fresh with no excess baggage.

If he'd stayed with Poppy, he would have ruined her.

He'd only needed to look to his parents' broken marriages to know he didn't have good genetics when it came to long-term relationships. Falling into the cycle of university life where some people encouraged a no-strings attitude had seemed simpler.

"I've been doing my part," Poppy said, dragging him back to the present. "Now it's your turn."

"I wouldn't say you've made it easy." To prove his point, he tightened his hold on her and brought her around so she faced him. Their hips pressed close together. She tried to wriggle away.

"You didn't say anything about mauling when I agreed to this." She continued wriggling. "Quit it," she whispered.

He moved his head just before she banged hers into his chin. "Quit what?" he teased.

"We're not dating, remember?"

"I remember." But he didn't loosen his grip. She was slippery and would scoot away if given the slightest opportunity. He knew his mother had one eye on them. All he needed was for her to see Poppy publicly end things. He'd spend the rest of the week fending off his mother's prying questions as to why things hadn't worked out.

"Then stop crushing me. I can't breathe." He wasn't sure if she was being truthful, but he eased up a little. She made a big show of inhaling, but didn't dart away. He figured that was a win.

Emmy and Jamie stared out at the lake, when they weren't staring into each other's eyes, and eventually called out they were heading back to the house because Emmy was cold. His parents followed suit.

Beck watched Poppy watch them. When they moved out of sight, she tried to shake Beck off again. But he was an immovable object. He could manage her weak attempts with one hand.

"What is the matter with you?" she asked once it became clear she wasn't getting away from him quite so easily.

"What do you mean?" He played dumb and turned her in his arms so they faced each other again. "All my parts are in exactly the right places." He leaned toward her so she could check for herself.

"That is not what I meant." She wedged her elbow between her body and his so he couldn't press up against her. "Why are you trying to convince everyone we're dating?"

"That was the agreement."

"No, the agreement was that I would act as a buffer and you would help me get some time with Jamie. A point at which you failed miserably."

Beck didn't think he'd failed miserably. He'd been the one to suggest Jamie head down to the dock to take a look at the view, and then casually mentioned to Emmy it might be chilly with the wind blowing. He'd even tried to prevent them all from coming down, but once his mother had mentioned going and his father had agreed, there had been no way to stop the entire group from making the trek.

But he shrugged in the face of her complaint. "If you think you can manage to get the time with Jamie on your own, that's fine."

It was a power play. A subtle one, but a play nonetheless. If she thought she could manage this on her own, she would never have joined forces with him.

"Maybe I will." She crossed her arms and shot him a challenging look.

He recognized her bluff. Beck had seen enough of them in boardrooms to recognize the signs. The way she held his gaze without even blinking was wholly unnatural and not something a confident person did. If they were to shake hands, she'd probably try to squeeze hard enough to rub his bones together. Plus, she had a pinched curve to her lips and held herself stiffly as though waiting for the anvil to drop on her head.

"Okay," Beck acceded to her statement. "Then I guess this is it. Good luck." He stepped back and removed his arms from her, pleased when panic flashed across her face before she replaced it with a tired, been-there-seen-it-all smirk.

"Are you forgetting that you need me to keep your mother from shoving you and Grace into a rushed engagement? You're trying to fake me out," she said, taking a step toward him, "but it isn't going to work."

"I'm not trying to fake anyone out. It's only a week. I can put up with anything for a week." True, but he didn't want to. This was much more fun. He met her eyes long enough to convince her and took another step toward the house.

She faltered, but recovered with a quick shake of her head as she followed him. "I don't believe you."

"Believe what you want." He moved down the steps, but instead of taking the path back to the house, stepped onto the small sandy beach.

"Okay, fine." She charged after him, waving the shoes she still carried. "I still need your help."

He stopped and faced her. "And what are you going to do for me?"

"I already said I would help with your mother, and I think I got off to a pretty good start today. By the way, what's going on with your parents? I thought they were divorced."

Beck stilled. "They are."

"They don't act like it."

"I know." The words tasted sour. They were acting like a couple of dopey teenagers.

"Are they getting back together?"

"I don't know." A lie. He did know. He grimaced. Not asking for outright confirmation didn't change anything.

She put a hand on his arm. "Does it bother you?"

He didn't want to think about it because thinking about it meant he had to face his own feelings. That he wasn't happy about his parents reuniting. That he didn't want to see them hurt each other again. "Yes," he said quietly.

He wasn't sure she heard him, until she slid her arm around his neck and hugged him. There was the sound of her shoes dropping on the sand and then the feel of her lean body wrapping around his. He liked that. Liked it a lot.

They stood that way for a minute. The wind tugged her hair loose so it draped across them. Her scent filled his head. Their bodies pressed together. Some of the ice inside him started to melt.

He pulled her closer. "It bothers me an awful lot." And let his hands slide up her back to tangle in her glorious hair. "I'm practically devastated, but this helps. You know what else would help?"

"What?"

"A kiss."

She shoved at his shoulders, but he wasn't letting go. "Beck."

"I'm not going anywhere." He dipped his head into the curve of her neck and inhaled. A quiver racked her body and caused an answering one in his own.

"I'm serious." She turned her head so she could see him, but all that did was bring their lips within touching distance. "I was being supportive."

"I like supportive." He ran a hand down her side. Her dress was silky smooth. He moved his lips closer to hers. If he stuck out his tongue, he could lick her.

"About your parents."

"I don't want to talk about them." He had other things on his mind, like seeing if Poppy's skin felt as soft as her dress and if she tasted as good as he remembered.

"Well, I do."

"No." Her evasive games didn't work on him. "You don't. So about this help you're offering me..."

"I'm not offering anything, you forced me," she reminded him, though she hadn't made a move to leave his embrace.

He took advantage of that by hauling her closer to him. "You don't seem to mind."

"I'm being polite."

He laughed. "You're going to have to do more than that."

"Oh?" Her eyes were wide. If he stared into them long enough he could lose himself.

"You're going to have to pretend you like me." He ran a thumb over her lips.

There was a small pause with only the sound of the waves lapping on the shore and the dock. And the occasional speedboat as someone zipped down the lake.

"I like you," she finally said.

A knot he hadn't known was in his belly began to unravel. "As I mentioned, my mother thinks we're dating." A notion he was increasingly glad he'd let her keep. He touched her lips again and Poppy's eyes darkened. "You'll have to play along."

"Seems like quite a hardship."

"Well, there's something hard about it."

"I've noticed."

Beck laughed softly. "So you won't have a problem acting like we're dating?"

He watched the decision play out on her face. She wanted to say yes, that was obvious, but something held her back. He placed a finger on the spot below her ear and pressed gently. She sucked in a sharp breath and closed her eyes. He drew little circles over and over.

"Exactly what would dating include?"

"I'm open to suggestions." He was open to pretty much anything at this point. He wanted to suck on that sensitive spot, but that was his money shot. And she hadn't said yes yet.

She opened her eyes. His heart hitched. "And you'll get me some time with Jamie?"

"Yes," he agreed before she finished asking. "I'll find some time for you to have a private conversation." He didn't know how, didn't care. He needed her to say yes. It was vitally important to his health because he was pretty sure if she didn't, he would be taking cold showers for the rest of his life. "In return, you'll start showing just how much you really do like me."

She nodded.

Good. He cupped her face, held her still. "I think we should seal it with a kiss."

"We should what?" Her tongue flickered out to wet her lips.

"A kiss." He ran a hand around the back of her

neck. "That expression of interest that two people who are dating share."

"You didn't say anything about kissing."

No, they'd just done everything leading up to it. The breeze kicked up again, blowing her hair around them and causing her skirt to twist around his legs.

"Part of the deal," he told her. "But if you're not into that…"

She wasn't going to turn him down. She couldn't. But she was thinking again. He knew from the small wrinkle between her eyes. "Just kissing?" she asked.

Beck flexed his fingers, massaging her neck, gratified when her eyelashes fluttered. She might not be ready to admit it, but she wanted the kissing as much as he did. "If that's what you want."

"Just kissing," she repeated. This time it wasn't a question. "And what if I don't agree?"

He couldn't believe she was bargaining. He struggled to keep his mind on the basics of their conversation and she hunted for loopholes. "I'm not going to force you," he said. He couldn't let her know she had all the power. But he did stroke that spot again.

She let her head lean to the side and Beck smiled. There it was. She was going to say yes. He started thinking of all the ways he planned to take full advantage of the *just kissing* portion of the agreement.

"So we have a deal?" She melted against him. He remembered how she used to do that. Let herself flow into him so their bodies touched everywhere. And then she stepped back. He frowned. She smiled. Her eyes darted to the right and the path that led back to the house.

Beck rolled onto the balls of his feet. She was going to try to sidestep him. His frown morphed into a grin. So she wanted to play, did she? He was game for that. "Unless you think the kissing will be too much for you." He nodded sagely. "Happens all the time. Women, they can't resist me."

She shook her head. "I'll do my best to manage. But—" she pinned him with a look "—just kissing." Then she smiled, catching him off guard long enough to make the dodge he'd been expecting.

Fortunately, he was tall, with a long reach, and he'd played football in college. His reflexes were still good. His hand snapped out and caught her by the wrist. "Aren't you forgetting something?"

"No." She put her free hand on her hip. He supposed she thought she appeared intimidating. He wondered if she had any clue how she really looked standing there in her bare feet, her dress blown by the wind, showing off all her curves. "You didn't say I had to kiss you now."

He pointed to her shoes lying in a heap on the sand. "I meant those—" he hadn't "—but I'm up for the kissing, too."

Her eyes flicked toward the shoes, then her feet, then the wrist he still held. Beck tugged, slowly reeling her in, not letting the fact she tried to dig in her heels have any effect. The sand was useless for bracing anyway and he continued to pull until she pressed right up against him.

"You seem to be thinking a lot about the kissing." He brushed away a piece of hair that had fallen across her cheek.

"I have not." But her voice was breathless.

He rubbed both her arms as if to ward off a chill, but mostly to touch her and keep her tight to him. "Maybe we should get it out of the way so you can stop thinking about me that way. I'm not a piece of meat."

"Nice try." Her eyes met his, their bright blue sheen putting the sky to shame.

"I don't hear you declining my generous offer." And before she tried, he lowered his head and covered her lips with his.

CHAPTER SEVEN

"WHAT DO YOU—" Poppy started to ask him what he thought he was doing, but the words never came out, swallowed whole as his lips descended on hers.

Oh. My. God.

It had never been like this at sixteen. No way. She'd remember this. A decade, two decades, a lifetime wouldn't have been long enough to erase *this* from her brain. It was as if he burned himself onto her. The searing heat, the way his tongue darted out to lick the inside of her mouth, making her body quiver and melt into his. She shuddered into him.

He growled, deep and possessive, which made her blood run even hotter. It was so, so wrong, but she didn't care and she didn't push him away.

Her hands clamped his shoulders, digging and marking. When his arm looped around her waist, slamming her body against his, she felt the outline of his muscles and couldn't help herself from running her hands all over them.

Hard, hot, dangerous Beck.

It was difficult to breathe. She felt as if she was sinking or floating. Something. Obviously, she was having an out-of-body experience, since she had lost her mind. This was Beck. The same man who had crushed her at sixteen and would no doubt do the same to her twelve years later without even realizing it. Which meant she needed to be strong enough for both of them.

And she would. In another minute. Or twenty.

His fingers played over the spot on her neck, the one that made her wild. Her legs shook as the sensations rolled through her. Oh, she wanted his mouth on it, on her. And once he did that, she would put a stop to this.

Okay, she would kiss him until her heart returned to its normal speed. It couldn't keep up this runaway-train momentum forever and it wouldn't be safe to stop before then. Yes, she was doing it for her health. The shock might do permanent damage. So would the loss of his body against hers.

He gripped her thighs, wrenching her up into his arms. She grabbed at his shoulders again, first for balance then because she liked it. She shouldn't like it. Somewhere in the functional part of her brain that recalled the awfulness of those weeks after he'd disappeared, a voice was telling her to take a step back and assess the situation. The voice sounded a lot like her high school gym teacher, Mrs. Parker, teaching them CPR.

She ignored it. No amount of prompting on Mrs. Parker's part had been able to convince Poppy to put her mouth on the dummy where her classmates' mouths had just been. And no amount of sound advice could convince her to let go of Beck.

Until he slid a hand beneath her skirt.

"Wait." She shoved at him, craning her neck backward until his mouth lost suction on hers. "What are we doing?" she asked.

"Kissing." He moved his head down to her exposed neck when she kept her lips out of reach.

"No." She wished the word had come out more of a command than a moan, but she wasn't about to be picky. It was a miracle she could speak at all with the way his lips moved across her neck.

He stopped, stared down at her. She swallowed and reminded herself she wasn't here to get her sex on. She wasn't even here to get her date on, the deal with Beck notwithstanding. She needed to make sure Jamie wasn't making a mistake, and Beck was simply a tool to make that happen. Poppy gathered what was left of her resolve, put her hands on Beck's chest and pushed.

He didn't move, so she pushed harder. He growled. "What?"

"Stop." She managed to put a bit of force behind the words this time.

"I already have."

"You're still holding me." She frowned, pretending she didn't like the way she felt pressed up against him. His hair was rumpled, messy, his shirt creased where she'd fisted her hands into it. Poppy was afraid to see what she looked like. Probably what she was. A woman who had been totally and thoroughly kissed.

"And you're holding me," he pointed out.

She glanced down, saw that her hands were wrapped up in his shirt again and let go. "Not anymore," she told him, knowing her statement would have more power if she wasn't shuddering like one of the tree leaves rustling around them.

"Don't even try to tell me you didn't like it." He lowered her to her feet, but his body remained plastered against her.

She backed away from him. He came with her.

"That isn't the point," she said. She pulled his hands off her body, but he only stuck them somewhere else on her.

"That's entirely the point."

"No." She had only two exit strategies. Shove hard and try to run, or play nice and convince him he wanted to let her go. Neither seemed promising. Or maybe it was just the kiss still fogging up her mind. She inhaled, trying to clear her thoughts. "This isn't part of the deal."

"You agreed to kissing."

That hadn't been kissing. That had been soul-searching, mind-blowing, change-your-life forevering. "Kissing only when necessary," she clarified.

He smiled. "This is necessary."

She stepped back instinctively and felt the cold water lap at her heels. It was the first time he didn't step with her. Perhaps she'd found his weakness.

She might get hypothermia, but it would be a small price to pay.

She let the cool water soak into her feet, hoping it would cool the rest of her as well. He studied her, but didn't move.

"When your family is around we can kiss." Her heart thumped when his lips curved into a smile. He liked that. She liked it, too. She must remember it was all for show. "But we don't need to pretend when we're alone."

His hot stare made her forget the icy waves washing over her. His eyes gleamed. A man on the hunt. She sensed she might be the prey.

"Beck." She held up a hand to stop him, but she might as well have sent him an invitation. Although preferably not one with sparkly hearts falling out of it. "Beck, what are you doing?"

It was like talking to a wall. He didn't answer, just kicked off his shoes and reached down to pull off his socks, his eyes never leaving hers. He was coming after her. A thrill zinged through her. It shouldn't have. She was an adult and she'd been around enough men to know many of them enjoyed the chase more than the catch.

There was no doubt he would catch her. She knew it and he knew it. He would reach out and wrap her in his arms and she would have that delicious body pressed against hers and her hormones would take over and she'd probably end up making out with him right here in the great outdoors where anybody could stumble upon them and she wouldn't even care until it was too late.

Another thrill washed over her.

"We should go back to the house," she said.

Beck tossed his socks aside and moved closer. Poppy took another step back. The ground beneath the water was rocky, full of pointy, sharp edges that threatened to break the skin.

He reached the border of the lake and held a hand out to her. "Come back to me, Poppy."

"No." She took a quick, jolting step and landed right on one of those bladelike rocks. It hurt. A lot. She winced—she thought she might have drawn blood—and tried to rebalance, but he'd already moved forward. Like a jungle cat, stealthy and certain, he was almost on her before she realized what was happening.

"Beck, don't." She reared back, trying to evade his reach. She didn't know if he was reaching to grab her or save her, but it didn't matter. She overcorrected and instead of getting her feet solidly underneath her, she slipped. She flung her arms out to regain her equilibrium, but it was too late and Beck was just far enough away that he couldn't help her.

She was going down into the chilly water with nothing to save her. Not even her dignity.

The last thing she saw before she hit the water was his shocked face splitting into a grin. She was not amused.

She came up spluttering and shaking. This was all

his fault. And she told him so when he hauled her out, shivering, and no doubt looking like a drowned rat. "You just had to prove your manhood and push me in the water."

"I didn't push you," Beck said. His pants were soaked up to the knee where he'd waded in to help her. "I didn't even touch you."

"Well, you were going to." She shivered again. The air was warmer than the lake, but hardly what she'd call comfortable.

"You're cold."

She might have thought he was being considerate until she noticed his gaze on her hardened nipples. She wasn't even wearing her faux-boob bra. She covered them with her arms and shot him a dirty look. But as she did, a flood of heat rushed through her. Stupid sexual attraction. "I need to go," she said.

Any further attempt to commune with Jamie would have to be put on hold. She was not having a serious conversation in soaked clothing. She'd probably catch pneumonia. Not to mention she wasn't about to stand around and participate in a wet T-shirt contest for Beck's amusement.

"I'll take you inside." His hand still gripped hers. He used the leverage to pull her into him. She would have complained, would have shoved him away, but he was warm, so warm, and her skin was already covered in goose bumps.

"I need to go home," she told him. "I need a hot shower and dry clothes." And to figure out how to avoid her mother who would want to know why she was soaked. "Could you lend me a towel so I don't ruin the car seat?"

"You can take a shower here," Beck said and curled his body so he surrounded as much of hers as possible, and began heading back up the path.

"No." Sheer desperation had her trying to tear herself away from his delicious heat. "Your family can't see me like this." What would they think of her? They'd want to know what happened and Beck would tell them. That they'd been kissing like teenagers. Her stomach flipped.

He didn't answer, just kept walking down the curved pathway. But instead of heading up the rise to the backyard and the pool, he turned to the left, down another path she hadn't seen earlier.

"Where are you taking me?" Her teeth chattered. She was going to crack a molar. Her dentist would not be pleased.

"My place," he said as they started down another pathway, much shorter than the one to the lake. Poppy glimpsed the main house through the trees as they walked by, but saw no sign of anyone. Probably inside, all toasty and comfortable, drinking another cup of coffee. She shivered again. She would love a cup of coffee.

But she would not love to get naked around Beck. "It's a short drive to my parents' house." And a necessary trip since she wasn't certain the lake bath had loused her hormones. Probably best not to be clothes free in his vicinity.

Beck didn't slow his pace, tucking her back into the crook of his arm so every inch of their bodies that could touch without causing them to trip was pressed together. A very perilous position.

"Beck," she tried again.

"No one will see you," he explained.

The main house was no longer in view, not even if she stretched her neck and squinted. So there was little chance of Beck's family discovering her in a less than flattering situation. Small mercies.

"You can take a shower here. I'll give you some clothes and then, if you still want to go home, I'll drive you."

She sensed him studying her, and wished she had a witty or even reasonable comeback, but his idea was sound, and forcing him to take her home when they were both drenched was petty. She'd be in and out of the shower so fast it would be almost as if she was never there.

"Fine," she conceded as the path opened up to a two-story house. It was a miniature of the larger main house, miniature being a relative term, since it looked as big as the house she'd grown up in. "This is the guesthouse?" she asked as they dripped up the steps to the porch and through a cheerful blue door.

"Yes." Beck, seemingly unaware or unmindful of the mess they made on the glossy pine floors, led her up the stairs and down a short hall. The inside looked like the main house, too. "When I was a teenager I told my mother I needed my own space."

"And she had this built for you?" Poppy was shocked. She'd known Beck's family was well off, but this seemed a little excessive in answer to a teenager's demands.

Beck snorted. "No. She built it for all the friends and family who were going to visit when she and my dad summered up here, but then their marriage fell apart. My dad finished it anyway."

He tried to cover the thread of pain in his voice with a factual tone, but Poppy heard it anyway. She wanted to ask why his parents reuniting bothered him so much, but held back. She and Beck weren't entering into a real relationship but a fake one, and then only in front of his family.

They reached the door at the end of the hallway. He opened it to reveal a large bedroom, obviously the master suite, and the one Beck used for himself. The king-size bed was made but disheveled as though he'd tossed the covers over the tumbled sheets without bothering to straighten them first. A buff-colored club chair sat in the corner of the room with one of Beck's shirts draped across it. But other than that, the room was spotless.

Until they left their wet and slightly dirty footprints behind.

"In here." Beck opened the door that led to the en suite, another large room that was nicer than Poppy's bathroom in the city. The walls, floor and counter were all covered in the same nutty-colored lime-stone and created a clean, masculine appearance. Glass accessories—jars filled with cotton balls, the soap dispenser and toothbrush holder—were offset by white towels and a bath mat. But mostly, Poppy was interested in the shower. A large walk-in that looked as if it could house six comfortably, and had eight—she counted twice—showerheads.

"I'll leave you some clothing in the bedroom," Beck said, and headed out leaving her in privacy.

Poppy only gave a brief thought to the idea that she might be disappointed he hadn't tried to talk his way into the shower with her before stripping off her dress and tossing it, along with her sodden undergarments, into the sink so they wouldn't leave a puddle on the pretty floor.

It took almost no time for the room to fill with clouds of billowy steam. Poppy stepped under the water flow. She enjoyed being sprayed from multiple angles, letting the showerheads do their thing until she felt warm and tingly all over.

She sighed as the water ran over her head and down her body.

A trio of clear plastic bottles sat on the wide shower shelf: shampoo, conditioner and body wash. She dumped a liberal quantity of shampoo in her hand and began to wash the smell of murky lake water out of her hair. Or at least cover it up with the scent of coconut.

She did the same with the conditioner, and then

lathered the body wash all over until she felt pink from the heat of the water and was satisfied she no longer smelled like a creature from the black lagoon.

When she stepped out of the shower, her clothing in the sink was gone. She hadn't heard Beck come in, but then she hadn't been listening either. Her skin, already pink from the shower, blushed a little hotter. She told herself the steam would have blocked his view anyway and hoped he'd liked her froggy rendition of Madonna's greatest hits.

He'd left a pile of clothes on the bed for her. A pair of faded jeans and a soft, white T-shirt. She didn't have anything to put on under the clothes, but she didn't have a choice. She could go commando or go naked. She chose the former.

The jeans were huge, but she finally made them stay up by rolling the waistband until it caught on her hips. She rolled the legs up, too. The shirt smelled like Beck, but she only permitted herself one quick sniff before slipping the soft cotton over her head. She had to tie a knot in the back to make it fit.

She eyed herself in the mirror, unwinding the towel from her hair and tossing it over the glass shower door. There was a hair dryer under the sink and Poppy finger combed her hair in an attempt to have it hold some sort of style.

When she finished, though she wished desperately she hadn't left her purse with its emergency compact and lip gloss at the main house, she traipsed out of the room and down the stairs in search of Beck.

She saw he'd wiped up their footprints and collected her shoes, which now sat by the front door, looking none the worse for wear since they'd managed to avoid the dunking.

She found him sitting in the kitchen, hunting and pecking away on his laptop. He glanced up and smiled when she came in. He'd changed into dry clothes, too. Another pair of jeans and a white shirt that matched the one she wore. It looked as though he'd taken a quick shower as well.

"Hey." He glanced up with a smile. "You want some coffee?"

Poppy normally would have said yes, but suddenly her stomach was all jittery. She placed a hand over it as though that would help. She wasn't sure how to deal with this smiling, considerate Beck. Didn't he know his role was to be overbearing, overpowering and just a little sexy? She could fend off that kind of man.

But this man? The one who pulled her out of the water, promised to help her with Jamie and made her coffee? This man was dangerous.

"No." She pressed her stomach in a silent command for it to calm itself. "I should probably head back." She needed some space before she did something stupid like decide to forgive him. She knew all too well where that might lead.

"You sure? I just made a pot."

And they'd sit down together, probably have some laughs and slowly but surely he'd wiggle his way back into her good graces. She pressed harder and managed a smile. "No, I really need to get back."

If she was lucky, Cami and her family would be gone, her mother would be out back tending to her flowers and her dad would be watching golf and no one would spot her sneaking in wearing clothes completely different from those she'd left in.

CHAPTER EIGHT

POPPY WASN'T THAT LUCKY.

Cami's car still sat in the driveway, which meant everyone was there. And while it was likely her dad and Hank were in the family room caught up in whichever golf tournament was on TV this weekend, her mother and Cami would definitely be hovering nearby. Even if they were in the backyard, Poppy knew they'd hear Beck's car pull up and would already be making their way inside to ask how things had gone.

And she had no way to explain it.

She glanced down at the jeans and T-shirt, which was quite the stylish combo with her nude heels and glitzy clutch. Beck had retrieved her purse from the main house during her shower. She didn't ask how, afraid he would tell her he'd explained to everyone she was back at his place, naked and wet. She wouldn't put it past him.

Not that it mattered what his family thought of her. After this week, they'd probably never see each other again. But Poppy had liked them, his mother in particular, and she wanted Victoria to like her back.

But she had bigger things to worry about right

now. Holding her breath, though it was probably a lost cause, Poppy carefully opened the front door, making sure to push slowly and only far enough to sidle inside. At the three-quarters mark the door had a tendency to let out a loud squeal announcing an arrival.

The door stayed silent and no one stood in the entryway to greet her. Poppy exhaled a little. Still plenty of bated breath in her lungs, but at least the welcome committee wasn't pulling out the brass-band stops. She heard the television coming from the back room, a low murmur of voices and the sounds of muted clapping. So Hank and her dad would be no problem.

She shut the door behind her and risked a glance into the kitchen. It was sparkling clean and empty. No one stood between her and the foot of the stairs only a few feet away. She slipped off her heels and padded forward, letting the rest of the air escape as she did.

"Auntie Pop-pop!" Holly's toddler voice had a massive boom for one so small. "You're home." She hurled her tiny body at Poppy's leg and hung on tight.

"Hi, Holly Hobbie," Poppy whispered, hoping maybe, just maybe, the entire house hadn't heard Holly's greeting. "I need to go upstairs. Do you want to come?"

She figured she could keep her niece busy in her bedroom with some of her shoes and purses while she hunted for something else to wear. Changing from her brunch outfit into something more casual for around the house wouldn't even merit a question, let alone require an explanation.

"No, come outside." Holly giggled and reached up to tug on Poppy's hand. "I want to play. Win."

"In a minute," Poppy said, prying the sticky little fingers from her hand and leg. "I have to change and then I'll come and play." And would let the little munchkin win because the joy in Holly's face totally made it worth being schooled by a two-year-old.

"No." Holly frowned and her rosebud lips wobbled. "Want to play now. I win."

"You go get things set up. I'll be right there." The stairs, only steps away, had never seemed so far.

"No, you come now." The lips wobbled again.

Poppy debated her options. Snatch up Holly and haul butt up the stairs before the toddler realized what was happening, then distract her with something shiny while she changed. Or disentangle herself from Holly's grasp and run up the stairs before someone heard them talking and came out to investigate or...

Stand there like an idiot debating her options until her mother and sister hunted her down, gave her the once-over, took note of her new outfit and turned their curious gazes on her full force.

"You weren't wearing that when you left," her mother said. "What happened?"

"Oh, I think it's obvious what happened." Cami

stroked Holly's hair when she ran over to explain she and Auntie Pop-pop were going to play. "She was corrupting my daughter."

"I wasn't corrupting," Poppy said. "I slipped and fell in the lake." She held up the plastic bag Beck had given her to put her wet clothes in.

"Who fell in the lake?"

Poppy raised her eyes to find one more person joining the party, but this time she grinned. "Wynn." Her best friend and business partner had never looked so good or been so welcome. Wynn knew her family well and was a master at distraction techniques. "I thought you weren't getting in until tomorrow." She hugged him, laughing when her wet bag swung around to slap him in the back and cause him to dart away.

"Please, Poppy. This is designer." He gestured at his suit, which appeared custom-made and expensive. His short strawberry-blond hair was perfectly coiffed and his pale green eyes were bright and searching. He didn't look like someone who'd spent the morning traveling.

"When did you get in?" she asked.

"Unimportant." He eyed her borrowed outfit. "What are you wearing?"

She glanced down at herself, embarrassed to admit she enjoyed wearing Beck's clothes. Pathetic but true.

"I fell in the lake," she repeated. "Beck gave me this to wear."

"Beck?" All three of them leaped on her comment in a flash.

Her mother got an excited gleam that spoke of weddings and more grandkids, her sister wore a know-it-all smirk, but it was Wynn, with his raised eyebrow and half smile, who said, "Details, please."

No, she was not going to stand here and be interrogated like a common criminal when she was simply an innocent victim of circumstance. But when she told them that, they all laughed. Even Holly, who said, "Play now. Win?"

But Holly's questions distracted her sister and mother long enough for Poppy to reach the first step. "I'm going to change," she called out as she rabbited up the stairs, knowing they wouldn't follow her. Wynn, on the other hand, climbed behind her, though he moved at a more leisurely pace.

"Don't think you can hold out on me," he said, pushing open her bedroom door and plopping himself down on her bed.

"If you think I'm changing in front of you, you're wrong."

To his credit, Wynn seemed as put off by the idea as her. "You aren't my type. Besides, I can tell you don't really want to change. You were just trying to get away from Rose and Cami." His grin widened. "Now, tell me what's been going on. How can you already be hooking up with someone after three days? I'm so proud."

"We're not hooking up," Poppy said, burying

her face in her closet under the guise of searching for something else to wear, in the hopes that if her cheeks flamed up, Wynn wouldn't notice.

"So you just happened to be wearing sexy heels by the lake in a pretty dress all alone when you fell in and some big, bad, handsome stranger rescued you?"

Poppy shot him a look over her shoulder. "You caught me. That's exactly what happened."

Wynn laughed. "Your sister was only too happy to brief me, so there's no point in trying to pretend. What's he like?"

Poppy turned back to searching through her clothes. Since she'd only brought enough for the week, there wasn't much to dig through, even though she'd packed at least twice as much as she'd need so she'd be prepared for any occasion. She started at the front of the rack and flipped through again, more slowly.

"I can wait here all day."

Wynn always said that, but Poppy had never put him to the test. She was a spiller, divulging all her secrets when asked. And she did want to talk about what was going on with someone who wasn't her mother or sister, but she wasn't sure how to start.

"Do you promise not to blab everything?"

Wynn pulled his best offended face. "Please, I am known for my discretion. Except when tequila is involved, but everyone has their weaknesses."

"I met him when I was sixteen." She shared all the details of that summer. How Beck had cruised into town in his Acura Integra, so different from the boys she'd grown up with. Or maybe just different because she didn't already know everything about him. He was smart and funny. They swam in the lake behind his parents' new house, and sneaked wine coolers in the guesthouse that was still being built. Actually, sneaking wine coolers was one of the less exciting things they'd done in that guesthouse.

The more she told Wynn, the more he sat up until finally he burst out, "How could I not know this? I thought we were best friends. You've been holding out on me."

"I wasn't holding out. It was a long time ago." And by the time she and Wynn had met in second-year university, it wasn't something she thought about much at all. "What would you have thought if I'd started crying about some high school relationship when I first met you?"

"I'd have thought you were a freak."

"Exactly."

"But after we became friends, you should have told me. The night a woman loses her virginity is an important one." He somehow managed to appear hurt by this, as though she'd let him down.

"It never came up."

Wynn got a sly look in his eye. "Is that what he said?"

Poppy threw a pillow at him. "No." Not at all, but that wasn't up for discussion. "Besides, it's not exactly like I've been pining over him for the last decade."

"Are you pining now?"

Wynn had always been too astute for his own good.

"Not pining," Poppy said. "A little confused." She pulled a clean dress out of the closet, a cute little shift that looked like something someone might have worn in the sixties, with a straight bodice, short sleeves and a hem that cut off about midthigh. She liked the friendly-dolphin print that from a distance looked like a herringbone pattern.

"You still like him," Wynn said, crossing his legs and running a finger down the sharp crease in his pant.

"I don't think I'd go that far." But she'd be lying if she didn't say something drew her to him. He intrigued her. Still. She *should* still be mad at him.

"I would. You're smitten."

"I'm not smitten."

"Such a smitten kitten."

She opened her mouth to argue and then closed it. Who was she kidding? Beck still made her weak in the knees. And, apparently, the head.

"I don't want to like him," she told Wynn, laying the dress across the footboard. "But there's something about him."

"About time."

Poppy glanced up. "What is that supposed to mean?" As if she didn't already know.

Wynn tilted his head and gave her a pitying frown. "Your attempt to play coy is a sad failure. We both know what I'm talking about."

Since she would only embarrass herself by continuing the act, Poppy dropped it. For months, Wynn had been hounding her to get over Evan, to get back into the dating world and see where life took her. He hadn't believed her whenever she tried to tell him she wasn't mourning Evan.

She still thought it had been a perfectly natural grieving process. Would any woman be okay after coming home from work to the apartment she shared with her fiancé to be told he had quit his job and was selling all his worldly goods so he could go to Thailand and find himself? Poppy didn't think so.

Of course, that didn't explain the fact that in the ten months since she hadn't gone on a single date, but Poppy didn't think she'd been avoiding anything. During that time she worked and grew the business—nothing wrong with focusing on the professional aspect of her life for a while.

"Anyway, it doesn't matter. I won't see him again after this week." And she was okay with that. Totally. She realized she was clutching the hem of Beck's T-shirt and let go.

"Why not?"

"He lives in Seattle, for one thing. Plus, I don't know if I'd want to see him again anyway." The abrupt way he'd left her all those years ago had left a mark. "He's helping me with Jamie," she said in an effort to change the subject.

Poppy had filled Wynn in on her concerns about Jamie's sudden engagement as soon as they'd received their invitations to the wedding. Though Wynn and Jamie had only met through Poppy they'd immediately hit it off and since Wynn spent his holidays with Poppy's family, they'd seen each other semiregularly.

Her ploy worked. Wynn's eyebrows lifted. "What did you find out?"

"Nothing." She sighed, flopping down on the bed beside him. "It's been incredibly frustrating. She doesn't work and doesn't seem to have interests outside of Jamie and the wedding." She sighed again. "But she seems sweet."

"She would though, wouldn't she? Seem sweet," Wynn mused. "What's the ring like?"

"Nice. Boring but nice."

"But it's not your ring."

"No ring is my ring except my ring." Poppy knew it was silly, but she'd picked out her engagement ring a couple years earlier. Not on purpose. She'd been out with a friend who wanted to stop into a jewelry store. Poppy, who had still been planning weddings at the time, couldn't think of anything she'd like to do less, but she'd gone along rather than make a fuss.

While her friend had ogled the sparkle and shine of the princess cuts, Poppy wandered into the vintage area. And there, staring back at her, was the piece that soon became known as her ring. She'd never seen anything like it before—art deco in style with a square-shaped center diamond surrounded by onyx and more diamonds.

"I still don't understand why you don't buy it for yourself," Wynn said.

"Because as I've told you a thousand times, buying it for myself takes the fun out of it."

"But finding it for yourself doesn't?"

"I told you, Wynn. The ring found me." And the right man would buy the ring for her and they'd both live happily ever after. Just as soon as she found him.

"Back to the point, what did you learn at the brunch?"

The vision of her beautiful ring disappeared. "Nothing. It's weird. They didn't share anything personal. She has a sister though."

Poppy and Wynn had done internet searches on Emmy and her parents, whose names were on the invitation, but hadn't gotten any relevant information. Her mother's name hadn't gotten any hits and her father only showed up on the board of directors for a charitable organization, but the site merely said he was a Seattle-based businessman. Grace provided a new and untried option.

"Then let's search for her."

Poppy dug her phone out of the clutch and opened a browser before typing in Grace Burnham. Maybe Grace would be one of those twenty-somethings who posted their entire lives online. Friends, enemies, loves and a stream of pictures displaying every activity she'd ever participated in from the age of fifteen on, hopefully with running commentary.

She got one hit, a single Facebook page that was definitely Grace. Poppy recognized the blond hair even from the minuscule photo, but access was restricted to friends only. Poppy sent a friend request.

"It'll probably come to nothing," she told Wynn. "Judging from the rest of the family, I find it unlikely she's going to list her workplace and income for public consumption."

"Probably," Wynn agreed, "but it won't hurt." He pulled out his own phone and punched the screen.

"Don't waste your time," Poppy told him. "I only got one hit." Not even a Twitter account or an old MySpace page.

"I'm not looking for her." He tapped the screen a few more times, then in his best news anchor's voice began to read. "'He dines at Seattle's finest restaurants, has a bachelor pad worthy of Bond and has a personal net worth in the millions.'" He glanced up at Poppy. "In case it wasn't obvious, I'm talking about your boyfriend."

"He's not my boyfriend," Poppy said, reaching for Wynn's phone. He was a little taller than her, but she was willing to fight dirty and she knew he wasn't. She grabbed the leg of his pants and twisted, leaving behind a mess of wrinkles.

"Poppy," Wynn said, handing over his phone as

he brushed his pant legs. "You're going to have to iron these now."

It was a small price to pay. "He's not my boyfriend," she reiterated even as she scanned the article Wynn had pulled up.

She wasn't researching Beck, not exactly. She was just reading what someone else had discovered. Like the fact that Beck had taken over running the family business the previous year and the hotel group had shown an increase of ten percent from last year's financial statements to this year's.

"Oh?" Wynn's sly smile returned. "You seem rather interested and you *are* wearing his clothes. Are you sure nothing happened back at the lake?"

Poppy closed the web browser on both phones and handed Wynn's back to him, hoping the prickling in her cheeks was nothing more than a healthy tingle because she'd used a facial scrub this morning. It wasn't.

"You're getting red. Something did happen. Tell Uncle Wynn."

"Okay, first off, *ew*. Don't call yourself my uncle, that's creepy. Second, there's nothing to tell. We kissed, that's all."

"You kissed?" Poppy appreciated that Wynn didn't throw himself into a paroxysm of joy or shock the way her mother and sister would have. But his excited grin was almost as bad. "And then what?"

"And then nothing. I slipped, fell in the water and had to change." She would not talk about the shower. "I'm not here to meet someone, Wynn. This is about Jamie, remember?" She twisted a strand of hair around her finger and let it unravel before pushing herself off the bed. She needed to change before she got too comfortable wearing Beck's things. "I need to make sure Jamie isn't being taken advantage of. Beck's helping me, that's all."

"It doesn't sound like that's all."

Poppy flipped her hair and grabbed the dress off the bed. "I can't help it if you hear things that aren't there. Now, if you'll excuse me." She turned to head to the bathroom since Wynn seemed happy to make himself comfortable in her bedroom the rest of the day.

"You may go." Wynn saw her out of the room with a gracious wave. "But this conversation isn't over."

And as she expected, he was waiting to pounce when she reentered her bedroom with Beck's clothing neatly folded in her arms. "Are you going to sleep with him?"

"Clearly, you've been letting Cami get inside your head and make herself at home." Poppy laid the clothing on top of her dresser. She'd have to contact Beck later to organize their return, and didn't that give her a lovely little rush.

"You didn't answer the question."

"Because there's nothing to answer. He's helping me with Jamie. Nothing else."

"I think you should," Wynn said, completely ignoring her explanation. "It would be good for you to get back in the saddle, as it were."

Since this was the same discussion they'd been having for months, Poppy didn't feel bad for tuning him out. He would say she should try out casual sex, she would explain she wasn't that kind of person, he would say she wouldn't know until she tried, and she would say she didn't need to try to know. Also, casual sex wasn't like trying escargot. It could have repercussions. Big ones.

No, she wasn't into casual sex. She didn't expect the guy to get down on one knee the first time he met her or anything, but there should at least be hope for a mutually satisfying relationship.

And for her, that meant more than just heating up the sheets.

CHAPTER NINE

BECK GLANCED UP when he heard the knock on the door. His muscles tensed for one second and then Jamie's blond head appeared. "Hey. Can I come in?"

"Sure." Beck closed the laptop he'd been working on. He wasn't doing anything, just checking his email. "Where's Emmy?" This was one of the few times he'd seen them separated. It was kind of odd, actually. Somehow with their golden-couple status, they'd become linked in his mind.

"She's with her mom and Grace, looking at magazines."

"And you're not looking too?"

Jamie frowned. "I'm not *completely* henpecked. Just a little."

Beck laughed, long and loud. He'd forgotten that despite his sweetness, Jamie was entirely capable of getting in a jab or three. It had been too long since he'd spent time with his cousin. "Want some coffee?"

"In a minute." Jamie took the seat across the table from Beck and folded his hands. "You coming to dinner tonight?"

"No." Brunch was enough. He was not doing the family dinner as well. Emmy's family wouldn't be around, so Beck's attendance wasn't mandatory. He told Jamie he planned to spend the evening eating pizza and watching the game on TV.

"Your mom won't like that."

"She'll get over it. Want to join me?"

"Absolutely." They grinned at each other.

"So the brunch and Poppy. You want to tell me what's going on?"

"Not really." He wasn't about to share with Jamie that Poppy was worried his fiancée was only after him for his money. And instead of telling her about Emmy's financial stability, he'd let her keep believing the worst.

"So it's nothing?"

"I wouldn't say nothing." It would be something if he got his way. But he had no guarantee of that, though the kiss they'd shared earlier certainly hinted it might be.

"Then what's going on?"

"She entertains me," Beck said, hoping it would be enough to get Detective Jamie off the case. He wasn't sure what was going on with him and Poppy. But it wasn't something he felt like figuring out now, with his cousin hanging on every word.

Part of it was he wasn't used to women turning him down. Not that he spent his time with a different woman every night, but he didn't do too badly in the dating sweepstakes. And perhaps that was part of the problem.

He was bored.

The women in his circles offered no challenge, throwing themselves into his lap, and their behavior didn't make him want to get to know them any better either.

It wasn't like that with Poppy.

Not only did she refuse to throw herself at him, she actively threw herself away from him. But he saw the look in her eyes and sensed the way she responded to him. That spark between them had never died.

"You know I love Poppy. She's one of my best friends," Jamie said.

"And?"

"And I don't want her to get hurt." Jamie's gaze didn't waver. "She's nice, Beck."

"Yeah." He smiled, thinking just how nice she'd looked in his shower this morning.

"She's not like the other women you date."

Beck blinked, losing the unannounced staring contest. How did Jamie know what kind of women he dated? And why did he care? "What does that mean?"

"It means she's not a bimbo looking for a spot on the social pages." Beck and his dates were often featured in newspapers and online.

"They're not *all* bimbos." Just some of them— and those ones he didn't take out more than once. Beck wasn't looking to make a deep and personal connection with the women he dated, but he needed them to talk about more than fashion and the latest celebrity gossip.

"Poppy's not like that."

"No? What is she like?" He'd lost touch with her, but Jamie hadn't.

"She's amazing. She'd do anything for someone she loved. She deserves that in return."

Beck was a little offended. Hard not to be when Jamie clearly didn't think he was up to the task. Not that he wanted the task, but he could manage. "I'm not going to hurt her, Jamie."

"You have before."

It was a slap, but one he'd earned. "I was young and stupid." And messed up by his parents' relationship. "I'm not going to do anything, Jamie."

Jamie tilted his head. "I've been friends with her a long time, Beck. I don't remember not having her in my life…" He trailed off and shrugged.

"I like her, okay?" And yes, he hoped they could spend this weekend learning about each other again, but he wasn't going to admit it under the gaze of the Golden Boy. Jamie could be as bad as his mother and Beck didn't need two people asking about his future plans. He didn't do future, and he was okay with that.

Jamie watched him steadily.

Beck decided it was time to change topics. "She mentioned you two haven't seen much of each other lately. She was worried you'd be too busy this week with wedding stuff. That's why I invited her to brunch."

Not entirely true, as it also provided the benefit of getting Grace off his mother's radar. Beck didn't stop to wonder why it didn't bother him to have Poppy on that same radar.

"Weird." Seemingly satisfied he'd gotten whatever response he'd been looking for, Jamie decided they both needed coffee. He pulled down a pair of cups and filled them, grabbed the cream out of the fridge and a sugar bowl from the cupboard. Beck hadn't even known he had a sugar bowl. "Why wouldn't she call me?"

"Maybe she didn't want to add any stress to the week?" Beck poured a dollop of cream into his cup, watching the white liquid bloom to the top.

Jamie added sugar and stirred, then took the cream from Beck. "Probably. I should call her. It's been so busy with the wedding." He stirred his coffee again. "Let me ask you something."

As long as it wasn't about his intentions, Beck was all for it. "Go."

"Do you think Poppy dislikes Emmy?"

Beck put his coffee down without taking a sip. "What gives you that idea?" he asked carefully.

"I'm not sure." Jamie tapped a finger against the side of his cup. "Just a feeling. You wouldn't know what I mean, since you and Poppy aren't close."

Beck took a slug of coffee to ease the sudden tightening in his stomach.

"But she's usually pretty open. She seemed a bit distant this morning."

"There were a lot of people at the house, Jamie." The coffee sloshed in his stomach. "I'm sure it was nothing."

"Maybe." But Jamie didn't sound convinced.

"If it's bothering you, why don't you try getting them to spend some time together." Beck thought of Poppy's concerns and realized he had a perfect way to solve them and earn some points, too. "Why don't you have Emmy invite her to the bachelorette party."

Jamie's face brightened. "You think?"

"Oh, yeah." Beck warmed up to the idea.

The bachelor and bachelorette parties were happening on the same night at different locations. The boys were going out for a round of golf and dinner, while the girls were heading to a spa for mani-pedis. But there was talk of turning it into a Jack-and-Jill party later. Beck would be a lot more interested in the idea if Poppy would be there.

"It'd be a chance for them to bond."

And a chance for him to figure out how to convince Poppy to take their dating ruse to the next level.

CHAPTER TEN

POPPY SELECTED A pair of bubblegum-pink jean capris, a black-and-white-chevron top, a fitted black blazer and the same nude heels she'd worn to brunch the other day to complete her outfit for Emmy's Wednesday night bachelorette party. She'd been informed by Grace that since Emmy's favorite color was pink, all attendees were expected to show appreciation for her by wearing something in the girlie shade.

No word on whether or not Grace was going to befriend her on Facebook. Poppy wasn't sure it mattered. If Grace had been the type to let it all hang out online, they would have discovered more than one tightly managed Facebook profile bearing her name.

Poppy was stuffing money and her ID into a black leather tote when she heard a car turn onto her street. She peeked out her bedroom window as a white stretch limo parked in the driveway.

She put an extra couple bills into her bag and hurried down the stairs. They were going to Penticton, a slightly larger small town only fifteen minutes away, for the mani-pedis and dinner.

Beck had also mentioned something about the two groups meeting up at the end of the night. Poppy hoped so, but if not, Wynn would be in attendance at Jamie's party and could get some intel.

She stepped outside into the sunshine. It was hot after the air-conditioned splendor of the house and she hurried to the car, which was full of pretty women in various shades of pink, from the lightest blush to the darkest magenta.

Emmy fell somewhere in the middle in a sparkly rose-colored dress made out of actual sequins. They scratched Poppy's cheek when Emmy leaned over to give her a hug. "I'm so happy you could come."

"Thanks for inviting me." She settled into one of the plush seats.

"Everyone," Emmy said as the limo started moving. "This is Poppy. One of Jamie's best friends." She was greeted with a chorus of friendly hellos and questions. Everyone wanted to know more about Jamie and figured Poppy was the one to ask

Poppy regaled them with the time Jamie had cut her hair in grade one because she'd accidentally gotten glue in it and had been afraid she would get in trouble. They'd both gotten a lecture about owning up to your mistakes instead of trying to hide them. Then there was the time in high school when he'd lost a single shoe at a party—turned out someone had stolen it, but only the one—and Jamie'd had to hop home. And she also shared that they'd attended prom together.

"Did you date?" Grace asked.

"No, no," Poppy assured them, sending Emmy a

worried glance. That was all she needed. For Emmy to think she wanted her man. "We were always just friends. I was actually getting over a broken heart and wanted to stay home, but Jamie insisted."

All the women aahed, led by Emmy. "That is so like him," she said and reached out to give Poppy a one-armed hug. Poppy eyed her silently, thinking she made it awfully hard to dislike her.

As the limo rocked down the curving roads leading out of the valley and into town, someone opened a bottle of champagne. The bar was also stocked with sparkling water and, in honor of the bride, pink lemonade. Poppy had a glass of the latter, appreciating the sweet tartness. The princess pop playing through the speakers she didn't appreciate quite as much.

Although she was unable to ask Emmy or Grace any questions about themselves, Poppy enjoyed the trip. And she enjoyed the spa treatments even more.

Emmy had booked the entire spa for the party, so they had the place to themselves. She'd provided nibbles for snacking and trays of drinks. Cosmos for those who wanted to indulge and an alcohol-free concoction served in a martini glass rimmed with, of course, pink sugar that tasted like fresh strawberries and chocolate. Poppy drank two while a cheerful woman buffed her toes and painted them an attractive shade of crimson, which, sticking with the theme of the party, was a kind of pink.

She would do well to remind herself it was Jamie's

money and Jamie's hard work paying for the day, but Poppy had to admit the party wasn't particularly extravagant. She knew the associated costs of doing something similar and this was a lot less than what most brides shelled out to celebrate their last few days of singledom.

They had dinner at one of the local wineries where each course was paired with a specific wine. And on the way back to Naramata and their final stop on the bachelorette-party wagon, Poppy finally managed to snag the seat beside Emmy.

She hadn't gotten an opportunity to talk to Emmy during the spa treatments or dinner, but thought maybe now would be her chance. She hoped she hadn't been too obvious, practically elbowing one of the other women out of the way, but time was drawing near and Poppy wasn't about to let another opportunity slip away.

She waited until they were on their way, as the other women showed off their newly painted fingers and toes, before broaching the subject. "You know, I don't think I heard how you and Jamie met."

Poppy figured if she eased into the conversation, chatted about unimportant details, letting Emmy think they were becoming friends, she'd be more likely to let something slip. Poppy didn't know what, but she was sure she would when she heard it.

Emmy smiled and blushed prettily. "Oh, it's nothing exciting. I came up with some girlfriends for a long weekend in April and we stopped in at his winery."

"And it was love at first sight?" Poppy wanted to believe Emmy's story sounded like a convenient cover excuse for the real version in which Emmy had researched and targeted Jamie, and the drop-in at the winery had been a planned approach. But Poppy didn't entirely buy that. Love at first sight happened. She only had to look at her own family for two examples.

"I'm not sure if it was love. But there was something about him." Emmy laughed. "He asked me to dinner and I accepted. When I went back to the city at the end of the weekend, we kept in touch."

Nothing shady about that. In fact, it was sort of sweet.

"He came down that next weekend and stayed with me." Emmy's whole face lit up at the memory. "By Sunday, we both knew we had something real and we wanted to be together. I was pretty surprised when he came back later that night. He had the ring." She spun the rock around her finger. "I said yes."

Okay, it wasn't *sort of* sweet. It was saccharinely, treacly sweet. And it sounded as if it was all Jamie's doing.

"Were you surprised?" Poppy asked.

"Shocked. I didn't expect it at all. But I didn't have to think about it." She laid a hand on Poppy's arm. "I don't want you to think I have any concerns about marrying Jamie. As soon as he got down on one knee I knew what I wanted."

"To get married."

"No, to be with Jamie. I don't really care about the wedding and all this. That's my mother's doing. I just want to be with Jamie."

Well, this wasn't going the way Poppy had planned at all. Was it possible Emmy and Jamie were a love match? That they were moving quickly only because they couldn't stand the idea of not being together?

"I was nervous to meet you," Emmy admitted.

"Were you?"

"Yes. Jamie's told me so much about you. How close you are."

Not that close, considering Poppy hadn't known how serious things had gotten with Emmy until the wedding invitation arrived.

"You've known Jamie since you were kids. You're important to him. I was afraid you might not like me and might not want Jamie to marry me."

A dull flush warmed Poppy's ears. "Oh, no. I'm just happy to be included in your big day." It was a lie, but Poppy was starting to wonder if it should be the truth. Was she creating something out of nothing?

"Me, too." Emmy smiled. "And I don't want you to worry. I'm going to take good care of Jamie. We have a deal." She leaned over to giggle in Poppy's ear. "He's going to make the money and I'm going to spend it."

BECK SMILED WHEN he spotted Emmy's bachelorette party troop into the Sundowner Bar & Grille at nine o'clock. The boys had been here for an hour, having finished up their golf game early and not wanting to linger over dinner. Most of them stood around in small groups, gold glinting on their ring fingers as they sipped their beer and talked about sports. Poor suckers.

Jamie seemed to be having a good time. Beck and Wynn had convinced him to take a shot of tequila as a final goodbye to bachelorhood and Jamie had taken it from there.

At last count, he'd downed three, which wasn't much for a tall, healthy male. But apparently, Jamie didn't do much besides taste test his own wine these days. He currently sat on one of the cheap wooden bar stools with a hand on Wynn's shoulder for balance. Probably saying how much he loved him, man.

It was good for him, Beck decided. Jamie didn't cut loose enough, and if a man couldn't cut loose at his bachelor party, then when? Still, he'd already signaled to the bartender to stop serving him. There was cutting loose and then there was making an ass of yourself. Beck would make sure Jamie didn't do the latter.

He watched Poppy as she separated from the group. She looked good enough to eat in a pair of tight pants, her red hair swinging and snapping as she moved.

He headed toward her, making sure to stay out

of her sight so he could pop up behind her before she tried one of her avoidance maneuvers. The bar was noisy—shouts of laughter, the clink of glasses as patrons toasted each other and the tinny country music that played through the speakers. Beck had to raise his voice to be heard.

"Miss me, Red?"

She whirled and frowned at him. "I'd tell you not to call me that, but clearly it isn't sinking into your Neanderthal skull."

He grinned and lifted a hand to her hair, running his fingers through the fiery strands. "You could try."

"I don't believe in wasting my breath."

"And yet you've been standing here chatting about everything but my question. Did you miss me?"

Heat flared in her eyes before she dropped her gaze and stepped back. "No."

"No?" He stepped with her. "Now, why don't I believe you? Maybe because you've been avoiding me."

He hadn't seen her since the brunch on Sunday. He'd called to tell her about the invite for the bachelorette party coming her way and asked if she wanted to get together, but she'd told him she was busy. He didn't know if that was true or if she needed some space after that kiss. He figured if that was the case, she'd had enough by now.

He'd certainly had enough.

He thought about her a lot. And not just at night. No, he found himself thinking about her during the day, too. Every time he glanced at the lake, he remembered the summer with Poppy.

He, Poppy and Jamie, and a big group of their friends had taken over a section of the main beach every day. It had been fun. The group had accepted Beck as one of their own and he'd soon come to think of them as his friends, too. He'd let his communication with them slide as well when he left. Yet another thing to blame his mother for.

His mother, who had taken to visiting him at the guesthouse on a daily basis. Every morning, as soon as he'd finished his first cup of coffee, she'd come waltzing in for one reason or another. Once to make sure he had everything he needed, another time to invite him to breakfast. Today had been to make sure he had things ready for Jamie's bachelor party.

Poppy frowned and a line appeared between her brows. "I haven't been avoiding you."

"You have." He rubbed his thumb over the line, enjoying the feel of her silky skin and the sharp little exhalation she couldn't quite hide. "You didn't call."

"Neither did you," she pointed out and brushed his hand away.

He captured hers and linked their fingers together. "I called once. I missed you."

"What are you doing?"

"We're dating, remember?"

"Just for your family."

"And my family is here." He stroked her cheek,

letting his finger lie there a moment. Skin on skin. He noticed she didn't brush his hand away. Maybe they *would* get to more than kissing before the week was over.

"I should go say hello to Jamie."

Beck gripped her hand a shade tighter. "He's busy."

She tried to peer over his shoulder, shot him a look when he shifted to prevent it. "Are you blocking me?"

He pasted on a hurt expression and put a hand to his heart. "Would I do that?"

The edges of her mouth curved. "Yes."

"Guilty." He leaned in. "And I didn't get my hello kiss. My family is probably watching." He doubted Jamie could see more than a foot in front of him, but Poppy didn't know that.

Their eyes met again, held.

Beck felt the deep, slow thump of his pulse. He suddenly wanted to carry her out of the bar to a private spot and stare into her eyes as he slipped inside her. "I should tell you I'm a champion at staring contests."

Another smile tugged at the corners of her mouth. "Are you?"

"Best in the world. I could watch you like this all night."

Color bloomed in her cheeks and she blinked.

He smirked. "I win."

She laughed. "Fine, you win. What do you want?"

"You."

She swallowed, the muscles in her neck moving up and down. "Well, that's bold."

They were so close his lips were almost brushing her ear. Again, she didn't brush him off. "I am bold." Her skin looked so creamy and soft. He wanted to dart out his tongue for a taste, but refrained, knowing the tease could be as delicious as the fulfillment.

Her hand flexed beneath his like a trapped bird fluttering its wings. He closed his fingers around her more closely. He liked having her here. With him. She wasn't getting away that easily.

"How was the party?" he asked. "Get any dirt on the bride?"

Poppy sighed. "Not really. I don't think she worked before she met Jamie, which makes me nervous. What normal twenty-something doesn't have a job?"

"One who doesn't have to," he suggested.

"Exactly. So how did she pay for things? A string of wealthy gentleman friends? I don't like it."

Beck didn't want to talk about Emmy. Probably should have thought of that before he introduced the topic. "So what's next?"

"I have no idea." She frowned, her lower lip pouted. Beck wondered what she'd do if he sucked on it. Probably like it and pretend she didn't. "I'm gonna go say hello to him."

Beck didn't like the idea of her leaving his side. "He's not in any state to listen." He nodded to the end of the bar where Jamie and Wynn still sat together, a pair of empty glasses in front of them, a half-filled bottle to their right.

"Is that a tequila bottle?" She craned her body, rubbing across his chest to check. He liked that—a lot. "You're letting him get drunk?"

"I'm not letting him do anything." He enjoyed the movement of her body as she shifted. So soft and warm. "I already told the bartender to cut him off."

"Seems you don't have as much influence as you think."

Beck followed her pointed stare and saw the bartender refilling the glasses in front of Jamie and Wynn. And not with water. "Let him have some fun. He's not hurting anyone." Jamie would feel that tomorrow, but Beck didn't feel like playing bachelor party police.

"Except himself. He can barely sit up straight." Poppy glared at Beck as if it was his fault Jamie was getting loaded. "Exactly how many of those did you let him drink?"

Beck looked over at Jamie. His cousin was beginning to list as he reached for the shot glass. He probably wouldn't be upright if he didn't have the bar to lean on. Damn.

"Well?" she said to him. When he didn't move immediately, she did, peeling herself off him and spinning on her heel. "I'm going over there." She yanked on his hand when he didn't automatically move with her. "Well, come on. You're not getting out of this so easily."

She dragged him past a group of Emmy's friends who had pulled the bride onto the extremely tiny dance floor to shake their bodies to the music.

"And don't let Emmy see him," Poppy said.

"Wouldn't she have already seen him?"

"No, thankfully," Poppy said over her shoulder, hurrying them to their destination. "She'd be mad or at the very least embarrassed if she saw him like this."

"It's a bachelor party," Beck reminded her. What was so wrong with getting a little happy? He glanced over again. Now Wynn was supporting Jamie, the only thing keeping him from crashing to the floor. Okay, maybe Jamie had sailed past happy a couple drinks ago, but it wasn't as if he was getting a lap dance or dancing on the bar.

Poppy sighed. "Trust me, okay. No woman would be happy to find her future husband getting drunk in public."

Beck wasn't sure why it was a big deal, but he didn't want to have a long discussion about it either. He had other plans, like how to talk Poppy into coming home with him tonight. And he had more than kissing on the agenda. "Why don't we leave them—"

She shot him a look that was on the verge of pitying. No, scratch that. It had dived off the edge of pitying and landed in a sea of contempt. "And let her get her gold digger hooks even deeper into him? No way."

"What?" Now Beck was confused. "How would this get her hooks in deeper?"

"If she's interested in his money, do you actually think a little drunken behavior will scare her off?" Poppy shook her head. "You have a lot to learn. It might have the opposite effect. He'd be so grateful she didn't hold it against him it would end up solidifying their bond. So let's get him out of here before she sees him."

They finally reached the long bar that ran the length of the room where the bartender had lined up another row of shots. Poppy swooped in and slid the glass away from Jamie, then spun on Wynn with a scowl. "What are you doing?"

"Tequila shots," Wynn answered. "It's my weakness, remember?"

Beck watched Jamie close one eye and try to navigate his hand the short distance to the glass. He sighed. Poppy was right. Jamie was way past his limit and now Beck would have to clean him up. He reached over Jamie's shoulder and deftly plucked the glass out of range. "I think you're done, pal."

"Beck." Jamie smiled sweetly, looking like a little boy. "Hi."

"Hi." Beck put his arm around Jamie's chest and helped him off the stool. "Time for us to go."

"Go?" Jamie's brow wrinkled. "But all my friends are here."

"They will understand," Beck said, casting a glance around. Poppy whispered heatedly into Wynn's ear. Beck wished she'd do that to him. He helped Jamie off the stool.

"Poppy," Jamie said when she crossed his line of vision, and he tried to give her a slobbery hug. Would have succeeded had Beck not been holding him.

"Hey, Jamie!" She finished whatever she had to say to Wynn and turned to Beck. "Let's go before Emmy spots him." She cast a concerned glance over her shoulder.

"Emmy?" Jamie lifted his head like a kid who'd just been promised a cookie for behaving. "You're not Emmy."

"No, I'm Poppy." She came around Jamie's other side, wrapped her arm around his waist and glanced at Beck. "Ready?"

He nodded and they made their way out of the pub. It was slow going with Jamie dragging his feet and people wanting to stop them every two feet to give him their best wishes, but they managed to get outside without seeing Emmy.

"Is she out here?" Jamie asked when the cool night air hit them.

"Who?" Poppy asked.

Beck tried to get his keys out of his pocket while keeping Jamie upright. The gravel crunched beneath their shoes as they walked toward his car. It had seemed a lot closer when he'd parked. But he hadn't been carrying a full-grown man who'd had one too many drinks then.

"Emmy." Jamie's blond head swiveled around. "I thought we were going to see her."

"Tomorrow," Poppy assured him. "Tonight she's out with her girlfriends."

"Yeah." Jamie slumped against Beck, smiling. "She's so great."

Poppy glanced over his head to Beck. "I can't believe what you did to him."

"I didn't plug his nose and pour it down his throat." Beck pulled the keys out and clicked the locks. The lights flashed in response.

"Emmy's great." Their conversation appeared to hold no interest for Jamie, who was in his own little Emmy world. "Don't you think she's great?" Jamie asked, tilting his head to stare at Beck.

"The greatest." Together, he and Poppy maneuvered Jamie into the backseat. Beck buckled him in, trying not to get a face full of tequila breath. "You doing okay?"

"The greatest," Jamie said then laughed before slumping against the backseat, that silly grin still on his face.

Beck closed the door. "Front or back?" he asked Poppy.

"Pardon?" The moon turned her hair a silvery red. He wanted to run his fingers through it.

"Front seat with me or backseat with the drunk guy?" He refrained from touching, but only just.

"You weren't planning to leave me alone with him, were you?"

"Well, I..." She turned back to the bar, the light blazing through the front windows. Everyone inside appeared to be having a good time, their departure barely noted.

"I need your help," he fibbed. Beck had managed plenty of drunk friends before, he could easily get Jamie from the car to the house and into bed, but he wanted Poppy to come home with him. It seemed the perfect way to convince her.

She sighed. "I'll sit in the back," she told him.

"Good. Need help getting buckled in?"

She climbed inside and closed the door in his face.

CHAPTER ELEVEN

"I'M GOING TO BE SICK," Jamie mumbled.

Poppy's heart raced as rapidly as the car they rode in. Oh, no. She was not spending the next hour cleaning up regurgitated tequila because Wynn had a weakness and Jamie couldn't hold his liquor. She tilted Jamie's head away from her pretty outfit and tossed her bag into the front passenger seat. "No puking allowed."

"No puking," Jamie repeated and hiccuped. She peered at him. It was hard to tell with only the moon for light, but she didn't think he was green. Not yet.

"Can you go faster?" she urged Beck.

"Already speeding," he said.

Poppy cursed herself for coming along. She'd only wanted to get Jamie out of the Sundowner Bar & Grille safely. She hadn't meant to be the one putting him to bed. Wasn't taking care of the drunk groom the best man's job?

She peeked at Beck and found him watching her in the rearview mirror. "Eyes on the road," she said.

Nothing about the situation was remotely appealing, she told herself as her entire body tingled. She still hadn't managed to have a conversation with

Jamie, and that was obviously out of the question tonight. She'd gotten nothing out of her little chat with Emmy and she was trapped in the back with a drunk about to blow.

But then she'd catch a glance of Beck watching her in the rearview mirror or recall the impression of his body smushed against hers and she'd experience a tickle of pleasure. Clearly, she needed to get out more.

"Do you need some air?" she asked Jamie, hoping to keep her mind on more important things.

Jamie smiled back. "Hi, Pop-Tart."

"Hi, Jamie." Poppy reached across him and pressed the switch to roll down the window so she'd have somewhere to aim Jamie's head in the event of an emergency. The cool air on her tingling skin didn't hurt either.

What was with her anyway? She wasn't seriously considering Wynn's advice to jump into bed with Beck, was she? No, of course not. Beck was a bad bet no matter how she looked at it. Lived in a different city. A different country. And no matter how attractive she found him, she did not do temporary relationships.

She glanced in the rearview again, found Beck still watching her and wondered if she should open the other window and stick her head out to cool off.

Jamie mumbled something and put his head on the window frame. Poppy rubbed his back and told him they were almost home. She glared at Beck. Did he see what his negligence had caused?

"How's he doing?" he asked over his shoulder.

"Drunk. Why didn't you watch him?"

"I did. And then you showed up."

Poppy snorted. The alcohol level in Jamie's blood had not been achieved in the limited amount of time she'd been at the bar. "Good one, but he was drinking before I arrived."

"He was, but he wasn't too bad. I stopped the bartender after the first three shots." She watched his eyes move toward her in the mirror. "You distracted me. Walking around in those tight pants and flirting with me."

Poppy raised her chin and rubbed Jamie's back harder. "I did not flirt."

"Yeah, Red, you did."

She had not. She'd simply answered his questions and done her best not to make a scene. Jamie groaned and Poppy realized she'd rucked his shirt out of his waistband. She shoved it back in and lightened her touch. Maybe she had flirted, but Beck had started it.

"And those pants."

"What about my pants?" Poppy loved her pants. They were cheerful and fun. She always got compliments when she wore them.

"They invite a man to flirt."

"There is nothing flirty about my pants." So what

if they looked as if they'd been painted on? That was the style.

"Oh, yeah, there is." She watched his slow smirk in the mirror. She shouldn't be flirting back. This was not a good idea. "Nothing to say to that?"

"Yes, hurry up before you have to clean your car."

He laughed and the car went a little faster, sleek as the cat it was named for. Poppy leaned back against the leather seat, wishing the smell didn't remind her of Beck, and rubbed Jamie's back in a calm, circular motion.

She glanced out the window as they drove past the turnoff to Jamie's place. "You missed your turn." Probably because he watched her more than the road. She shouldn't like that as much as she did.

"I didn't miss it." The car hugged the road as they flew past the tall trees that abounded in the region.

"Where are we going?"

"You said Emmy would be pissed." He drove down the twisting road that led to his neighborhood. "Figured it was safer to bring him here."

Poppy realized he was right. Emmy finding a drunk Jamie and caring for him all night like a kind and soothing fiancée would also strengthen their bond, leaving Jamie in no state to listen to any of her concerns. "You have to call her though," she told Beck. "And don't tell her he was drunk. Make something up."

"Like what?" Beck steered into the curving driveway. "That we picked up a hot woman, so he can't come home?"

The car bumped slightly as Beck cut the wheel to park and Jamie groaned. Poppy put her hand on the back of his head to keep his mouth facing out the window and away from the car's interior and her. "Obviously not. Tell her you're bonding, having some guy time."

"You think she'll buy that?"

"Why wouldn't she?" Poppy left Jamie, head hanging out the window, and climbed out her side of the car. Beck did the same. They walked around to Jamie's side. He slumped over, head out the window, eyes closed. "How are we going to do this?"

"We're not." Beck leaned down to talk to Jamie. "Hey, Jamie. Sit up. I'm going to open the door and I don't want you to fall out."

"Okay." Jamie opened his eyes and grinned. He wobbled a little as Beck helped him out, and Beck ended up taking most of his weight.

Poppy tried to help from the other side, but Beck waved her off. "I've got him."

The three of them walked up the steps to the front door. She felt like the fifth wheel. "What can I do?" she asked.

"Come over here and get my keys out of my pocket."

"Nice try." She hoped her jolt at the image of dipping her hand down the front of Beck's pants hadn't been obvious.

"What?" Beck was the picture of innocence, or as innocent as he could appear. "You asked if you could help."

"I didn't mean giving you a quick feel." She crossed her arms over her chest and tried not to shiver at the idea.

"Not up for it?"

"No." She didn't ask if he was. "I'll hold Jamie and you get the keys."

"You can't." Beck shifted, the movement causing him to almost drop Jamie's sagging body. "He's too heavy."

What? Did he think she couldn't hold her own? "I can, too." She lifted her chin and reached out again. "Hand him over."

Beck's low chuckle wafted through the air. "Red, he'll fall on you and when he pukes you won't be able to run away."

She hadn't thought of that. "Well, I do like this outfit."

"Grab the keys." He tilted his hips toward her. Poppy told herself he was not coming on to her no matter how much it seemed like it. "Just reach in my front pocket. I promise not to enjoy it."

She didn't think she had another choice. She reached in his pocket, searching for the keys, which had fallen to the lowest point, of course. Her skin tightened, everything becoming highly sensitized. She took a breath and dipped farther, trying to keep her fingers as far from his body as possible as she probed.

Something moved beneath her palm and she shot him a dirty look. "Really?"

"It has a mind of its own."

"I'm sure it does." Her fingers finally closed over the sharp metal ridges of the keys and pulled them free. "Why did you put them in your pocket anyway?" She held up each key one at a time until he nodded that she had the one for the front door. "Didn't you realize we would need them to get inside?"

"I had a plan," he said.

She flipped the lock open and glanced over her shoulder at him. "Oh? And what plan was that?"

"To get a quick feel."

"I should have known."

"You did, Red. And you went for it anyway."

Poppy declined to respond to that loaded statement and followed Beck up the stairs and down the hall to one of the bedrooms. She flicked on the light while Beck, now practically carrying Jamie, got him onto the bed.

The groom's eyes were half-closed, but they popped open when he landed on the bed. "Emmy?"

"Emmy's not here," Poppy said. "She's out with her girlfriends tonight, remember?"

"Right." A beatific smile appeared on Jamie's face. "She's so sweet. She has nice friends. I like them. They like me." He mumbled something else then grabbed the pillow and hugged it.

Poppy turned to Beck. He shrugged. "Beats me." He made Jamie sit up and take off his coat and shoes.

They both watched silently as Jamie yanked at the covers, twisting them into a ball. Poppy grinned. "I don't think I've ever seen Jamie drunk before."

"Never?" Beck glanced at her. "He never got you drunk in the woods and tried to take advantage of you when you were teenagers?" He helped Jamie untangle the covers.

"No." Poppy pulled the sheets back while Beck maneuvered Jamie under them. "That was you."

"And I've ruined you for every man since." His eyes darkened as he faced her, and Poppy felt the dangerous pull in her blood.

She snorted. "Hardly." But she backed off.

He took a step toward her, closing the distance between them. She didn't move. "You sure?"

"Yes." *No.* She reminded herself Jamie was only two feet away. "Is he going to be okay?"

Beck kept his eyes on her as he called over his shoulder, "You going to be okay, Jamie?"

"I'm good, really good."

"He doesn't know what he's saying," she murmured to Beck. She ducked around to check for herself, feeling safer with the drunk guy than his cousin. "Jamie? Do you need anything?"

"No." He sighed, a blissful smile on his face. "Pop-Tart?"

"Yes?" she ignored Beck's snigger. Pop-Tart was better than Red. At least Pop-Tart made sense.

"Do you think I'll be a good dad?"

"Of course you will." Jamie was probably worried since his dad had died when he was a baby, but she had no doubt he would be a great one. She smoothed his blond hair off his forehead. "When you decide to start a family, you'll be an amazing dad."

"I can't wait to be a dad." He hugged his pillow again. "Emmy's not showing yet. We haven't told anyone, but we're having a baby."

Poppy's hand stilled. Emmy was pregnant? Already? Poppy swallowed the bile rising in her throat. Now was not the time to get pukey. This explained the big rush to get married. Had Emmy gotten pregnant immediately, causing Jamie to go into good-guy mode? She knew he would. It was in his DNA. He would never walk away from his baby, even if he barely knew the mother.

"She's going to be a great mom. She's amazing. I love her." More pillow hugging.

Poppy forced her hand to move. "You'll both be great parents." She glanced at Beck, who was frowning. He didn't seem thrilled by the idea either.

"Did you know?" she asked under her breath as they headed out of the room.

"Not a clue." He flicked out the lights and put his arm around her shoulders.

"Good night," Jamie called.

But only Beck answered. Poppy was too busy

worrying. Had Emmy gotten pregnant on purpose? To trap him? And what could they do now? If Emmy was pregnant, Jamie was not going to be open to the discussion of calling off the wedding.

They were halfway down the dark hall when Poppy heard a woman's voice call out, "Beck?"

Her eyes still hadn't adjusted to the dark, but she recognized the sudden tension in his body. She stopped walking, too. He didn't respond.

"Beck?" she whispered, and sensed him turn toward her. "Aren't you going to answer?"

He leaned down so his mouth was right next to her ear. She trembled, glad he couldn't see her. "No."

He started moving her down the hallway, back toward the stairs and away from the voice. "Wasn't that your mom?" Poppy persisted.

"Yes."

"And?"

"And I don't want to explain why Jamie is drunk in one of the guest rooms."

"We should tell her." Poppy stopped halfway to the bottom of the stairs. Since Beck's arm was still around her, he stopped, too. "Someone should check in on him."

"He didn't have that much to drink," Beck assured her. "He just needs to sleep it off."

"Still, what's the harm in telling her?"

Beck started walking again, tugging her with him. "The harm," he said when they reached the ground floor, "is that she wasn't sleeping alone."

Poppy had figured out some sort of reconciliation was going on between Beck's parents. And that he didn't want to discuss it. But he should. It wasn't healthy keeping everything bottled up inside. "Do you want to talk?"

"No." He closed the front door and locked it. They stood in the shadows of the porch. There was enough light to illuminate their faces. It added an intimacy to the moment. A trickle of desire crept through her. Dangerous. But she didn't move.

"Are you upset they're getting back together?"

He shot her a look. "Wouldn't you be?"

Poppy considered his question. It wasn't something she'd had to think about. Her parents had always been happy. Of course, they had the occasional disagreement, The Wallpaper Incident of 1993 sprang to mind, but those instances were rare. "I'm not sure," she admitted. She'd never pictured her parents not being together.

"You would be if you'd lived through it."

Anger reverberated in his tone, but she suspected it masked a deeper pain. Her heart went out to him. "Beck."

"I'm fine." The tightness of his jaw said otherwise. She ran a hand along it, the bristles scratching her skin.

"Want to talk about it?"

"Nothing to talk about. They'll go on doing what they always do."

"Which is?"

"Loving each other for now." He closed his eyes. When he reopened them, they were clear but sad. "We don't need to talk about this."

Poppy thought he did. "You'll feel better letting it out, and I'm a good listener."

"Maybe later." He took her hand and led her down the stairs, their steps echoing through the crisp night. Instead of going straight toward his car, he turned left and led her across the front lawn.

She had to walk on her tiptoes so her heels didn't sink into the sod and send her sprawling. "Where are we going?"

"My place."

Her heart froze and then accelerated. "I'm not sure that's a good idea."

He slowed and studied her. "Why not?"

Why not? Because if she went into that house, she couldn't be sure what would happen. If she were being honest with herself, she knew she'd stopped being mad at him a couple days ago, but that didn't mean she was ready to take anything to the next level either. "I don't want us to do something we'll regret."

A smile curved his lips. She liked seeing it and knowing she was the one who'd put it there. "Don't think you can control yourself?"

"No, I don't think you can."

"Guilty." He caught her chin in his hand and kissed her. "Definitely guilty."

"Which is why I should go home." And not think

about that kiss, which had her wanting to throw herself into his arms.

He stopped smiling. Although they were under the cover of the trees, she could see the disappointment on his face. She could have gotten over that. But his sadness got to her.

"Stay with me."

"Beck."

"Just to talk."

"I've heard that before." From him, the night they'd slept together for the first time.

"Yeah, but this time I mean it." He stepped into her, so his chest brushed against hers. Her whole body turned into one big tingle.

"Beck." This wasn't a good idea. She didn't trust herself around him. Especially not when he was looking at her with such naked openness.

"One drink, and then I'll take you back." He caught her hand and brought it to his cheek again. "I don't want to be alone right now."

She should say no anyway. It was risky. But he'd asked for her help. How could she turn him down? She sighed. "Okay, but just one drink."

Agreeing was probably the wrong thing to do, but the relief on his face made it seem right. That and the way his hand fit into the small of her back. Large and warm and protective.

They settled in the family room, which held a comfy chocolate-colored L-shaped couch with a soft, white blanket tossed over the back, a glass coffee table and enough stereo and TV equipment to keep any techie happy.

He offered wine, she asked for coffee, even though the caffeine would probably keep her up half the night.

"Thanks." She accepted the steaming mug and took a sip. It was the way she liked it, a splash of cream, enough to change the color without making it too milky, and no sugar. He'd remembered. She was pleased, then had to remind herself he'd served it to her at brunch only a few days ago, so it wasn't as though he'd tucked the knowledge away for years in the hopes he'd get to prove his love to her one day.

"So?" she started.

"So." He sipped and studied her. They sat on the short side of the couch, which still gave them enough personal space. But only just.

"What did you mean about your parents loving each other for now?"

He shrugged. "Do you really want to talk about that?"

"It's why I'm here," she said, though that wasn't the complete truth. But she knew where it would lead if she told him her other less altruistic reasons.

He leaned back against the couch. "What do you want to know?"

"Why don't you want them back together?"

His fingers tightened around the mug and his lips pursed as he forced his hand to relax. "They don't have a good track record. They've already been divorced twice."

Poppy blinked. "From other people?"

"No, each other. If we include their other spouses, that brings the total up to seven marriages. Three for Dad and four for my mother." He put his coffee on the table. "So you can understand why I'm not too thrilled about them going for marriage number three."

"They're engaged?"

"Only a matter of time."

They were both quiet for a moment. His shoulders looked tight, his lips still pursed. "Have you talked to them?"

His laugh was more of a bark. "No. My mother wouldn't want to hear it and my dad and I don't have that kind of relationship."

There was a bleakness to his voice that made her want to gather him into her arms and soothe all his hurts away, but she didn't think he would appreciate that. So she waited and watched as the tension in his posture slowly seeped away.

"Can we talk about something else?"

"If you want." She wasn't going to force him to discuss his family situation if he didn't want to. But she was a little discouraged he wouldn't open up to her. "Would you rather talk about Jamie?"

He nodded. "Quite a surprise."

"Not a good one." Poppy's insides twisted. "Do you think that's why he's marrying her?"

Beck's sour-lemon expression sweetened a little. "Knowing Jamie?" He tilted his head. "Yes. It's exactly the kind of good-guy thing he'd believe was required."

Poppy rubbed a thumb along the heated ceramic cup. "I think so, too. I'm worried. What if she planned it all out?"

"I'm pretty sure the pregnancy wasn't planned."

"I don't think Jamie planned it. But she might have." What better way to ensure she'd have access to Jamie's money for at least the next eighteen years. "What if she wanted to trap him? They'll be tied together for life now."

"They're going to be tied together through marriage anyway." Beck picked up his coffee again and edged toward her.

Poppy aimed her knees in his general direction. "Not the same at all," she argued. "People get divorced and move on with no further contact. But a child connects you for life."

"I know."

She realized he was talking about his own life. His parents had never been able to move on from one another entirely because of him. "You shouldn't feel guilty about that," she told him.

"I don't."

But Poppy didn't think he was telling the truth.

He exhaled. "Look, Jamie's a grown-up. I don't think a baby is reason to get married, but he would. And all we can do is support him."

"I disagree. People don't have to get married because they're having a baby. Plenty of people don't."

"Jamie's not one of those people." He reached out and ran a finger down her shin.

The tingle went all the way down to her toes. "No, he's not." Which is what worried her. She was beginning to doubt there was any way to convince Jamie to postpone the wedding, even if it was in his best interests. She moved her legs back to the floor.

"Then we should focus on the positive. They seem to love each other."

"You think that's enough?"

"No, but if they do…" He plucked her coffee out of her hands, put both cups on the table and slid over so their legs touched. "I'm not saying it's what I would do."

"What would you do?"

"I don't know. I've never found myself in that situation."

He'd do the same thing. She could tell. Beck might put on a show of being distant, but he'd be as quick as Jamie to commit when he met the right woman. She let out a soft breath when he placed a hand on her knee.

"Tell me what I need to do to convince you to give in to this attraction." He leaned over, his hand wandering up her thigh. "I know it's still there between us."

"Beck." She placed a hand on his chest, wanting

to push back and gain some breathing room, and felt the thump of his heart. "I don't—"

"Poppy." He stopped her before she could try to pass off a lie as truth. "I want you. And you want me, too."

She ducked her head. His heart beat faster now. Hers sped up to match. She did want this. Badly. To fall into his arms, let him lead her upstairs to his king-size bed and crawl all over his naked body.

But what then?

She would be back in Vancouver in less than a week, and he'd be in Seattle. Chances were they wouldn't see each other again unless he started spending his holidays in Naramata. As that hadn't happened once in the last decade, she thought it unlikely.

He wouldn't call, wouldn't send her sweet emails or texts, wouldn't take her out on dates, and win over her family and buy her the perfect engagement ring and get down on one knee in front of a thousand people to ask her to spend the rest of his life with him. Whatever this was would just be over.

"Tell me you're at least considering it." He placed a finger under her chin and pressed up until she looked at him.

She was. She thought of Wynn's words that this was the perfect opportunity to get back into dating. No strings attached meant she could work out all that awkwardness on someone she wouldn't have to see again. No uncomfortable run-ins where she'd have o wonder why things hadn't worked out. No stilted conversations where they had to act as if they had never seen each other naked.

But those were just excuses she told herself. She wanted him. Beck.

Had it actually been almost a year since Evan? For the first time, she thought it had been too long. Way too long. Poppy missed the closeness of sex, of having someone sleep in the bed beside her.

A frown turned down the edges of her lips. "Depends."

His eyes narrowed. "On?" She didn't answer, just ran her hands through his hair. He reached back, stilled her fingers. "Depends on what?"

"On whether or not you're going to drop off the face of the earth afterward this time." She wasn't saying he had to pledge his undying love, but acting as if she existed was required.

"I didn't drop off the face of the earth."

There was no smirk on his face or teasing gleam in his eyes, which was good because she might have had to kill him. "It seemed like it to me."

"Poppy."

"It did." She forced a smile. "I'm sorry if you don't want to hear that, but it's the truth. You hurt me, Beck." It was as close as she was going to get to telling him about the two-week crying jag, and only going to prom because Jamie made her, and the stupid fantasy she'd had that Beck would walk through

the doors of their tackily decorated gymnasium and
ask her to dance.

"I wanted to call." The air around them got heavy.

Poppy had some trouble sucking enough into her
lungs to breathe, but managed to raise an eyebrow
at him. She refused to let him see just how much he
had hurt her. "And there were no phones in Seattle?"

"There were phones." He cupped the back of her
head. "I was stupid."

"Good answer."

"Do I get a prize?"

"No." He slowly inched toward her. She was either
unable or unwilling to stop him. She didn't want to
think about which one was the truth.

"I'll call this time."

"Not enough." Little tremors rippled through her
body. "Why didn't you call? Besides being an idiot."

"It was a bad time, Poppy."

"So tell me about it."

He sighed. "This is going to ruin the moment."

"No, Beck." She placed both hands on his chest.
"It's the only thing that's going to save it."

He brushed her hair away from her neck, his finger hovering over that sweet spot there. "My parents
separated that night." Surprise speared through her,
but she didn't say anything. "I dropped you off and
when I got home, they were arguing."

She lifted one hand and let it curve against his
cheek. "You should have called me. I would have
listened."

"I didn't want to talk about it." He pressed his face more fully into her palm. "It was hard. They were breaking up again and I was caught in the middle. I wanted a fresh start." His dark eyes stared into hers. "I should have called. But I didn't want to drag you into the mess, too."

Her heart pumped. He'd been trying to protect her. "I could have helped."

"It was better this way."

It wasn't, but she didn't explain that. In his own wrongheaded way, he'd been trying to protect her. Her heart swelled. "And now?"

"Now?" He bent his head and let his lips play along her neck.

"It seems we have the same situation." She was amazed she could form coherent thoughts, let alone sentences, when he was working her over like a master.

"No." He pulled back and his eyes were hot on hers. "This is nothing like then."

And all the reasons why she thought this was a bad idea melted away.

She shouldn't believe him. She'd been through this before and come out bruised. But she wanted to trust him. He looked so sincere, so sweet and so sad. She put both hands on his face.

His eyes got dark and he pressed toward her. "Are you sure?"

No, she wasn't sure, but she couldn't deny the building need inside her. This might be a mistake and after tonight he'd never call her again. Maybe she'd have to face the wedding knowing she'd been a complete fool. But she'd have tonight. And right now, that seemed like enough. She kissed him.

His hands threaded through her hair as he kissed her back and dragged her onto his lap. She placed her hands on his shoulders for balance. Her head swam. She was doing this. Nothing and no one could stop her. And she didn't want them to.

She sucked in a sharp breath when he ran a hand along the side of her neck. She loved his hands on her, his lips, his tongue, lighting her up from the inside.

"Is that a yes?"

She rotated her body against his, liking the low groan that rolled out of him. "I haven't decided yet."

"Good enough." He kissed her again, a long, hot kiss.

She realized he was right. This was nothing like it had been back then. This was so, so much better. She ran her hands down his back, tracing his bunching muscles, pulling at the back of his shirt.

He placed his hand under her butt, settling her more firmly against him, and stood, lifting her with him. Instinctively, she wrapped her legs around his waist. He kissed her harder and started toward the stairs. "Speak now or forever hold your peace."

She linked her hands around the back of his neck and smiled. "Now."

CHAPTER TWELVE

POPPY WRESTLED WITH the neck of her blazer as he carted her up the stairs. It was too tight and she was too hot. Everything was in the way of getting closer to Beck. She tried to loosen it, not caring if the stupid thing ripped under her yanking. She had plenty more at home. But the material was trapped between them. She pulled anyway.

Beck laughed. "No need to rush. Plenty of time for that."

She scowled at him, intending to inform him she was just a little warm and maybe her actions had nothing to do with him at all, but the words caught in her throat when she caught a glimpse of his eyes. They radiated hunger and all the delicious ways he planned to satisfy her. Maybe it had a little to do with him.

He kicked open the door to his room and lowered her onto the bed. His dark hair was mussed and silky to the touch. A sharp curl of pleasure radiated through her as he hovered over her body. "Much better." He braced his arms on either side of her and drew closer. "I've missed you, Poppy."

He'd missed her. The words whispered across her

neck, making promises she intended both of them to keep, but his lips didn't touch her. Longing poured through her. She wouldn't say it out loud, probably wouldn't have even dared to think it had he not brought it up, but she'd missed him, too. A lot.

Slowly, he eased her up, slid her arms free of her blazer and tossed it across the room. She shivered and reached out for him.

He brushed his cheek across hers, his beard bristling and tickling against her skin, before kissing her softly. It surprised her, the gentleness and how natural it seemed. Evan had always mashed his mouth against her, trying to get to the main event as quickly as possible, as if it was something to be hurried instead of savored.

Beck was all about the savoring. He nibbled the corners of her lips, while his fingers stroked the sides of her face before sliding down, along her neck, over her shoulders, along her arms to her waist. She sucked in a breath, felt him smile against her lips.

"I like this shirt." He fingered the filmy material. "But I'll like it better off."

She'd like it better off, too.

His hands moved beneath the hem, leaving goose bumps across her skin. The shirt landed with a flutter beside the blazer and she lay in front of him in only her bra. Her excellent, lacy push-up bra that created cleavage where none should exist.

A wave of shyness swept through her. What if he'd been thinking she'd filled out up top since high school? That her chest was all natural instead of thanks to the miracles of underwire and well-placed padding?

Beck captured her hands and pulled them away from her body when she tried to cover up. "No, I want to look at you."

She let him draw her arms open and look his fill. She still wished she had larger breasts, but she liked her flat stomach and the slight curve of her hips. Years ago, she'd come to the conclusion nature had a way of evening things out.

"You're more beautiful than I remember."

She blushed with both pleasure and embarrassment and tried to cover herself again.

"Not yet."

His fingers circled her wrists, preventing her from moving them. He was bigger and stronger and the fact was, she enjoyed knowing he wanted to look at her. She watched a small smile curve his lips as his eyes took in everything. His voice was gritty when he spoke again. "God, you're gorgeous. I could eat you up."

"Please do." Her breasts—small though they were—puckered under his gaze, and she sighed when he took that for the invitation it was and flicked his tongue across them through the lacy material. She arched against him, sparks of heat dancing through her.

She hadn't been fooling anyone pretending she didn't want this, didn't want him.

She wasn't usually like this, but every time her brain tried to engage, Beck licked or teased or touched and she'd be lost again. She loved every minute of it.

She ran her hands through his hair, loving how the strands flowed through her fingers. Even though it was longer than she liked, it suited him. She wrapped her fingers in it and closed her eyes as he expertly unhooked her bra and flicked his tongue across her bared nipple.

Desire shot through her. She wanted out of her clothes. And she wanted him out of his clothes, too, so his bare skin rubbed against hers for the first time in too long.

Beck was only too happy to oblige, sitting back when she began unbuttoning his shirt and helping when she slowed to kiss him. He shrugged it off. Poppy thought she heard a rip, but then he pressed against her, the light matting of hair on his chest rubbing her sensitized nipples, and she didn't care if his shirt was ruined.

Their mouths locked together, reaching and straining as they found each other's rhythms and adjusted to match. His tongue toyed with hers, playing and tracing, leaving little fires in its wake. She clutched his shoulders, wanting him closer, needing to crawl inside him so they were bonded completely and nothing could get between them. She ran her hands down his back and slid her hands into the seat of his pants.

He had a world-class butt. Round and firm. She slipped her hands beneath his underwear and smoothed her fingers over the bunched muscles. She would tear off his pants, too, in about 1.2 seconds, if he didn't get them off.

Beck's fingers fumbled at the front of her pants, popping open the button and dragging them over her thighs. His breath came faster, harder, rasping against the side of her neck when he pulled back to work her pants off. But the tight denim wasn't as ready to give in as Poppy was. It clung to her legs and caught around her left knee. He yanked and yanked again.

"What the hell did you do to these?" He looked completely flummoxed. His hair stood up where she'd run her fingers through it, a low flush on his face, his brow furrowed as he finally quit pulling on her jeans and stared at them as though by sheer will alone he could convince them to remove themselves.

Poppy started to laugh. "They're twisted." She reached down to loosen the material, but Beck brushed her hands away.

"No." He tugged, letting his hand run the length of her bared thigh. "I want to do this. If I have to chew through them, these pants are coming off now."

So Poppy lay back and let him work. Enjoying the view of his broad chest as it flexed and the delicate way he handled her, even as he fought with the tight denim. She sort of liked the idea of him removing her pants with his teeth. He grinned when she told him.

"Oh, yeah?"

She nodded and sucked in a loud breath when he finally pulled the jeans the rest of the way off and trailed his mouth along the inside of her leg.

"Much better." He tossed the jeans onto the floor and returned to licking his way up her body.

Her heart tried to pound its way out of her chest and her breath came in gasps. Why had she ever considered turning him down? She'd have missed out on all this. His beard scraping against her tender skin. Hands clutching her hips to hold her in place.

His mouth left a heated trail as he climbed back up her body. He tongued her nipple, slowly at first in long, lapping circles then faster. Caught it between his teeth and tugged. An answering pull emerged between her thighs. Her eyes drifted closed as need swamped her.

He laced his fingers through hers, dragged her arms over her head, exposing her body to him. She wrapped her legs around his hips. He still wore his pants. The material rasped against her. She wanted them off. Now.

"Beck." She barely heard her own whisper over the thundering of her pulse.

He didn't move from his careful exploration of her body. His tongue was doing magical things and she returned to letting him, writhing under the soft strokes. She should have agreed to this earlier. At the beginning of the week. She could have spent the last few days in his bed letting him worship her with his body.

She raised her knees, rubbed her toes on his legs. Only she got a light wool blend instead of skin contact. "Beck."

Her voice was loud enough to get his attention this time. He lifted his head. Even though the light was dim, only the moon shining through the window, she saw the gleam in his eyes. And he was hungry.

"Don't tell me you've changed your mind."

"No." She shook her head slowly, wondering if the same naked need shone out of her face.

He didn't give her the chance to say why she'd called his name, shucking off his pants and boxers in one smooth move and resettling between her thighs.

His hands cupped her breasts. His lips seared to hers. She moaned into his mouth. She'd waited far too long for this.

Beck responded by catching her bottom lip between his teeth and licking his way into her mouth. He tasted as good as he smelled. He hooked his thumbs under her panties, so she was naked, too. His hard body brushed against hers. There was no going back. Not that she'd want to. Her body was screaming for him. This was so right.

When he stripped off her underwear, she only wanted him inside her.

But Beck had other things in mind. His tongue dipped into the hollow of her stomach and swirled a slow, liquid pattern. His hands were on her knees, spreading them wider.

Her head fell back against the bed when at last he put his head between her thighs. His tongue traced the tiniest loops. Her fingers tangled in his hair. She would die a very happy woman.

He licked again. A very, very happy woman.

Seriously, that tongue. His was a tongue for the ages. An amazing, fantastic, should-be-bronzed-for-posterity tongue that flicked and teased, drawing out every breath of air in her lungs until she wanted to cry from the pleasure and the agony.

And then she did.

"Oh, God."

He simply smiled. She would have been embarrassed by the intimacy, but the overwhelming waves of release were too good. Her limbs wobbled, loose and relaxed, all the previous tension gone in a throb of heat.

Part of her wanted to curl up like a well-fed kitten, nestle her body against his, tuck her head into the crook of his arm and rest. But Beck rose before her, his body hard and proud. Adrenaline pulsed through her, and suddenly Poppy was wide awake and hungrier than she'd ever been in her life. She sat up and when Beck made to move on top of her she said, "No," and pushed him onto his back.

She wriggled over top of him, her body still buzzing, and lowered her head to return the favor. His skin was velvety. She kissed her way down from his neck, over his rock-hard abs, until she snuggled between his thighs. Then reached out to stroke him once.

"Christ." It was a strangled gasp from above.

Now it was her turn to taste. She drew him into her mouth, felt the length of him grow and swell as his hands tangled in her hair. His knees began to sag as she stroked and sucked. Poppy sensed the pressure building inside him, loved being the one in charge. She knew he was close when his fingers gripped tighter and his breath turned harsh. His hips began to jerk back and forth.

But he stopped her, placing pressure against her shoulders until she had to pull back. "Not this time," he said, flipping her on her back again. He rose above her, reaching into the nightstand to grab a condom. She helped him roll it on, wanting his body joined with hers.

He moved between her thighs, nudging her knees farther apart, and sank inside her. She gasped and welcomed the filling sensation. He began to move against her, a slow, steady rhythm that made her heart skip, her blood heat and her body long for more. Her nails scored his back as she pulled him closer, pressed herself against him.

This was so good, better than good. She let her head fall backward as they moved. His hands bit into her hips, anchoring her in place while he moved inside her. And then she was calling his name and breaking apart. He growled something in her ear, but she only held on until the waves subsided.

His head rested against her neck, his breath floated across her skin. She was safe and sated and pretty sure she wouldn't be moving for at least a week. So it was a good thing she already knew Beck was up to the challenge of carrying her.

"I'm glad you came to the wedding."

Poppy let her fingers twirl through the ends of Beck's hair. "Oh, yeah?"

"Yeah." He shifted his head to study her, his gaze intense and hot. "Don't say you don't feel the same way."

She did, but she didn't want to give him a big ego, so she shrugged.

He rolled and pinned her body beneath his. "Playing hard to get now?"

"I'm not playing anything." She met his gaze and her stomach clenched. "Are you?"

His expression grew serious. "No." He leaned up on one elbow, running one hand down the side of her body. She trembled under the onslaught. "There's something I should tell you."

Poppy swallowed, all that lovely languorous warmth slid away. Had anything good ever come of someone saying they needed to tell you something? Still, she tried not to jump to conclusions. Maybe he wanted to say this was the best night of his life. Or that he'd never felt like this about anyone before.

"Oh? What's that?" If he said he had a girlfriend, she would have to kill him. And she did not look good in orange.

"It's about Emmy."

Poppy frowned, trying to compute. Emmy? What did Emmy have to do with this?

"She's not a gold digger."

Poppy blinked at him. "How do you know?"

"We do business with her family." He paused. "They're rich."

"Oh." She should probably be angry he hadn't told her this immediately. That he'd tricked her into acting as if they were dating for no reason at all. But she was too satisfied to work up much of a mad. "Why didn't you tell me this right away?"

"You're not upset?"

"I'm relieved." It was a load off to know Emmy had no designs on Jamie's bank accounts and vineyard. "I'm still not crazy about the idea of them rushing into marriage, but…" She trailed off. "Why the big secret?"

"You mean, why didn't I tell you everything when the first time you saw me you pretended not to know who I was and ran away?"

"I did not run. I walked." A smile flitted around the edges of her mouth. "And you deserved to be forgotten."

"You didn't forget me." He traced a finger around her lips. "But you tried." He laughed when she tried to bite the tip. "And the reason I didn't tell you is I needed a way to make you talk to me."

"I talked to you."

"Only when I chased you down and trapped you in the hallway." He kissed her again. "I didn't want to come to this week of wedding festivities." She'd already gotten that impression, but this was the first time he'd said anything aloud. He was sharing. Her heart thumped. "When I saw you, I started to think it might not be so bad."

Her pulse skipped a beat. "And what about Grace? Was that all a lie, too?"

"No." He ran his hand through her hair, twisted his fingers in it. "My mother really does want me to settle down and get married. She loves weddings. And she definitely thought Grace and I might be a match." He stroked a finger down her neck. "But it was mostly a convenient way to get you to spend some time with me. If I'd told you that you didn't have to worry about Emmy, you never would have looked at me again."

"True."

"You would have peeked at me from the side whenever you thought I wasn't paying attention." She smothered her laugh. "I'm not sorry I didn't tell you," he said. "But I didn't want that hanging between us anymore."

"I'm glad you told me." More than glad, but she

didn't want to think about that now. Not when she had this big, yummy, delicious man in bed with her.

"How glad?" There was a devilish gleam in his eye.

"Enough." It seemed Beck had a similar idea. Her body shifted toward his, already they were moving and thinking as a unit. How delightful.

"Care to show me?"

He cupped the back of her head, tugged her closer so their bodies were tight together. She was aware of every glorious muscle.

She smiled. "I would."

CHAPTER THIRTEEN

BECK WOKE UP with the scent of lavender surrounding him and Poppy's hair tickling his nose. He was crazy about the way those long strands tangled around him, like his own personal blanket. He tugged her closer and inhaled.

While he didn't normally consider himself a cuddler, he was all too happy to wake up with Poppy in his arms. The way her body molded itself to his, so soft and pliant. She sighed against his neck and he imagined bringing her awake slowly. With his tongue.

But before he could make good on his thought, she turned and elbowed him in the ribs. "Ouch."

Her eyes opened and she blinked at him, a mixture of surprise and desire in her gaze.

"Good morning." He might not be able to wake her up slowly, but he still had a vision of how to greet the day. And like all men with an excellent plan, he moved to implement it. He pushed the covers out of the way and slowly descended down her body. She was a vision, indeed.

Poppy sighed and grabbed at his shoulders to halt his progress. "Stop that."

Not quite the greeting he'd been expecting. He paused, halfway down her sweet body, her skin smooth against his. She wasn't regretting last night, was she? Because as far as he was concerned, last night was only the beginning. They still had the rest of the week, and Beck intended to enjoy their remaining time to the fullest. He pressed a kiss to her torso.

She breathed in sharply and trembled under his touch. He continued his trail of kisses.

"Beck," she whispered. "No."

"Yes." Oh, yes. And possibly *more* and *now* and *take me, stud.* He had a personal preference for the last one.

"I'm late." She tried to push him off, but he wasn't going anywhere. He liked where he was just fine.

"It's early," he corrected. Sun filled the room, but it rose around five this time of year. He'd neglected to close the blinds last night, distracted by other, more important things. He skimmed a hand over the curve of her hip.

"It's almost six," she said. Beck knew that. He'd seen the alarm clock himself, but he didn't know what it had to do with anything. "I have to go."

"I want you to stay."

The tension left her for a fraction of a second and he thought he had her. But then she pushed herself into a sitting position, sliding her delicious body out from under his.

"You don't understand," she said, swinging her legs over the side of the bed. "I have to go."

It was a first for Beck. Not once in his life had any woman been so eager to get out of his bed. He'd become used to giving them a verbal nudge. He studied her backside as she rose and walked across the room.

"Go where?"

She didn't answer. "Where is my underwear?" She checked behind the chair where the rest of their clothing had ended up last night. Beck spotted something lacy sticking out from beneath the dresser but didn't mention it.

"Go where?" he repeated, tossing the covers off and climbing out to stand beside her, pleased when she glanced up and stopped hunting. Much better. He circled his arms around her waist and began dragging her back to the bed.

"Beck."

"Yes." He loved the sensitive spot below her ear.

She moaned when he licked it, then pulled away again. "I *have* to go." She spotted the underwear and snagged them from under the dresser. "I have plans this morning."

Irritation flickered in Beck's gut. What did she have to do that was so all-fired important she couldn't spend a leisurely morning in bed with him? "Like what?"

"I have a golf date with my dad at eight." She glanced at the clock on the bedside table. "I have to shower and change and—"

"You can shower here."

"You never quit, do you?" Her expression made it clear she'd read the intentions in his offer.

Beck didn't see what was so wrong with a little morning shower sex. It was good for the soul.

Still talking, she slipped into her pink jeans—he had good memories of those jeans. "If we leave now, they might not realize I didn't come home last night. I'll sneak in and—"

His eyebrows shot up. "Embarrassed?" He didn't care for that. Not one bit.

"Of course not." She ran her fingers through her hair. "But I don't particularly want to answer a lot of nosy questions from my mother. If you'd like to do so in my place, you're welcome to come along and explain why I'm walking in wearing the same outfit as last night."

And why her skin glowed. A glow he'd put there. It was a pleasing thought. Beck leaned back against the headboard and folded his arms behind his head.

"Get up," she told him, not at all impressed by his show of manly pride. His pants landed on the bed beside him. "You have to drive me."

He tried to convince her they had a little more time, but Poppy remained adamant. And in under ten minutes, he found himself dressed, behind the wheel of his car, driving her back to her parents' house.

"What are you doing tonight?" he asked as he pulled into the driveway.

"Spending time with the family."

He parked the vehicle and leaned across the console. "So, I'll pick you up after. What time should I be here?"

Last night was one of the best times Beck had had in recent memory. And not just because of the sex. Because of Poppy. She made him happy.

She wasn't the kind of woman Beck usually went for. She was a good girl from a nice family. Not that he picked up streetwalkers or broken birds, but he tended toward women who were familiar with the less pleasant side of life, who knew what they were getting into when they dated him. A couple weeks of expensive dinners and hot sex. Well, he and Poppy had the last part down.

It was too bad he only had a few more days with her, but he didn't intend to waste them.

She met his lips head-on, a soft sigh escaping as he showed her what she'd be missing by insisting on leaving his bed so early. "Is this your idea of asking me out on a date?"

"I'm not asking." He kissed her again. "I'm telling you." Some dessert, maybe a walk by the lake and breakfast in bed. He brushed a thumb along her cheek. "You don't have plans tomorrow morning, do you?"

"No."

"You do now."

He left Poppy, pretty pleased with himself and life in general.

The drive back was peaceful. A few runners and

cyclists were out, but most people were still in bed getting a little more shut-eye.

The main house was silent, staring with empty eyes. He slipped past and headed down the path to his own enclave of privacy. He'd have to go over there later, check in on Jamie, but not yet. Jamie likely needed a bit of a lie-in and Beck didn't want to make small talk with his parents while he waited for his cousin to get up.

The day was going to be another gorgeous one. So rather than spend any more of it inside, Beck grabbed a cup of coffee and his laptop and headed out to the porch to work.

He had a couple emails from his lawyer and real estate agent regarding the purchase of the hotel, but their concerns were minor and in the vein of making certain the contract of sale was completed soon. Beck answered what he needed to and emailed the company they'd hired to do the renovations.

The hotel was a grande dame who'd been allowed to go to seed. But her bones were great and he intended to return her to her former glory. Fortunately, most of the work was surface only and he was confident they'd be open for business by the end of October. That would give them three months. Even figuring in issues, because issues cropped up on even the smoothest projects, they should make their deadline.

He put the laptop on the slatted table between the chairs and stretched out his legs. Although the sun beat down, the trees created a canopy, leaving a dappled trail of light.

He was half asleep when the sound of someone on the front steps broke into his respite. He pictured Poppy wearing only those pink pants and returning for that shower. But when he turned his head, he found his mother smiling at him instead.

He sighed. Her regularly scheduled visit.

"Good morning." She looked crisp and clean, wearing a flowered skirt and white blouse, her hair brushed into its usual tidy bob.

"Morning." Beck had changed into jeans and an old white T-shirt he found in the dresser after dropping Poppy off.

His mother poked at the hole in the sleeve. "Really? You couldn't find a shirt that wasn't motheaten."

"It was clean." He was careful not to appear too welcoming, recalling the parental love nest he'd stumbled upon last night. The good feelings soaking through his body started to dry up. Of the many things he didn't want to think about, his parents getting it on topped the list.

"I see Jamie enjoyed himself last night."

"He did."

"Was that you I heard getting him settled?"

Beck nodded. "I thought he'd be more comfortable here than with Emmy."

"That was thoughtful." She sat in the empty chair

beside him. "Does this mean you're coming around to your cousin's getting married?"

"I'm around," he told her. It was true. He might not be searching for marriage personally, but he thought Jamie and Emmy were doing the right thing. Especially in light of the baby bomb Jamie had dropped last night.

"Good." Her smile, so sure and vibrant, faltered. Only a fraction, but Beck picked up on it. She was nervous. "Beck, I'd like to talk to you about what's happening with your father and me." Her hand fluttered to her bob and back down.

He exhaled. "I know. You're getting married."

"Well." Her hand fluttered again before settling in her lap. "Yes. He's asked me and I've accepted."

All his old sourness rose up the back of his throat, looking for an outlet. He forced it back. "Congratulations."

She didn't smile. "Beck, I know this has been difficult for you."

He'd known it was happening. Everyone, even people who didn't know them, knew it was happening. But knowing it logically and seeing it in action were two different things. "This is your life. You two can do whatever you want."

He wanted to ask what, if anything, had changed, to demand they examine their reasons for doing this. Because, as far as he could tell, they were the same as they'd always been and this was simply the latest chapter of their continuing saga.

He did not understand them. They dated, claimed they were in love, got married, acted as though they were utterly blissful and then divorced. After some time apart, usually years and often with marriages to other people, they'd find each other again and the cycle would repeat like a sick version of *Groundhog Day*. Beck was unclear how or why the ecstasy turned to agony, but the pattern had remained the same for as long as he could remember. Thankfully, he was old enough now not to be roped into their drama. He pressed his lips together.

"Beck." She reached a hand out to touch his. "I understand how you're feeling."

He was pretty sure she didn't. She'd never had to choose where to spend holidays so no one got bent out of shape. She hadn't grown up not knowing if this time things would last. And she'd never been expected to pick up the pieces when it didn't.

"We love each other."

"I'm sure you do." It didn't seem like love to him. Her hand remained on his. He thought about shaking it off, but figured he would come off as surly and undermine the point he wanted to make: his parents were entitled to do whatever they wanted, but they couldn't force him to be a part of it. "So again, congratulations."

Some more of the bitterness leaked through then, but he couldn't help it. Marriage wasn't something a person should dive into because it seemed fun. There were vows and promises that should be honored.

"Beck." Her fingers tightened, squeezing his wrist. "I realize you might have some concerns about the relationship your father and I have had."

Some concerns? He'd have laughed if his throat hadn't closed up, making it difficult to even breathe.

"It hasn't been typical." Try messed up. Completely and utterly messed up. "But we both want to try again and we hope you'll be happy for us."

Beck stared at her. He hoped she wasn't going to ask him to walk her down the aisle and give her away. He'd be expected to attend the wedding and he would, but he drew the line at participating in the farce of it all.

He crossed his arms over his chest. "If you're happy, does it matter what I think?"

Hurt flashed in her eyes before she masked it with another smile and carefully folded her hands in her lap. "Of course it matters, Beck. We're a family."

He raised an eyebrow. He didn't have a lot of first-hand experience, but he understood families stayed together through bad times as well as good. They certainly didn't create tales of lust and adultery and end marriages without proof.

He didn't remember much about their first divorce, he'd only been five. One day his father had been living in the house, the next day not. Mostly he recalled his father taking him to the park and buying him greasy hamburgers and his mother crying in her bedroom with the door closed.

When he was six, his father got remarried to his

secretary. She'd smelled like cinnamon and always gave him those hot candy hearts, which he'd thrown away when she wasn't looking. His mother had gotten remarried the following year. Both relationships had lasted less than a year and when Beck was eight his parents reconciled and retied the knot while they were on vacation in Hawaii.

He'd liked that wedding. The sensation of the sand beneath his feet, the ocean breeze blowing across his face, his tiny chest puffed out in pride and hope while he stood beside his father. Because they were together again, a family, the way they should be.

Bliss lasted ten years until that awful night here when everything fell apart. His mother explaining in a tight voice that she wouldn't put up with his cheating and his father arguing there was no one else.

"We've both changed, Beck. Things are different."

He wasn't sure about that. The years after their second divorce had been hard on him. His mother had called him regularly, wanting his support and a shoulder to cry on. He'd wanted nothing to do with her.

His father remained unwavering. He hadn't cheated, but his mother was equally sure he was lying and proceeded with the divorce. And then she'd wanted to cry about how things hadn't worked out. As if she hadn't been the one to tear the family apart.

"Are they?" He leaned his head against the chair back and watched her from beneath half-closed eyes.

"Yes."

His father had never gotten over her. It was one of the reasons Beck had begun to distance himself from the family. Throughout university, family dinners and holidays had been less than palatable. Whenever Beck spent time with his father, he'd ask how his mother was. But the year he graduated, the same year he'd started working for the family company and seeing his father every day at the office, his mother had gotten married again.

His father had been crushed. He'd tried to hide his pain behind a jovial expression and acted as if it didn't hurt to hear that his ex had moved on, but Beck knew better. It had become unbearable having his father drop by his office looking for all the details of the latest family sit-down. So Beck had stopped going.

And life had gotten easier.

He'd become used to the distance and even grown to appreciate it. Christmas in the city at a beautiful restaurant with his latest fling was a marked improvement over the awkward turkey dinner conversation at his mother's home.

"I hope you're right."

"Beck." She reached over to hold his hand, but he refused to allow her it, keeping his hands tucked under his arms. She rested her hand on his biceps instead. "I know this hasn't always been easy for you. I'm not perfect, and your father and I have both made mistakes."

"Yes, you have."

"I love you. What can I do to make things better?"

Like he was a little boy with a scraped knee. Back then, she'd swabbed on stinging antiseptic and blown on the injury until it didn't hurt anymore, then sent him off with a bandage and a kiss. But this pain wasn't so easily negated and he wasn't six anymore.

"You can't do anything."

"I want us to be close again."

He shrugged. That wasn't going to happen, but he didn't want to get into an argument with her. He'd do what he always did. She'd call or email, and he'd respond, explaining he was busy or it wasn't a good time but he'd get back to her later. And then he wouldn't.

"I hoped this would bring us closer together." She leaned back in the chair. "It's not just a fresh start for your father and me. It's a fresh start for all of us."

He wanted to believe her. He was desperate to believe her. But having his family cut off at the knees twice before made that innocent naiveté impossible.

"I don't expect our relationship to get better right away."

He found his voice. "It can't."

She blinked. "It can, Beck. *If* that's what you want."

"And if it's not?"

She clasped her hands in her lap, gripping so hard her knuckles turned white. "I'll still do my best to change your mind." She pasted on a cheerful smile that didn't reach her eyes.

He'd hurt her. Good. Why should he be the only one affected by this? And then he felt guilty. This was why he tried to keep his distance from his family. Getting involved meant getting mixed up in their needs and emotions, which always led to pain. At least, it always had in the past. He didn't understand how this time would be any different.

"I don't want to change my mind," he said. "I'm fine with how things are."

"Beck."

"You can't come here and dump this on me and expect everything to be okay." His breathing grew raspy and he clutched his coffee cup hard enough to break the handle. He exhaled, loosening his grip. "I don't want to talk about this."

"Do you think we—"

But whatever she'd been about to say was abruptly cut off by the sound of someone or something crashing through the woods. Though the area was well developed, they were still in bear territory. The beasts had been known to lumber into vineyards and eat up all the grapes or stumble into a backyard, prowling for food. They both rose immediately. Beck pushed her behind him. He might be angry, but she was still his mother.

"Beck, what is—"

"Get in the house."

And he'd be right behind her. He was strong and not afraid of much, but he wasn't about to go toe-to-toe with a bear. Even if it was only a cub, because cubs had mamas, and they didn't trust anyone around their babies.

His mother didn't question him. They both turned, leaving the coffee and laptop on the porch.

He could afford to buy new ones. He couldn't replace his life. Or his mother's.

But it was Jamie who came tearing up the path instead of the growling animal Beck expected. He paused and put his hand out to stop his mother.

She spun to see what the problem was. "Jamie?" Her face changed from pinched to smooth in an instant.

His cousin's usually tidy hair stood on end and his eyes were still bloodshot from his overindulgence last night. He looked like hell. Beck grinned. The bachelor party had been a hit.

"Need a little hair of the dog?" He had tomato juice in his fridge and vodka.

"What?" Jamie turned a wild-eyed gaze on him. "No, no. Thank God, you're here."

But he wasn't looking at Beck anymore, he was looking at Victoria. Beck tried not to take it as an insult.

Victoria stepped out from behind Beck. "Jamie. What's the matter? What happened?"

"Help, I need help."

Beck swallowed and clasped his hands behind his back. Of course, Jamie wouldn't ask him. Hadn't that been his goal the last ten years? To make sure the family didn't turn to him with their needs? But still. He ran a multimillion-dollar company. He had skills. He could help.

"It's Emmy," Jamie said. "Something about her dress. I'm not sure. She was crying." He ran a hand through his hair, making it even messier. "I think she said she wants to postpone the wedding." His face crumpled at that.

"Oh, Jamie." Victoria had moved down the steps before Beck managed a blink. With a soothing murmur she gathered Jamie into her arms, already in full romantic-crisis mode. She was, after all, an expert. "What's wrong with the dress?"

Jamie hugged her back while Beck stood awkwardly on the porch. He didn't want to be in the hug, but an offer of inclusion would have been nice.

Finally, Jamie pulled himself together and explained. "I think it's too short. It was hard to understand her through the crying." His eyes got a dangerously wet sheen to them. "What if she calls the wedding off?"

"She won't call it off," Victoria assured him, giving Jamie another supportive hug. "Will she, Beck?"

"No." Beck had no idea, but it seemed the right thing to say because when Jamie turned to him the awful wetness was gone, which made Beck feel a little better. Maybe he wasn't giving hugs, but he still had support to lend.

"We'll figure this out, Jamie. Don't worry." Victoria gave her nephew a brisk rub. "I think I should talk to her." She held out her hand for Jamie's phone.

Beck was surprised when his cousin handed it over without an argument. Beck would have told his mother he was fully capable of handling his own problems and this was none of her concern. Of course, Beck wouldn't have come running up the path and shared the problem with his mother in the first place. He moved down the steps so he could listen in on the phone conversation.

"Emmy? Hello, dear. It's Victoria." Beck heard Emmy's wails through the receiver while Victoria clucked sympathetically. "I understand. I don't blame you for being upset. But we'll fix everything. I don't want you to worry." She listened some more. "I want you to rest up. You've got a big weekend, so you leave this to me. I'll make sure you have a beautiful dress." She smiled. "Of course, I will. We're family now, Emmy, and that's what family does for each other."

After another minute of soothing and comforting, Victoria hung up and handed the phone back to Jamie.

"Well?" Jamie watched her with a hopeful expression. Beck shook his head. Had Jamie not heard the wailing?

"The dress is four inches too short." She looked back and forth between the two of them. "It can't be salvaged. We'll need to find a new one."

"But what—"

"Jamie, you come with me. You're a fright. You'll have some coffee and a shower and you'll feel better."

Beck thought Jamie required more than some coffee and a quick dunk under the water. The tequila fumes were obvious from where he stood. But Jamie looked so relieved to have someone taking over, Beck couldn't bring himself to make the cheap joke.

"Beck?" his mother called. He snapped to attention. He wasn't used to his mother like this. "I'd like you to speak with Poppy. I'm sure she's got some contacts. Maybe she can help with the dresses."

"Good idea." Actually, he thought it was an excellent idea. He was rewarded with a smile from his mother.

"You'll call to update us?"

"Yes." He smiled back. He would have done it for Jamie anyway, even if it meant spending the rest of his morning with an old lady who smelled like peppermints, but the fact it was Poppy he'd be hanging out with sent a roll of pleasure through him. Now he didn't have to wait until tonight to see her. Getting him out of the line of fire of his mother's wedding conversation was pretty great, too.

"Thank you." Jamie shook his hand. Hard. "Thank you." He blinked rapidly and Beck pretended to find the treetops particularly interesting while Jamie got his emotions under control. "I'll see you later?"

Beck nodded. "I'll call you when everything is sorted." He started back toward the guesthouse and assumed they were heading to the main house, when he heard his mother call his name.

"Yes?" He turned. Jamie had disappeared through the trees and it was just the two of them again.

"I'm proud of you," she said. He shrugged, but that didn't slow her. "I know you're upset with me, but you put that aside for Jamie."

"It's not Jamie's fault I'm upset," Beck pointed out.

"I'm proud of you," she repeated and gave him a quick hug.

He let her. It felt good.

CHAPTER FOURTEEN

POPPY PULLED HER eight iron out of her golf bag on the back of the cart and eyed her lie. It was about ninety yards to the pin, and straight. No sand traps or water hazards in the way.

The course was quiet today, unusual for a sunny June morning, but Poppy was grateful. Often, they'd be paired up with another twosome to play, and she didn't relish making small talk with strangers. She preferred the comfortable silence of being with her dad, bonding over putts and drives, and letting her mind flicker—as it did frequently—to Beck.

She lined up over her shot, loosening her grip on the club slightly, and swung. The ball made a sweet thunking sound when she connected and flew straight down the fairway, landing on the edge of the green.

"Nice shot," her father praised as she slid the club back into her bag and climbed onto the golf cart. In the city, she often walked the course, but it was too hot today. She was already tired and she didn't need to add sunstroke to the mix.

When Beck had dropped her off, she'd been certain her mother was tucked behind a curtain, watching as she made her way up the front walk and onto the porch. She'd braced herself for the pointed comment when she opened the front door, but she'd been met with silence. And not the kind of silence indicating people lurked in hiding, waiting for the opportunity to jump out and ambush her, but the kind of peaceful silence that told her no one was stirring.

She'd actually made it all the way upstairs without alerting anyone. She'd taken a shower and changed into a plaid skirt and collared golf top in pale blue, tying her hair into a low ponytail. By the time she headed back downstairs, ready for her golf date, she'd had the audacity to think she might have gotten away with it.

Until her mother turned from the coffeepot, and after asking if she'd like a cup, said, "Did you have a good time last night?"

From another mother, the question would just be a curiosity, a polite inquiry into her daughter's life. Rose Sullivan was not that mother. And Wynn, sitting at the table, his hands wrapped around his mug while he snickered, hadn't helped.

Poppy had been nothing short of exulted when her father had wandered down a minute later and said they needed to go if they wanted to make their tee time. Her father didn't ask about the intimate details of her life. He probably didn't even listen when her mother tried to share them. She appreciated his stoicism.

She wasn't sure what was going on with Beck,

what her suddenly changed feelings meant, but she knew she didn't want to talk about things. Not yet.

Though her family didn't usually keep their privacies—they unloaded even the most banal minutiae onto each other and liked it—Poppy sensed this was different.

Her father parked the cart to the side of the fairway and they both climbed out. Her father's shot had landed only a few feet short of the pin, so he held back while she lined up. She'd never be able to get her ball into the hole in one shot, so she simply aimed to get closer.

There was nothing worse than trying for the glory putt, overshooting and ending up with an even worse shot on the other side. And this green sloped down, so she had to be careful. She gripped her putter over top of the ball and swung, an easy pendulum motion her dad had taught her when she first learned the game.

The ball rolled toward the hole, past her father's and stopped on target, about six inches from the lip of the cup.

She smiled, pleased with her shot and herself as she walked over and tapped her ball in. Her father made par on his shot. "Show-off," she said, which earned a smile.

Poppy closed her eyes and lifted her face to the warmth as her father navigated them to the next tee box. Since her work schedule was fairly busy over the next couple months—it was something of a miracle she and Wynn had both been able to get away this week—there was a good chance this would be her only chance to make hay while the sun shone. Or in her case, make tan.

A little color would be welcome. She couldn't manage much more than a light beige with her fair skin that had a tendency to freckle and burn, but it took the edge off her glow-in-the-dark paleness.

They finished the round in companionable silence. Her father parked the golf cart outside the pro shop and went inside to return the keys while she stayed with the bags. Even the shade was hot, but it might be the only sun she got this summer, so she tried to appreciate it even though her shirt was stuck to her back.

She should go for a dip in her parents' pool when she got back to the house, float around, cool off and figure out what seeing Beck tonight meant.

She almost thought she'd conjured up his voice when she heard her name.

"Poppy."

Her eyes sprang open. That wasn't her imagination. She turned toward the source and saw Beck coming over the rise from the parking lot.

A long, excited tickle rose up her chest. She didn't know why he was here or who he was with, but she was glad. "Hello." She tried to play it cool. He reached her side and pulled her into a hug followed by a kiss. It was an exceptionally nice greeting.

"You're distracting me again."

"How am I distracting you?" He still had his arms wrapped around her waist, which were awfully distracting indeed. "I'm not wearing the pink jeans."

"You don't need the jeans to distract me." He pressed another kiss on her. "But that's not why I'm here."

"I figured that." She tried not to let her disappointment show. It was silly, but she liked the idea that he hadn't been able to stop thinking about her this morning and had been sidetracked so completely he'd had no choice but to hunt her down immediately. "So why are you here? Golfing?"

She didn't glimpse anyone with him or a set of clubs, but he might have left them in the parking lot, which wasn't visible from the pro shop. She liked thinking even if he'd had another reason for showing up at the course, he'd made a point to come and find her.

"I need your help. Actually, Jamie and Emmy need your help. Something happened to her dress and she's in a panic."

"What happened?" The dress was an integral part of any bride's dream wedding and the crises that surrounded them were legendary. She could only imagine how Emmy was doing.

The last wedding Poppy had ever organized had involved a dress dilemma. After being delayed and delayed, the owner of the bridal shop had finally admitted she was bankrupt and had never ordered the dress. Poppy had managed to pull off finding another gown—luckily the bride had been sample size—but it had been the final straw in her decision to stop planning weddings. The money wasn't worth the headache or the worry of being responsible for the big day someone had been dreaming of since they were seven.

"It's too short."

Poppy frowned. Not ideal. Better if the gown were too long, but length could be added by letting down the hem. Most dressmakers left some wiggle room for last-minute alterations. "Did you talk to Jamie's mom?" Georgia Cartwright was an excellent quilter and could be counted on to fix any small tailoring issue.

"She looked and said she can't fix it. According to my mother, it's about four inches too short."

Poppy stared at him. "You're kidding."

"No. And now Emmy wants to postpone the wedding until she can get a dress that fits, and Jamie is in an uproar. Can you help?"

Poppy paused. She still had plenty of wedding contacts in Vancouver, including Missy, who owned a bridal shop. Although they didn't do regular business together anymore, they still got together every couple months.

She briefly considered saying no. Postponing the wedding would give Jamie the chance to think about whether or not this was something he was ready for. But Poppy knew there was no point. Everything

Jamie had said and done not only indicated he was ready, but also that he was willing and eager.

How could she say no? Besides, this life was Jamie's and as a friend, she needed to support him. Maybe Jamie and Emmy were meant to be together and would have a long and happy life full of laughter and babies.

"Of course, I can help." She pulled her cell out of her golf bag. She'd turned it off during their game and it buzzed to life when she powered it on. She ignored the emails and texts that had come in and scrolled through her phone book until she found Missy's name.

BECK CALLED HIS mother to tell her Poppy had sorted everything out and would be in touch. She told him she was proud of him again. He didn't know what to say to that, so he didn't say anything.

His mother had never been shy with her praise, but he didn't usually give her a chance to shower it upon him. But he kind of liked it, which was unexpected. He'd spent so long focusing on keeping himself a separate entity, he'd forgotten how good it was to be part of a group.

After updating his mother, he'd happily accepted the lunch invitation to join Poppy and her father. Clearly, her entire family was close. Poppy and her dad had a comfortable teasing relationship Beck envied. Although he'd seen his father every workday over the past few years until he'd recently stepped back from the company, they'd never had this casual closeness. He wasn't sure whose fault that was, or if it was no one's. The Lefebvres might not be built for that.

"You okay?" Poppy leaned over to whisper in his ear.

They were on their way back to the car without her dad. A group of Bob's friends had shown up as they were settling the bill and he'd decided to stay and have a beer with them. Beck was in charge of taking Poppy back, which was a task he was up to. He'd been trying to think of a way to make it happen naturally the entire lunch.

"I'm fine."

She slipped a hand into his, but didn't say anything.

"My parents are getting remarried."

"Ah." The sun beat down on them, causing drops of sweat to bead around his hairline. Poppy looked cool and fresh. He wanted to sink into her and bury his head in the curve of her neck until he felt better. He settled for squeezing her hand.

"I'm not thrilled."

She squeezed back. "I got that."

"They're just…" He trailed off. He'd been trying not to think about it. "They're making a mistake."

"Maybe they're not." Her voice was soft but sure. He looked at her. "It's been a long time, Beck. They might love each other."

"They've done this before." Twice, in fact.

"And maybe this time is different." They stopped at his car. Beck hit the button to unlock the doors, but neither of them moved. "Give them a chance."

"I don't want to." He sounded petulant, like a crabby three-year-old who needed a nap. He felt like one, too.

Poppy rose onto her tiptoes and kissed him on the mouth. "You should anyway."

"I'll think about it." He bent down and kissed her more thoroughly. None of this hunt-and-peck stuff for him. She wasn't getting off that lightly. *Especially not if she wanted him to give his parents' relationship a chance.*

Since that thought put a damper on the whole kissing-her aspect, he shoved it away. He didn't want his parents tainting what the two of them had, even if their little tryst did have a built-in end date. Her hands slid up his back and tangled in his hair, curling the ends around her fingers.

He groaned into her mouth. He loved when she played with his hair. She responded by pressing up against him more tightly. If it got any hotter they might burst into flames in the parking lot.

"It's hot," she murmured against his mouth.

His temperature spiked. "So hot." She was smoking, scorching. He couldn't think of any more adjectives, and he didn't want to. He wanted to stay here, kissing Poppy and not thinking about anything.

"No." She pulled back a little. "It's hot. I'm going to burn."

He looked down. Her shoulders were a little pink. "Ready to accept the redhead banner yet?"

She poked him in the chest. "Auburns can burn, too."

"I like redheads." He nipped the little spot under her ear, gratified when she shivered against him. "They're sexy."

"That's fine. My hair is still not red."

He laughed. "Come on, Red. Let's get you out of the sun before you turn into a flamingo."

"A flamingo?" She laughed and got into the car when he opened the door. "All the pink things in the world and you come up with a flamingo?"

"What should I have said?" He started the car, enjoying the low purr of the engine. He revved the gas once before putting it into gear. "Hello Kitty?"

"No, but surely I'm more attractive than a flamingo. Also, I'm not burned yet."

"So you're up for a swim at my place?"

She sent him a coy glance—she was thinking about it. "I don't have my suit with me."

"So?"

"So I am not skinny-dipping in your parents' pool."

"We'll stop and get your suit." He placed a hand on her thigh, running his fingers up and down the creamy smoothness. "My vote is for a bikini. Preferably a pink one."

"Sorry to break the news, but you don't get a vote. Also, my bikini is not pink."

"Blue? Yellow? Green? I'm an equal-opportunity kind of guy when it comes to bikinis."

"How unusual. Most men are very particular about the hue of a woman's swimsuit. And really, anything in spandex."

"I'm the easygoing type." He slid his hand a little higher. "You're the one who said you needed a swimsuit."

She laughed but didn't move his hand. "Appealing as getting caught in the nude by your mom is, I can't." She sounded disappointed, which pleased him. "I need to get back. Spend some time with my mother."

He was disappointed, too. Now that he had the image of Poppy in a string bikini swimming through his mind, it wouldn't go away. "You sure?"

He liked that she considered it. Liked it a lot. Her answer, he wasn't such a fan of.

"Yes. She misses me. I don't get back often, only a few times a year, so she likes to jam in as much togetherness as she can."

There was a funny pinch in his chest. She thought a few times a year wasn't often? "But I'll still see you later?"

"Sure." She reached out to run a finger along his jaw. "Or…what have you got planned this afternoon?"

Besides hide out from his family? Even though the wedding-dress drama was over, the big house would still be a busy place. According to Jamie, the whole group had gotten together for lunch and wanted him to join them. He could try to seek shelter at the guesthouse, but it would be a temporary solution. Someone would notice his car in the driveway and come down to drag him up.

"Not much." He should probably drive into town and set up at a coffee shop. He didn't have his laptop, but his phone would allow him to check his email and read the paper.

"Did you want to hang out with me?" She turned her head to face him, her red hair fanning out on the seat. The sun caught in the bright strands. "You're welcome to join us."

"Yes." He didn't have to think long. The choice between dealing with his family and Poppy's was a no-brainer. He navigated the car around one of the twisty corners, edging over when a car coming in the opposite direction veered slightly into his lane. "Sounds great."

"Really?" He glanced over and found her smiling. Did she honestly think he would turn down the chance to spend time with her?

"Yes, really. Sounds like fun." He placed his hand back on her leg after his nifty driving maneuver, letting it drift higher.

"Okay." She crossed her legs, trapping his hand between them. "So you're up for the challenge?"

"I'm up for something."

She laughed. "I mean my family. They can kind of be a lot to take."

He thought about her family. He didn't know them well, but from what he'd seen he liked them. They were cheerful and noisy and involved in each other's business. Pretty much the opposite of his own.

"I can take it," he assured her. Was looking forward to it, he realized with a little bullet of shock. He didn't spend time with families. Not his own or others. He'd like to observe how a functional, happy one worked.

"Don't say I didn't warn you."

He insisted on stopping in at a little grocery store that sold homemade pies when Poppy mentioned they were her mother's favorites. He thought the gesture might win him an invitation to stay through dinner.

He was right.

"Oh, Beck. These are my favorites. How did you know?" Rose's smile was as open and affectionate as her daughter's.

"I told him, Mom," Poppy said. "Did you think he was psychic?"

Rose laughed and put the pies off to the side so they wouldn't get damaged. Or eaten. "It was very thoughtful, Beck. I hope this means you'll stay for dinner."

"I'd love to," Beck answered. Poppy smiled at him, a smile that did something to his insides. He'd have grabbed her and kissed the smile right off her face if her mother hadn't been watching.

"We're doing casual. Bob will barbecue and I'll

make sides. Nothing fancy." Rose had a mound of vegetables on the counter beside a wooden cutting board. "Why don't you two go and sit out back while I finish." She shooed away their offers to help, insisting she would be quicker on her own but promising them cleanup duty.

"You won't have to do that," Poppy said as she led Beck out the backdoor of the kitchen and onto a wide stone patio. "She meant me."

"I don't mind helping." Okay, he hadn't done a whole lot of cleaning up in his life. By the time he'd been old enough to help around the house, the family company was well in the black and they had a service come in twice a week. He had a similar setup in his penthouse condo in Seattle now.

The Sullivans' property wasn't as large as the one Beck's family held down by the lake, or Jamie's up on the bluff, but it was big compared to city living. A small vineyard ran down the slope away from the house. Poppy said her dad used the grapes to make his own private reserve. "You'll know he likes you if he brings out a bottle. He treats that stuff like gold."

"I'll be sure to be on my best behavior."

She sent him a teasing look. "Not too good. I might not recognize you."

Between the grapevines and the house was an inground pool surrounded by a glass wall, and an expansive lawn that rolled around the side of the house. As Beck took it all in, a tiny redheaded girl came tearing around the corner, Wynn hot on her tail. The pair of them had their arms out to their sides and Wynn made loud zooming noises while she screamed in delight.

Her screams increased in pitch and volume when she spotted them. "Auntie Pop-pop!" She flung her little body at Poppy's legs, almost knocking her down, and then did the same to Beck. "Hi."

He wasn't used to being around kids, but he said hello.

"This noisy beast is my niece, Holly. She takes after her mother." Poppy reached out to tickle her niece, who screamed, giggled and ran behind Beck's legs.

Beck was afraid to move in case he stepped on her and crushed her. But he shifted quickly when Holly tried to wedge her head between his thighs to see what her aunt was doing. "Whoa." He put a hand on her head to hold her in place while he stepped around.

Clearly used to this type of attention from the adults in her life, Holly turned her face up to him, her blue eyes shining with happiness, and began a garbled explanation of planes and Wynn.

"We were flying," Wynn clarified as he walked over. Despite the fact he'd been running in the hot sun, his white pants and matching blazer looked as if he'd just stepped out of an air-conditioned office.

Holly tugged on Beck's pant leg, demanding his attention, and continued her cheerful account. It seemed her dad had taken her to watch the planes land and now she wanted to *be* a plane.

"I can fly planes," Beck told her, pleased when her tiny face lit up. She clambered into his lap when he sat down on one of the loungers and commanded he tell her more.

"Holly," Poppy chided. "You don't tell people what to do, you ask politely." She tried to pull Holly off him, but Beck shook his head he didn't mind.

"Planes," Holly said. "I like planes."

"Me, too." He tried not to bore her with details of plane dimensions or the equipment a pilot relied on if visibility was bad, instead focusing on how much fun it was in the air, free of constraints, where it was only him and the sky.

He glanced over at Poppy, who smiled at them, and felt a tug in his chest.

CHAPTER FIFTEEN

"Wow."

Poppy blinked when Wynn spoke, suddenly aware she'd been watching Beck and her niece far too closely. She seriously considered checking her chin for drool, but that would be admitting she'd been gawking. She went for polite interest instead. "Yes?"

"Don't 'yes' me." Wynn rolled his eyes and sent her an I-know-you-too-well-to-be-fooled-by-your-pathetic-attempt-at-nonchalance look. "I see you."

"I'm not hiding." She hadn't even changed out of her golf clothes yet.

"So we're playing it this way, are we?"

She nodded. "Though I feel it's my duty to tell you I'm not playing anything."

"No need to tell me. It's plenty obvious." Wynn's eyes saw far too deep into hers and she dropped her gaze, pulse pumping. "What are their names?"

"Whose names?" Poppy lifted her ponytail off the back of her neck and fanned.

"The hypothetical children you're going to have with him."

Poppy fanned faster and forced a laugh. "I have

no idea." But she totally did. Oliver for a boy and
Eloise for a girl.

"Right."

She hadn't fooled Wynn. Not even a little. But she
shrugged anyway. It would be worse to own up to
it, because he'd tell her family everything and she'd
never hear the end of it. Though there was a chance
that would happen anyway.

Fortunately, whatever other bit of wisdom Wynn
was poised to share was cut short when her mother
came out the backdoor carrying a massive tray with
a full pitcher of lemonade and glasses.

"Let me help." Beck was already out of the
lounger, careful to put Holly down safely, and res-
cuing the laden tray before it smashed all over the
patio.

"Thank you, Beck." Rose beamed at him. Poppy
wondered if Beck was aware how many points he
was scoring. Judging from the pleased curve of his
lips? Yes.

They sat together under the shaded back. Her dad
had built a pergola years ago and her mother had
grown vines up and over it, creating a scented overhead garden. It was nice to be back there now, sipping lemonade and watching Holly race around.

Her niece had convinced Beck to join her plane
games and the two of them were rushing from one
end of the yard to the other in a race to finish first.
It wasn't much of a contest, but occasionally Beck

fell over or pretended to get turned around so Holly could hustle past him, little legs and arms pumping.

"He seems nice," her mother said, shading her eyes as she watched them.

"He *is* nice," Poppy said.

"Poppy's in love," Wynn added to the conversation, only raising an eyebrow when Poppy glared. "What? Do I lie?"

"In fact, you do. Often and not well." She rose from her chair, not willing or able to have this conversation right now. Not when she wasn't sure what she *or* he wanted from this. "I'm going to change." Her golf clothes were sticky and she wasn't up to facing the duo of her mother and best friend.

Upstairs, she ran some cold water over a facecloth and laid it on the back of her neck before she went into her bedroom to find something to wear. Too casual and Wynn would think she was overcompensating. Too dressy and he'd think she was trying to get Beck's interest.

She settled on a loose off-the-shoulder number in aquamarine with an elastic waist so the top bloused out. It showed off a lot of leg, but it was hot today. And she was only too glad to strip off the bra and let the girls run free.

When she let herself back outside, hair twisted into a knot on top of her head, Beck glanced over. It was like being blasted directly by the sun. She was glad to have the outside temperature as an excuse for why her cheeks were so rosy. Not that either her mother or Wynn asked. They just assumed.

"See?" Wynn said when Poppy sat back down. "Love."

"Stop it," Poppy said, and fixed the edge of her dress. "You're putting visions of wedding gowns and bouquets in her head and she's only going to be disappointed."

Wynn looked from Poppy to Beck and back. "I'm not so sure about that."

Poppy ignored the birdlike flutter of possibility in her chest. She hadn't come up here to find a husband. Of course, it would be nice, but she was practical. "We're friends."

"Friends?"

Even her mother snorted at that. "You spent the night with him."

"Seriously? I was quiet. I made no noise when I sneaked up the stairs."

"Not that quiet."

Well then. Poppy took a long sip of lemonade and prayed her face didn't look as red as it felt. She was glad when they seemed to drop their interrogation, but she should have known better.

They were stealthy, stealthier than she was, and simply changed tack. Instead of trying to pin Poppy down on what her future plans were with Beck, and whether her colors would be Blush and Bashful or pink and pink—as if, she was all about black and white—they indulged their curiosity by picking Beck's brain.

He impressed her with how he managed their questions. He didn't get ruffled or irritated, but answered them thoughtfully and thoroughly. Everything from where he lived and how he spent his free time, to how excited he was about Jamie's upcoming wedding.

"They seem happy," Beck said as he slung an arm around Poppy's shoulders. They were all on the patio now, including her father, who'd finally returned from the golf course, and Cami, who'd shown up refreshed from a nap with Hank in tow.

All of them, save Hank and her father, had their faces turned eagerly in Beck's direction as though he was about to tell them the secret to success. That, or they were taking note of the casual arm over her shoulder and drawing certain conclusions.

Since Poppy worried shrugging it off would only draw more attention to it, she allowed the arm to stay put. She was such a pal, taking one for the team. And when her own wispy sigh tried to creep up and out, she reminded herself that she and Beck hadn't talked about the future.

The problem was, she wanted to believe they had one, and that his arm around her shoulders meant something. They'd created this ruse to fool his mother, but that didn't explain why he perpetuated it here at her house where they had no chance of being seen by anyone else.

She got her chance to ask him about it after dinner when she and Beck were cleaning up the kitchen. Cami and Hank had packed up Holly and headed for home. Cami was tired and uncomfortable and only wanted to soak her feet in a cool bath, while Holly had barely been able to keep her eyes open. Too much flying, Poppy suspected.

She'd sent Wynn off to visit with her parents since he'd already helped grill, while she and Beck washed the dishes that couldn't go in the dishwasher and wrapped up leftovers.

He had fit in so well with her family. Seamlessly, as if he'd been one of them for years. It was dangerous, letting him get too close to them and to her. She tried to keep her tone light.

"So, what's with the love act?" she asked, securing plastic wrap over a bowl of potato salad and carrying it to the fridge. The cool air from the appliance rushed across her skin, eliminating any flush that might have resulted from her bluntness.

"Act?" He paused, holding one dish in hand, the other wrapped in a tea towel.

She nodded and made room for the bowl, sliding it onto the bottom shelf. "You don't have to pretend around my family. You can just be yourself."

"I was being myself." He placed the dish in the drying rack after a quick swipe with the towel and turned to face her.

Poppy reminded herself it was in her best interest to clarify what was going on between them.

"I meant, you don't have to keep up the pretense we're dating."

He raised an eyebrow at her. "Are we not?"

"Are we?" She smashed down the bird of hope that tried to fly through her chest. Beck was an attractive and powerful man. He had plenty of women walk through his life and had surely learned the ropes of what to say and do to get what he wanted. It didn't mean anything.

"What would you call it?" One half of his mouth flickered up as though he was too lazy to put the effort in to lift the whole thing. Too bad it had the added effect of making her knees wobbly.

She locked them and closed the fridge with a snap. "I have no idea. This isn't something I do all the time." In fact, never. She only brought home men she thought were going to be in her life for a while. She lifted her chin.

He met her challenge with another half smile. "Me neither."

That took her legs out from under her, or would have, had she not locked her knees. Still, she braced a hand on the fridge for good measure. "So what is this?"

He covered the distance between them in three long strides and backed her into the fridge. Cold metal pressed against her legs, the hum of the motor buzzed over her skin. He leaned forward, creating a protective barrier between her and the world. "What do you want it to be?"

Her mouth dried out, all the liquid in her body pooling in her core. His eyes were dark and fathomless. She could dive into them and sink below the surface forever if she wasn't careful. "I asked you first."

He brushed her hair off her shoulder, sending a beat of longing through her blood. She should sidestep him, slip out of this almost embrace and switch topics to something safer, like whether or not he'd like some coffee. But she didn't.

"I want you to come home with me," he said, lowering his head to lick a soft line up the side of her neck.

She bit back her disappointment. Sex. Of course, that's what he wanted. And she hadn't given him any reason to think there was anything more to it. She'd pretty much thrown herself into his bed last night. Had she really thought anything would be different today?

Yes, she had. She felt silly admitting it, but the way he'd looked at her when he thought she wasn't paying attention, the fact that he'd wanted to spend time with her family, and how he'd insisted on acting like a boyfriend around them made her think this was more than sex.

"Not tonight," she told him, putting a hand on his chest and trying not to notice the delicious sensation of his muscles bunching beneath her palm. "I feel like I've barely seen my family."

She wouldn't act like a softhearted lovesick teenager again. She'd spent her entire senior year mourning the loss of what she'd thought they'd had. Now she was a grown woman of twenty-eight. She'd dated. She'd had two serious relationships.

"Can I stay here then?" There was a longing in his gaze that surprised her. "I don't want to leave yet."

It struck something in her and she moved her hand to rest on his arm. "Really?" Her heart flopped.

"Yes." He leaned over and touched the tip of his tongue beneath her ear and made her all melty. "We could do it in your childhood bedroom. Kinky."

She angled her head away with a laugh to cover her disappointment. He wanted sex. Not a lifetime together. Just sex. "No. Not happening."

"Why?"

"Because I'm not that kind of girl."

"Let me convince you." He ran a hand up her arm and along her shoulder. "We'll be quiet. No one will hear us."

"No." She was only a little tempted.

He kissed her once. "All right." Then again. "I wouldn't want to get on your family's bad side."

"No, you wouldn't," she whispered back, her heart swelling once more. He didn't want to upset her family. He liked them. That had to mean something, right? She forgot they were supposed to be cleaning up, forgot her family was only a couple rooms over and could hear everything if they really wanted to listen.

"Your dad even brought out the wine."

"He did." One of his own private reserve bottles. "They like you."

"Good. I like them, too."

Her heart sparked even as she told herself it didn't matter if he liked her family. There was nothing serious going on between them.

He lowered his head to whisper, his breath whooshing across her sensitive skin. "My family should take a few pointers."

She flattened her palm against his chest. It was dangerous, but she'd been wading in dangerous waters from the moment she'd recognized Beck at the welcome barbecue and hadn't told him to never speak to her again. "What do you mean?"

"Your family is great." His tongue doodled rings around her ear now. She found it difficult to stand. "Not like my family at all."

"Your family seems very nice." Her hand slid up his chest to curl around the nape of his neck. It had a mind of its own. Bad hand.

He pushed closer, nestling a thigh between hers. "I don't see much of them." His words rumbled against her neck. "After my parents' second divorce, I figured it was easier not to get involved."

There was no self-pity in his tone, not a single call for sympathy, which made it one of the saddest things Poppy had ever heard. Her heart broke for him. "That would have been a difficult choice."

"It didn't seem like it at the time." He sighed. "But yeah. I think it was."

"Do you miss them?" Their foreheads were pressed together. He closed his eyes and for a moment Poppy worried she'd pushed him too far.

He nodded. "Sometimes."

She wanted to curl over him, protect him from the world even though he probably wouldn't appreciate it. She already knew he was one of those manly men who popped a broken finger back into alignment without making a face. "Have you tried reaching out to them?" she suggested, stroking the back of his neck.

"No." He opened his eyes and pressed a kiss to one cheek, the other, then her mouth. "I'm not sure there's a point."

"Of course there's a point…." It was hard for her to focus when he teased her like that. "If you want things to be different, you have to change."

"What if they don't change? What if it only lasts a month?" He feathered light kisses across her lips, eating his way to her ear. She shivered.

"Then you tried." She clutched at him, wanting him closer. His hair was so soft. She ran both hands through it. *Very* bad hands.

He ran his tongue along her shoulder. "I'll think about it." He put his arms around her and yanked her against him. "Come home with me."

"Beck." He held her so tightly, she couldn't draw a full breath. "I should stay here." And she should probably take a step away from him before her mother walked in and found them in this compromising position. But she didn't.

"You should come." He cupped the back of her head and kissed her until she forgot what she was going to say.

She wanted to go with him. She so badly wanted to. She'd already slept with him and introduced him to her family, but part of her shied away. He didn't have all of her—not yet. But it was close. "Tomorrow," she told him.

"I don't want to be alone tonight."

Her throat got dry, very dry. They were on treacherous ground. "Why not?"

He shrugged, but she recognized the concern in his eyes. "I'm not ready to be around them yet. My family." She stroked his face but didn't say anything. "I need you."

Her heart quivered. She remembered what he'd told her about coming home and finding his parents fighting. She was unable to imagine what that must have been like, to have his whole life turned upside down in one night. No wonder he'd avoided all personal entanglements with people.

"I wouldn't normally ask." He leaned his cheek into her palm. "But I'm asking, please come home with me."

But he was changing. And he wasn't avoiding her. Beck might put on this big-bad-male disguise, but underneath he was searching for love. Like they all were.

The guard around her heart faltered. "Poppy?"
And then shattered under his worried expression.
He needed her. He needed this.

"Yes, I'll go home with you."

CHAPTER SIXTEEN

BECK STAYED IN bed watching Poppy dress. He'd already tried to convince her to stay. Multiple times.

"I'm sure Jamie would be happy to pick up the dresses for you." He tried again, snaking out an arm to loop around her waist. He wasn't ready to let her go. The wedding was tomorrow and she was leaving the day after that. Spending today with other people wasn't part of his plan.

He tugged and she landed on the bed beside him, which was exactly where he wanted her. The morning sun slanted through the windows and blanketed the bed. The bed where they'd spent a good chunk of last night doing everything but sleeping. And it had been good, very good. But the lying together and talking had been wonderful, too.

It was comfortable with her. She made him feel as if he could be himself and didn't have to rise to anyone's expectations. She got that from her family, who had the knack of making a person feel entirely welcome without effort. He bet it served her well as a party planner.

"Beck." She laughed and placed a hand against his chest. "I have to get them. Emmy is expecting me."

"Jamie," he reminded her, nuzzling the side of her neck the way she liked. As anticipated, she softened under the strategic assault and sighed. Beck slid a hand along the length of her body. She'd managed to get her pants on before he captured her, but the top still sat on the chair. It would take him less than thirty seconds to strip the pants off her.

But before he even got a finger on the button, she sat up, for real this time. "It can't be Jamie," she explained, adjusting her bra strap. He pulled it back down her arm. She pushed it up. "Emmy doesn't want him to see the gown she chooses before the wedding. And she'll need help getting in and out of them."

"Won't her mom and sister be there?" Beck asked, still looking for a way to get her to hang around. He liked having her here. Not just in his bed, though that was pretty spectacular, but being around her. She made him more relaxed, less tightly wound. He hadn't even checked his email yet this morning. "Come on. They can handle it. Jamie can pick up the package without looking inside and the ladies can take it from there."

She was tempted, he could tell by the way she stopped moving and sank back into his side. "I'll bring you coffee in bed," he said, and ran a finger over her shoulder, pushing down that lacy bra strap again.

She sighed, but it wasn't the consenting kind he'd been banking on. "I can't." She eased the blow by kissing him before putting her bra strap back in place. "I'm needed." She pushed herself off the bed, shooting him a sultry look over her shoulder. "Guess you should have thought of that before you roped me into helping."

"If I'd only known." But he wasn't upset about it. It made Jamie happy and that was important to him. "How long will this take?" He leaned back against the headboard, enjoying the view as she bent over to dig out her shirt.

"I have no idea." She stood up, something delicate and silky looking in her hands. She slipped it on, smoothing the fabric against her body. Beck's fingers itched to do it for her. "Depends if Emmy likes any of the dresses and how many alterations will need to be done." She smoothed her hair where his hands had mussed it.

"Later then. I'm taking you out." Somewhere fancy where she might wear those high, high heels and show off those sleek legs.

"Is that a command?"

He smirked. "Depends if you like it." She'd only taken one step from the bed, so he reached out and slid his hand up the inside of her thigh. "Let me take you out for dinner."

"For food?"

"There'll be food. Although—"

She put up a hand. "Don't say it."

"I'm insulted. Would I be so cliché?"

She eyed him, considering, then nodded. "Absolutely."

He laughed, because he would have said it if he'd thought of it. "There will be food. Real food." Plenty of wineries in the area had restaurants on their grounds. Many of them considered world class. He'd ask Jamie for any recommendations. "So, you in?"

She nodded and let him pull her back to bed for another kiss. Her body fit perfectly with his, molding and curving without effort so they blended into a single unit. It was a while before they separated.

Beck got up after Poppy left and once he'd showered, he fired up his laptop. The only thing of importance was a meeting scheduled for next Tuesday, during which he'd be signing the papers to make the purchase of the hotel in Vancouver official. Beck sent an email off to his project manager, instructing him to start lining up the construction team and other laborers.

As this was the first project they'd run outside the U.S., they couldn't use their usual crews, but Beck was confident that wouldn't be an issue. And he wanted to be ready to start the renovations as soon as possible. But he wasn't merely concerned with hiring workers—there were permits to acquire, plans to approve and materials to choose.

Beck left most of the exploratory work up to his team but liked to have final say himself. They would narrow down the types of flooring and he would pick from them. It worked well. If he didn't like the end result, it wasn't because of someone else's decision.

He finished with his email in under fifteen minutes, and while there were other things to do—look over budgets, projected sales and future projects—he turned off the computer instead. His mind wasn't on work.

It was barely past ten. He wondered if Poppy was already at Jamie's house. He guessed it was Jamie and Emmy's house now since she'd been living there for a while. He should probably take a drive over there to check in on Jamie. His role as best man practically insisted on it.

And if Poppy should already be there and they had to say hello, that would just be a happy coincidence.

JAMIE WAS COMING out of the house when Beck pulled up. It was a long way from the road to the main house to keep the private residence separate from the business portion. Cars turning into the property went straight for about ten feet to the parking lot for the wine shop. Those heading for the house turned right and weaved through rows of grapes before following a winding driveway up the bluff.

Beck recognized his mother's car and his aunt Georgia's. There was a Cadillac that probably belonged to the Burnhams, but there was no sign of Poppy's little blue convertible. Too bad. He liked watching her tool around in it. He'd made her drive in front of him last night when they'd left her parents' place, afraid he'd drive off the road otherwise because he'd be checking her out in his rearview mirror the whole time.

"Beck." Jamie waved and jogged over as Beck parked and turned off the engine. "What are you doing here?"

"I thought you might want some company." He'd made up the excuse on his way over. "Poppy mentioned this was a ladies' day."

Jamie nodded, his blond hair shining in the morning sun. "They kicked me out." From anyone else it might have sounded petulant, but Jamie made it sound pleasant, as if being kicked out was an aspiration to be held by all.

Beck thought about offering to go inside on his behalf, but Jamie had already climbed into the passenger seat.

He buckled himself in. "Have you eaten?"

"Not yet." Unless you counted the kind Poppy had put in his mind. "You hungry?"

"Yes." Jamie explained he'd been out in the vineyard this morning, unable to sleep and looking to burn off some energy. Though he'd had breakfast with Emmy, he had room for more.

Beck navigated the car back to the main road and went left according to Jamie's direction. Although they didn't talk about anything of a serious nature, Beck enjoyed the conversation. Sometimes it was satisfying to spend time with loved ones. Something he hadn't done enough of the past ten years.

They arrived at a small diner that looked like the kind that served the greasy fare small towns were famous for. There was a Formica counter that ran along the front of the diner, old circular bar stools and booths covered in the same shiny, red vinyl. Even the waitstaff in bowling shirts and shorts fit the ideal diner, as did the sizzling kitchen, apparently manned by someone named "Mel."

But the food, when it came, bore no resemblance to the oily mess Beck had been expecting. His eggs were light and fluffy and sprinkled with fresh herbs. The coffee was strong, hot and fresh, and the side of fruit was most definitely not from a can.

"Thanks for this," Jamie said.

Beck looked up from a piece of pineapple he'd speared. "No problem." And it wasn't. This was nice for him, too. "I hadn't eaten breakfast yet."

"I didn't mean breakfast. I mean, coming to the wedding and acting as best man. I know you weren't crazy about doing it."

Beck had thought he'd put on a better poker face than that. "I was glad to do it, Jamie." It was true now, so it wasn't a complete fabrication. "Family supports each other."

That sounded dangerously close to something his mother would spout at him, so he didn't elaborate. He didn't think he'd need to. Jamie was a guy, he would get it.

Jamie nodded. "So how did you know I was getting the boot this morning? Your mom tell you?"

Beck swallowed. "Ah, no." He could have let Jamie believe that, would have been easy, but it felt a little like they were regaining the footing in their relationship and Beck didn't want to sully that.

Jamie grinned. "So how is my dearest and oldest friend?"

"She's fine." Better than fine. He grinned and forked up some eggs.

Jamie watched him with a discerning eye. "I'm glad."

Beck didn't say anything and concentrated on his eggs. He was glad to be repairing some of the distance with his family, but one step at a time.

"I've had a great time having you around this week. Think you might come up for Christmas this year?"

Beck hadn't thought much beyond the next couple months with work. He nodded slowly. "I suppose." What else was he going to do? Have another lonely Christmas in Seattle with whoever was around? "I'd like that."

"Great." Jamie took a bite of pancake and swallowed. "It'll be nice to have you and Poppy up," he said, his expression a pathetic attempt at casualness. He did not do subtle well. His face was too open and displayed everything he thought in vivid color. "She's usually in town for the holidays anyway."

"Poppy?" Beck's fingers clenched around his fork.

"Is this a dual invite?" He was certain he did a better job than Jamie at hiding the sudden flood of emotions coursing through him, but not by much.

Jamie blinked. "I thought you two were…" He frowned. "Actually, I think everyone thinks that."

"Everyone doesn't know my business." And Beck intended to keep it that way. He was all for building closer relationships with his family, but they didn't need to hear all the intimate details of his life. "I like spending time with her." It didn't mean they would still be seeing each other at Christmas, although the idea did have possibilities.

Naramata often had snow around the holidays. He liked the idea of drinking coffee in front of a roaring fire with a naked Poppy beside him. Come to think of it, he had a soft rug in front of his fireplace that needed christening.

He shook the thought away before it took root. The holidays were a long way off and he wasn't ready to be roped into anything permanent. Who knew how things would play out. He might not see Poppy again after the wedding. They'd gone more than a decade between meetings before. What made this time any different?

"Interesting," Jamie said, a little smirk playing around his mouth.

"What?" Beck set down his fork. A stone made itself at home in his gut. A very unpleasant stone he attempted to dislodge with a blast of caffeine.

"Nothing." Jamie mimed innocence, but that

smirk kept peeking out around the edges. It pissed Beck off.

"It's not 'nothing.'" Beck's cup rattled against the saucer. "And you sound like a chick."

"How do I sound like a chick?"

"I ask what's wrong and you say 'nothing.' But it's never nothing and next thing you know I'm buying you a diamond bracelet to make up for something." He scowled across the table at his now fully grinning cousin. "I'm not buying you diamonds."

Jamie laughed.

"What's so funny?"

"Isn't it obvious?"

"No. Enlighten me."

Jamie shot him a "duh" expression. It reminded Beck of when they were kids, poking fun at each other with good-natured insults. Jamie leaned forward. "I don't think I'm the one you want to buy a diamond for."

Beck reared back. Diamonds? No. Hell, no. "Don't you think you're getting a little ahead of yourself?" Weddings and marriage were the beginning of the end. All he had to do was look at his parents for proof. Which was why he was never getting married. "Be serious."

"I am." The smirk was gone. "You clearly have feelings for her."

"That doesn't mean I'm ready to get married." The back of his neck prickled. He reached up to swipe a hand over it. "We've only known each other a week."

Jamie shook his head. "Not true. You were tight that summer when we were teenagers."

"That was a long time ago." He'd changed and so had she. It was ridiculous to think whatever had happened back then still meant something.

"You telling me you forgot about her?"

"Of course I didn't forget." He wouldn't lie to his cousin. "But I haven't spent the past decade waiting for her either."

"Yes. But—" Jamie tilted his head like a curious dog "—don't you find it interesting that all your girlfriends have been kept at arm's length until now?"

That stone was back, along with its good buddy, Stiff Neck. "How would you know?"

Jamie looked surprised. "I keep up with your life."

Beck wasn't sure if he was pleased or perturbed by this bit of information. He didn't flaunt his personal life, preferring to keep it private. "Just because I never proposed marriage doesn't mean I kept everyone at arm's length."

The simplicity of a no-strings relationship was something he'd been clear about from the start with every woman he went out with, and if a few of them had wanted more than Beck had been willing to give, well, that wasn't his fault. He'd been honest and up front, and in the end had parted amicably with all of them. Usually with a gift of diamonds.

"Who are you trying to convince?"

"You. No one." Beck pressed his lips together. Why was he engaging in this ridiculous argument?

No matter what he said, Jamie would twist it to suit what he wanted to believe. "How did we get on this topic anyway? Shouldn't we be talking about your wedding? Flowers or dresses or something?"

The prickling had crept down his spine. Beck rolled his shoulders. This was stupid. There was nothing to be getting bent out of shape about. Jamie was allowed to believe whatever he wanted. It made no difference to the facts.

"Yep, definitely hooked," Jamie diagnosed.

Beck felt the need to take one last swing for the fences. "This week has been nice. Better than I expected. But it's not that serious."

Jamie gave him a knowing look and reached across the table to punch him in the shoulder. "That's what we all say."

CHAPTER SEVENTEEN

POPPY BEAT THE box of dresses to her parents' place by about twenty minutes. Enough time to shower off the scent of sex with Beck and tame her waves into a semblance of professionalism.

While this wasn't a typical work meeting, Poppy wasn't comfortable showing up in casual dress with her hair flipping every which way either. She twisted it into a knot at the back of her head and selected a simple, fitted dove gray dress, which she accessorized with a scarf in pale pink and matching earrings.

She considered checking over the gowns before leaving but decided not to. Missy had exquisite taste and would have sent a variety of options to suit any bride. It would be a nice surprise for Emmy to have the excitement of opening the oversize box. And Poppy figured Emmy would need a little boost after the stress of worrying whether or not she'd have anything to wear at all.

The box was too big to fit in Poppy's trunk—her little car was low and the trunk wouldn't close over it—so she belted it into the passenger seat instead, not wanting to crush the precious cargo.

Wynn had declined to come. She couldn't blame him. Dress selection, especially on a tight timeline, was not a lot of fun. She started the car and headed to Jamie's.

Funny, it was only a week ago she'd been on this exact route planning how she would break up the wedding, and now she was making sure it went off without a hitch.

There were three cars in the driveway at Jamie's house. Poppy parked beside a black Cadillac and hopped out. She hadn't even gotten around to the passenger side when the front door opened and a mass of excited women poured out.

"Poppy!" Emmy was first across the driveway, her blond hair pinned up into an elegant chignon, which was perfect for trying on dresses. She hugged Poppy tightly. "Thank you so much. I can't even tell you how much this means to me."

Since she sounded on the verge of tears, Poppy patted her back. "It's my pleasure. I'm happy to help." And she was.

Grace stepped forward to help pull the box out of the car. She carried it back to the house with her mother and Emmy trailing behind while Poppy shut the car and tossed her keys into her purse. Georgia and Victoria waited by the door, their arms linked together. Poppy hadn't realized how much the sisters looked alike until they stood beside each other.

Victoria may have spent more money maintaining herself, but the family's good genes were plenty evident in Georgia's high cheekbones and smooth skin. She'd allowed her hair to silver naturally and kept it in a short cut that suited her face. Both women were trim and well dressed, though Georgia was more casual in khaki pants and a matched grass-green sweater set, while Victoria wore a georgette cream silk blouse with a black pencil skirt.

"You're a lifesaver," Georgia said with a smile.

Victoria greeted her with a warm hug. "I'm glad to see you again."

Victoria linked her other arm through Poppy's and the three of them traipsed through the entryway, past the kitchen, down the hall and into one of the guest bedrooms, which had been transformed into a bridal boudoir for shopping.

The bed had been shoved to the wall and a floor-length mirror had been dragged into the middle of the room. A trifold screen was set up in a corner and there were shoes lined up along the wall. Grace dealt with the packing tape on the box while Emmy stood to the side, watching, with her hands clasped behind her back. Poppy had a sudden fear none of the dresses would work.

She needn't have panicked. From the moment the first gown—a confection of flowers and silk—was pulled free the sighs and aws made it clear Missy had done it again. She'd even remembered to include veils, gloves and other accoutrements Emmy might want.

They spent the next ninety minutes trying on the

gowns with a variety of shoes and styling choices. It was difficult, but not because they were running out of time and had to pick something, but because tall, elegant Emmy looked amazing in pretty much everything. And she'd look even better once Georgia adjusted the seams and hems.

After retrying on her favorites, Emmy settled on a strapless gown in soft white with delicate beading along the top. The material was pleated along the bodice and came to a point on her left hip before spilling into a waterfall of flounces and a small train. Georgia pinned the waist of the dress, which bagged a touch. Was there another woman alive who, while pregnant, would require a wedding dress to be taken in?

Victoria convinced Emmy to try her hair down, and the blond locks spilling across her shoulders lent sultriness to the look. A pair of borrowed diamond dangling earrings and a matching tennis bracelet completed the outfit.

"You're gorgeous," Poppy said. And she was. Really, every bride should be so fortunate. She glowed. And while Poppy figured some of that was due to the new life she carried, most of it was Emmy. The glow of a happy woman about to take the next step in life.

Poppy's heart stuttered, but she covered it with a cheerful smile and set about packing up the dresses and other bits of paraphernalia that hadn't made the cut. She could ship everything back to Missy tonight, but Poppy preferred to drop it off in person when she arrived back in town on Monday, along with the sizable check Emmy had written from her own account.

She'd tried to pay Poppy, too, but Poppy had insisted it wasn't necessary. Though she and Emmy weren't quite friends, she'd started to think it was inevitable. And even if it weren't, she'd never take money for Jamie's wedding.

Everyone except Victoria left. Emmy and her family off to have a last day together before she started her new life. Georgia with the chosen dress, carefully wrapped in plastic and on a hanger, to make the necessary adjustments.

Victoria, though, stayed around helping Poppy check to make sure nothing had been left behind. "You're very good at this," she observed.

Poppy brushed aside the flicker of conceit. She was good at it, which was why she did it for a living, but she didn't want Beck's mom to think she was a braggart. "It's just a matter of being organized and staying calm."

"It's more than that." Victoria fluffed the duvet cover and smoothed where it had gotten rumpled from being sat on. "I can see why my son likes you."

Poppy's heart stuttered again. Actually, it almost slammed to a complete stop, but she breathed through it. She glanced at Victoria, who only smiled back. Exactly where was this going and did Poppy want to take the trip?

"I like him, too," she finally said. It was a neutral statement, but the only one Poppy was willing to share.

"I think you're good for him."

It was a good thing her heart had strongly started back up again, because otherwise Victoria's statement would have stopped it.

"He tends to keep to himself. With me, at least." There was a sadness to her smile before it brightened again. "But this week has been different. He's been different. You're the first girlfriend he's introduced to us."

Poppy found her voice. "Really?" She didn't want to believe it. Scratch that. She wanted desperately to believe it.

"Yes." Victoria came over to hug Poppy. "And I want to thank you. He likes to keep his emotions to himself, but you've brought them out. He's bloomed."

Poppy stifled a smile at the image of Beck as a flower. He'd hate that. But his mother meant well.

"I want him to be happy and this is the happiest I've seen him in a long time."

Poppy swallowed. She longed for Victoria to be right. But there had been no discussion of a future, no hint at what would happen once the wedding was over and everyone went back to their respective lives.

But Beck would be in Vancouver with his new hotel. That fluttery anticipation flickered through her again. Maybe, just maybe, he had plans for them.

"Speak of the devil."

Poppy followed Victoria's gaze out the window and discovered Beck's car pulling up in front of the house. She watched as the man himself climbed out of the driver's side. Jamie's bright head popped out, too, but Poppy spared him only a momentary look.

She probably shouldn't enjoy gaping at Beck. Especially not with his mother in the room, but she couldn't help drinking in her fill of him. His confident gait. The smirking grin he shared with Jamie. The way his eyes roamed the area and zeroed in on her. Her pulse thumped.

She'd fallen for him again.

The realization swept through her like a windstorm, blowing out every other thought in her head. Oh, no. No.

She stepped back and would have groaned if Victoria hadn't been beside her. This sudden awareness wasn't something she wanted to share with the mother of the object of her affection.

Poppy tried to shake off the thought. It was crazy. How well did she actually know Beck? She knew what he liked in bed, knew the sound of his laugh and the way his hair felt. But did she really know him? Sure, they'd been close as teenagers, but a decade was a long time and they'd both changed.

So it was insane to think she'd fallen for him. She hadn't, she simply lusted for him. It was totally different.

So why had she introduced him to her family and let them think there was more going on than friendship? Why was her mind already whirring with ways to keep this going once they returned to their respective cities?

By the time Poppy got herself together, Victoria had exited the bedroom. She heard the older woman moving down the hallway and her cheerful greeting when she reached the front door.

She should go and join them. She made her feet move, then slowed and wondered if she should take the dresses with her. There was no point in leaving the box behind, and it would give her a few more seconds to regain her cool.

Lifting it in front of her, she entered the hallway. There was nothing to be nervous about. Nothing had changed. Except her heart.

But all her best intentions to act as if this was an everyday meeting evaporated when she reached the entryway and saw Beck smiling at her. He shouldn't be allowed to look at her like that. Her fingers went numb and she quickly put the box down before she dropped it.

"Is that it?" Jamie came over to peer curiously at the box. Poppy had already taped it back up for travel, so there wasn't a strip of satin, bead or sequin to be seen, but that didn't stop Jamie from trying.

"It's not in there," she told him, nudging it behind her with a foot, glad for the distraction. "You'll see the dress tomorrow."

"The dress is beautiful, Jamie," Victoria said. "Emmy looks stunning."

Jamie's face got that moony, glazed expression again. Beck was still looking at her, studying her as though he was searching for the answer to a question that hadn't been asked. Poppy got warm all over.

"Beck?" Victoria spoke again.

"Yes?" He didn't look away from Poppy.

"Will you be joining us for dinner tonight? It's Jamie's last one as an unmarried man."

"I'm not sure. Poppy and I have plans."

Poppy was reminded of their conversation this morning. Her cheeks burned brighter. "That's okay. You should have dinner as a family." And she should leave before she embarrassed herself. She turned and hefted the box of dresses back into her arms. "See you tomorrow."

"Let me." Jamie started forward to take the box from her, but Beck beat him to it.

"I've got it." His fingers sliding across hers brought up more thoughts of this morning's conversation and activities. She brushed them away. Plenty of time for that later, when Victoria and Jamie weren't around.

"You should join us," Victoria said as the four of them tromped out the front door to the driveway. Beck stowed the box in Poppy's passenger seat as directed, while Victoria flitted about on the sidelines. "We'd love to have you."

"Thank you." Poppy smiled. "But it sounds like a family event. I wouldn't want to intrude."

"Don't be silly, you wouldn't be intruding."

"I'd love if you came, Poppy," Jamie said.

The only person who didn't say anything was Beck. He kept staring at her. She didn't know what that meant. "No, really. It'll be nice to have dinner with my family." Her parents were playing cards with the neighbors and Wynn was babysitting Holly so Cami and Hank could have an adult dinner alone, but only she knew that.

"If you change your mind," Victoria said, "you're more than welcome."

Beck continued to stare. Poppy began to feel uncomfortable. And overheated. Had he seen her step back from the window? Did he know what she was feeling? Was it written all over her body?

She fussed with her hair even though it was already tidy and then fiddled with the seat belt for the dress box. She needed to go home, have a cold shower and figure out what to do about all this, but Jamie stopped her.

"Poppy, can you stick around for a bit?"

She paused. "Um, sure." She moved to follow him inside, but Beck caught her arm.

Silently, they watched his mother drive off with a wave and Jamie head back into the house. They were alone.

"What is it?" She looked at him, into those dark, dark eyes, and felt herself slip a little further.

"I didn't want to do this in front of everyone." He bent his head and laid down the hottest, sexiest kiss

Poppy had ever experienced. Seriously, she was surprised her head didn't pop off.

She poured everything she felt into it. All those emotions newly risen to the surface, the ones that told her to trust him, trust this, because something this good should not be temporary. Even his mother thought they were a good match.

He smiled against her mouth. "Remind me to do that again later."

"Later?" She was breathless but still managed to form a somewhat coherent thought. Okay, fine, so it was only one word. At least it made sense.

"You're coming to dinner." It wasn't a question.

"But it's family."

"You're coming." He kissed her again and with one last look that practically scorched her clothes right off, he got in his car and drove away.

Poppy stood there for another minute until her pulse returned to normal and she had control of the goofy smile that kept trying to stretch across her face.

"You look happy," Jamie said when she entered the kitchen.

Okay, not so controlled. "I am." She hopped up on one of the stools around his breakfast bar and took a long sip of the lemonade he'd poured. He'd used the tall skinny glasses his mother had always used for lemonade.

They'd spent many hours as kids after school drinking milk and eating cookies in this kitchen.

They'd never gone through that awkward point in their relationship where puberty hit and they'd started thinking of each other as more than friends. It had always been easy with him, friends forever.

"I want to thank you for everything you did for Emmy," Jamie said as he sipped from his own glass. "I don't know what we would have done without you."

Poppy put her glass down carefully, recalling they'd been Jamie's grandmother's, and as kids they'd been taught to respect them. "I was happy to do it, Jamie. I want you to be happy."

"I am happy." His face was serious when he spoke again. "I know you had some concerns about Emmy—"

"I don't. Not anymore." Emmy was lucky to have Jamie, but Poppy was coming around to the idea that Jamie was lucky to have Emmy, too. There was no mistaking the love they had for each other. And so what if they were getting married after only being together a short time? Plenty of long and successful marriages had started out that way. "I like her," Poppy said. She meant it, too.

He reached out and gripped her hand. "Thank you."

She squeezed back. "You're going to be a great husband and father." It felt a little like this was goodbye, but it didn't make her sad. She was happy Jamie had found someone. Nerves fluttered in her belly.

Maybe she had, too.

"I hope so." He gave her one more squeeze then let go. "What about you?"

"What about me?"

"You and Beck. You like him," he said. It seemed it was obvious to everyone. Poppy wondered if she should have been more discreet. "And he likes you."

Sparks flickered. Poppy clutched her glass and did her best to look cool. She would not get all giddy like a schoolgirl. She and Jamie didn't have that kind of relationship. She'd save that for Wynn.

"I haven't seen him like this before," Jamie went on, apparently unaware she had lit up like a parade float. "He's different. Happier."

It's what Victoria had said, too. And the surge of possibility crested through her again.

"I talked to him about it." Jamie smiled and shook his head. "He tried to play it off, but you're important to him."

"He's important to me, too." She almost didn't get the words out, trapped behind the *woo-hoo* happy shout rising in her throat. And the hope rising in her heart.

"So you'll have dinner with us tonight?"

She couldn't think of a reason not to.

CHAPTER EIGHTEEN

THE WEDDING WAS gorgeous. The sun was out, the grapes were ripe and Emmy looked as if she'd stepped out of the pages of a glossy magazine. Seriously, the models and actresses who graced the pages of those publications had nothing on her.

Poppy stood and sighed as the bride came down the aisle with her father. Emmy's beautiful blue eyes were damp, her lips curved in excitement, and her dress was exquisite. Georgia had managed to take in the waist without affecting the draping of the gown.

Jamie looked pretty radiant himself waiting at the end of the runner for his bride. While they looked at each other, hands clasped as they spoke words of eternity and love, Poppy only hoped something similar might be in her future. She couldn't help her gaze straying to Beck, who stood beside his cousin all tall and dark and hers. He looked as good in a tux as he did in jeans. She envisioned peeling him out of it later.

The ceremony ended and everyone filed into the large backyard where only a week earlier they'd hosted a welcome barbecue. But the two events couldn't have looked more different.

Tonight the music was classical only, servers carried flutes of champagne and platters of prawns on ice and a chef worked a station serving rack of lamb. There were tables spread out across the lawn, crisp linens fluttered in the breeze and the centerpieces were crystal buckets filled with grapes.

Poppy sat with her sister at one of the tables. There were no place cards and people milled about, enjoying predinner cocktails and canapés. Holly bounced in Poppy's lap, asking every ten seconds if she could go and play now.

"Not yet, honey," Cami said. She rubbed her belly. "Wait for Daddy."

"Okay." Holly giggled happily and bounced some more.

"You feeling okay?" Poppy glanced at her sister's distended belly. "It's not coming out tonight, is it?"

"It's not an it."

"Well, we don't know the sex and I thought he-she sounded weird. Like you were birthing a drag queen."

"Very funny." Cami snorted. Poppy figured since she was well enough to snort, she must be okay. "Speaking of S-E-X."

"Not sure how you found yourself in the family way?" Poppy grinned. "Well, see the man—"

"You're quite the comedian today."

"I try."

"So it's good?"

"Very." Really, there were no words to describe

it, so she didn't bother trying. But she couldn't help the smile from spreading across her face. It wasn't only the sex—it was also the talks they shared, and just being together. And, yes, it was the conversations she'd had with Jamie and Victoria. Those conversations had given her permission to admit what was in her heart. That she was already half in love with Beck Lefebvre. Again.

"As in great?"

"As in I could die happy."

"I knew it." Cami clasped her hands awkwardly around her belly. "That smolder you've been wearing totally gave you away."

"I don't smolder." Though she thought she might like to. Smolder sounded so adult and powerful. A woman in control who did whatever she wanted and left men trailing along behind her, caught up in the wake of her smoldering. She tickled Holly, who squealed and pointed to her dad before leaping down to go and play with some other kids her age.

"So what does it mean?" Cami asked after checking that Hank was watching to make sure their daughter didn't pull off a tablecloth or cause other trouble.

Poppy shrugged. She'd only recently come to the conclusion she didn't want this thing with Beck to end. She hadn't talked to him about it yet. She'd considered bringing it up last night after the family dinner at the main house when Beck had insisted she stay the night with him. But things had been light and fun. They'd laughed, played cards and then Beck had insisted they needed to play strip Go Fish, which had been even more fun. Having a heavy-duty conversation about where this was going hadn't seemed right.

Besides, she was pretty sure she had an idea where things were going.

"Is it a fling?"

"No." Poppy's voice was quiet. She didn't have an official announcement to make. Not yet. But it wasn't a fling.

"Oh, wow." Cami sat back, looking smug. "You've fallen for him."

"How can you tell?" She didn't bother to deny it.

"Um, the smiley glow all over your face. You always look like that when you're in love. And believe me, I've seen that face enough times to know."

"You're talking as if me falling in love is an everyday occurrence. Ridiculous." She was too practical for that to be true. But her cheeks flushed in spite of her protests. She pressed the back of her hand to her face. And anyway, she wouldn't say she was *in love,* just that there was a possibility.

"Seriously?" Cami rolled her eyes. "You fall in love all the time."

"I don't," Poppy said. She'd only had two serious boyfriends. Jason, her university sweetheart, and Evan.

"Yes, you do." Cami waved Wynn over. "Doesn't Poppy fall in love all the time?"

"All the time," Wynn confirmed, settling in at the table with them.

"Two times," Poppy reminded them. "Two, and I'm not even sure they were love."

"Ooooh. Because it's different this time?" Wynn wanted to know.

Poppy scowled but didn't answer, because that was exactly what she'd been thinking. The emotions were different with Beck. She was different with Beck. Regardless, Wynn and Cami were still wrong. She did not fall in love all the time.

Even if she counted Jason and Evan, that was only twice. And twice was not all the time.

"Are you going to tell him?" Cami asked.

"And say what? 'I love you. Let's be together.'"

Cami laughed. "Yeah, because that won't scare him away."

"Exactly." Poppy looked down at her skirt, which her hands were busily smoothing. She was going to wear a hole through it. "I'm going to see how it goes."

She didn't have to look up to identify the look Wynn and Cami shared.

"Stop it," she told them. "I'm not putting any pressure on him. Or on me."

Wynn smiled sadly. "She actually believes that," he said to Cami.

"I know. Isn't she the cutest?"

"I'm right here." And she was getting annoyed. "I don't know why you think I can't be casual."

She *could* be casual. Hadn't she been casual this whole week?

Wynn patted Poppy on the hand while Cami continued to rub her belly. "You're not the casual kind," he told her. "There's nothing wrong with it. Own your romantic little soul."

"You think I'm a romantic?" When they both nodded, she was shocked to the soles of her feet. "How so?"

Wynn started. "You think *The Bachelor* is a viable way to meet a spouse."

"They've had at least two marriages." Poppy felt obligated to point that out. "More if you include *Bachelor Pad*."

He continued. "You cry when you watch Hallmark movies."

"Because they're sweet." How could she not cry when the guy and the girl got together at the end? She wasn't a robot.

"She used to cry at Hallmark-card commercials, too," Cami interjected.

"What are you two made of, stone?" Everybody cried at Hallmark commercials. Everybody.

"You sniffle over sunsets and going for long walks in the rain." Wynn was on a roll now. "You find out your man's favorite foods and cook dinner for him. You've even picked out your own engagement ring."

"That doesn't mean I'm romantic. I'm organized and I have a heart that beats." They both smiled at her. "Fine," Poppy told them. "It's clear you're not willing to listen because you've already made up your minds."

LATER THAT EVENING, Poppy decided to wait until they were at the house before broaching the subject of the future with Beck. She needed to look him in the eye, search his expression. Or that's what she told herself. She pressed a hand to her jumpy stomach as they drove back through the starry night.

His hand was warm over hers as they traversed the path she'd come to learn quite well. He'd placed his jacket over her shoulders earlier and she drew it close around her throat, inhaling his scent. It made her all hot and bothered and a little dizzy.

"Beck." Her voice carried through the stillness as they climbed the front steps to the guesthouse. He turned, smiled at her. "About tomorrow."

"Let's worry about that later. Tonight, I just want you." He tugged her across the threshold and closed the door behind them and suddenly his hands and mouth were everywhere, peeling off the single shoulder of her peach gown, tugging down the side zipper and leaving the chiffon material in a puddle around her feet.

She moaned when he scooped her up, now down to her silky panties, matching strapless bra and gold heels. Yes, tomorrow would be plenty soon enough. They wouldn't be able to have any kind of conversation anyway, since she could barely remember her name. When he lowered her onto the bed and wrapped himself around her, she forgot even that. And it was a long time before she thought about anything at all.

BECK LAY ON the bed, Poppy's head cradled in the crook of his arm. He didn't care what Jamie said, he wasn't hooked. He enjoyed her company. And what was wrong with that? They were adults, they knew what this was.

He looked down at her. She slept, her breath feathering against his chest. He tightened his hold. He didn't think he was ready to let her go. But he didn't think he could hold on either.

She wanted more. He'd known from the moment she'd said his name last night as they'd neared the house. He had no clue how to answer, so he didn't. Instead, he kissed her until they were both distracted and breathing hard. And told himself he'd done the right thing.

He wanted to believe it, but he wasn't so sure, lying here in the darkness.

Maybe they could take it slow. See each other casually. No promises. No rings. And definitely no wedding plans.

She snuggled against him more fully, twining her legs through his.

Or maybe he should let her go.

She wanted all those things—the wedding, the family, the house with the backyard where the kids and dog ran around. Beck's lungs got tight at the thought and he struggled to breathe.

He lived in a penthouse apartment that overlooked the city. He worked late and liked it. He couldn't stand the thought of putting some innocent kid—his innocent kid—through the same things he'd had to endure. Because there were no guarantees.

It was a general statement about life, but to Beck it seemed even more fitting for love. Relationships had end dates. And those ends were painful and affected more than just the two involved.

He sucked in another breath. He couldn't do it. He wasn't cut out for it and it wasn't fair of everyone to expect him to change. They should appreciate he knew himself, knew his failings and didn't try to drag anyone down with him.

Tomorrow, he would take Poppy back to her parents' place, kiss her goodbye and never see her again. It was the right thing to do. The noble thing.

But it didn't help him sleep that night.

CHAPTER NINETEEN

"WHERE'S POPPY?" HIS mother looked behind him as though expecting to find her hiding there. As if Poppy's hair could ever be hidden.

"She went home," Beck said, and ignored the pull of disappointment in his chest at the memory of seeing her off. He'd done the right thing. A relationship between them had no chance of working out. It wouldn't be fair to make her hope it might. She deserved better than that.

When his mother had come over this afternoon and insisted he come to the big house for dinner since it was their last night in Naramata, he'd agreed. But no one had told him it was supposed to be a couples performance.

"I hoped she'd join us. I like her."

Beck did, too. But he didn't voice that thought as he pulled the front door closed behind him. It was odd being here. He'd managed not to spend any time alone with both his parents this week, always begging off or making sure someone else would be in attendance.

That old familiar prickling crawled up his spine. He paused at the threshold to the kitchen. The table was set for four. There were lit candles and one of his mother's floral arrangements. Wine was open and breathing. Romance was clearly in the air. "I should go. I don't want to intrude on your dinner."

"You're not intruding." His mother came around from behind the kitchen island, wiping her hands on her apron. "It's a family dinner and you are part of this family."

She hugged him. She'd started doing that the last couple days and he'd started letting her. Then she took his hand and dragged him farther into the room, pushing him onto one of the bar stools.

He was trying. It wasn't easy breaking a decade-long habit, but he was trying. However, that didn't extend to having a couples meal where his parents made eyes at each other. "You sure? Because if you and Dad need some alone time…" He couldn't bring himself to finish the sentence or look his mother in the eye. Christ, this was embarrassing. Perhaps dinner together was one step too many. He should head back down to the guesthouse and eat the leftover pizza from the night he'd had Jamie over.

His mother reached out and put her hand over his. "You're not leaving. Harrison?" She turned her head to call upstairs. "Please come down here and tell your son he's not leaving."

His father came downstairs, his mustache twitching happily, and proceeded to wrap his arms around his ex-wife's waist and plant a kiss on her cheek.

Then frowned at his son. "You're not leaving." He looked at his ex-wife for approval.

Beck frowned. "I'm telling you right now, if you start making out in front of me, I am leaving." And quite possibly never coming back. Ever.

"We're not going to make out," his mother said. "Offer your son a drink, Harrison."

So Beck stayed and had a beer with his father while his mother put the finishing touches on her lasagna and poured herself a glass of wine. He even started to relax. His parents didn't avoid touching each other, not exactly, but they didn't cuddle or make kissy noises at each other either, for which he was truly grateful.

The meal was delicious. The lasagna was hot, the bread fresh and the wine full-bodied. By the time they'd finished, Beck felt better. He even agreed to stay for coffee. They settled in the great room, in front of the massive stone fireplace. His parents sat on the couch while Beck took a chair across from them.

"That's too bad Poppy couldn't stay," his mother said, sipping her coffee. "Did she have to get back to the city for work?"

"I think so." He stirred in some cream, stirred again. He hadn't asked.

He'd taken her back to her parents' place this morning. At first, he'd thought he was off the hook. She hadn't brought up the future after her attempt the night before, and the little bundle of nervous energy in his stomach eased. They were on the same page. She got it, got that he wasn't a good risk. He'd even begun thinking they could reconnect when he headed up to Vancouver next month.

They were both adults, both single. There was no reason they couldn't enjoy one another's company while he was in town. Much as they'd done this week.

And then she'd said, "So when do you think you can come up for a weekend?"

He'd stuttered like an imbecile and mumbled something about lawyers and real estate and needing to spend some time at the hotel in Seattle, which was a joke. The Seattle hotel could run itself and had been doing so for years.

She'd smiled and looped her arms around his waist. "Well, I'll have to check my schedule with Wynn's, but I think I could come to you instead."

It was a perfectly nice, perfectly lovely offer. She wasn't saying she expected a house and a dog and an offer of marriage. But Beck saw it in her eyes. She wanted more. She was telling him she wanted more. And she was nervous he didn't feel the same way.

His heart had sunk. Because he'd known then. Known what he should do. Known what he owed her. And he'd still said, "Yeah, that sounds great."

Because he was too cowardly to tell her he wasn't a good bet, wasn't a good choice and wasn't the right guy for her. He was afraid she might convince him to try anyway.

She could do it. She was the only person he'd ever met who had the capability to make him question his choice to stay single, which scared him. Because things wouldn't work out and then he'd really have ruined her.

He wished he were more like Jamie, the eternal optimist, who looked for and found the best in everyone and every situation. Jamie had dived right into the marriage game without any doubts. Even Beck's parents, who overlooked the multiple failures in their pasts, went for it. But he was too cynical for that and too aware of the damage those failures could cause.

He wouldn't be the one to dim the light in Poppy's eyes.

"Well," his mother said, "it'll be nice for you to spend time with her when you come up to oversee the hotel renovations."

He planned to spend the three months necessary to get the hotel into shape living in the city. His parents had informed him over dinner they intended to settle in Vancouver permanently. His mother had lived there during university and had moved back after the demise of her last marriage. Beck wondered if *that,* more than wanting to slow down, had been the reason for his father's retirement last year. He didn't ask.

"I don't think I'll be seeing her again," he said,

recognizing it was futile but hoping his mother would let it drop anyway.

His hope was wasted. "Oh, Beck. Why?" She put her cup down on the coffee table and leaned toward him.

Beck kept his tone easy. He didn't want anyone to learn how much it had hurt him to say goodbye, knowing it was for the last time. And telling himself it was for the best wasn't helping. Not yet. "We have different lives in different cities. It was never going to work."

His mother studied him and for a moment Beck was sure she knew everything. That he'd never dated a woman longer than two months. That his most memorable relationship had taken place here, the summer he was eighteen. Which was pathetic.

"Are you sure?"

No, he wasn't sure. The selfish part of him wanted to call Poppy tomorrow like he'd promised before jetting off. Wanted to tell her she was more than welcome to come down for the weekend. That he'd take her to his favorite restaurant and lounge. But that wouldn't be fair. Incvitably, the relationship would end. They always did. And he didn't want to be responsible for hurting Poppy.

"I'm sure." He hoped in time he would mean it.

"Are you?" She watched him with careful eyes.

"I said I was."

"Victoria." His father laid a hand on her shoulder.

"I know, Harrison. But I can't help thinking he's

letting go of a good thing." She turned her attention back to Beck. "What happened?"

"Nothing." He wished he hadn't stayed for the coffee.

His mother opened her mouth again, all ready to insist on family togetherness and sharing and every other trope put forward on sitcoms about families who lived and loved together that didn't exist in the real world. Except for the Sullivans. But she stopped, sat back and didn't say a thing. And it wasn't only because of the pressure his father's hand placed on her shoulder. Though it probably helped.

She was trying. Beck's throat loosened and he took a sip of coffee without feeling as if it was about to choke him. His mother was trying.

He coughed, awkwardly. His mother couldn't be the only one making an effort. He recalled Poppy's advice that if he wanted things to be different, he had to change his patterns of behavior, too. "I'm not ready to talk about it yet."

She nodded.

It wasn't much. But it was a start.

CHAPTER TWENTY

One month later...

HE WAS A tool bag.

It wasn't the first time he'd had this thought. Probably wouldn't be the last either.

Beck watched the needle on his odometer climb as he left Seattle behind and headed onto the I-5. The tall evergreens that lined the freeway whizzed past. The sun shone bright and hot on this Friday August morning. He had his sunglasses on and the car window down, the breeze blowing through his hair.

His mother would tell him he needed to get it cut, which was exactly why he hadn't bothered. She also wanted him to live with her and his father for the next three months, which would not be happening.

Beck glanced at the folder on the passenger seat, which contained the information for the apartment he'd rented in Vancouver. He was picking up the keys tomorrow and had decided to stay with his parents tonight.

His mother gave him plenty of grief when he'd told her that her dream of one big happy family all living under the same roof was not to be. But what did she expect? He was a grown-up. A man. He had needs, and staying under his parents' roof was not likely to meet them.

Still, things had improved in their relationship. Not the massive, bounding improvements that his mother hoped for. But improvements. For one, he wasn't staying in a hotel tonight.

But shutting down his mother's dream wasn't why the pang of guilt radiated through his chest. No. That was all about Poppy.

Leaving her alone was the right thing to do. She wanted something he wasn't capable of giving and it was cruel to continue to lead her on. But that didn't make him feel any better about himself.

According to Jamie, she was fine. Beck hadn't been able to bring himself to call her. Cowardly, he knew, but he thought a clean break was better. His fingers tightened around the wheel. Now he was heading into her neighborhood, her hometown.

He didn't expect to see her. Vancouver was home to more than half a million residents, and the chance of stumbling across her should be small. But he couldn't help wondering *what if.*

He cranked the music and pressed the gas pedal a little harder. He shouldn't be wondering at all. He'd severed that contact. He had no place in her life.

The drive went smoothly and Beck arrived at his parents' home ahead of schedule. That didn't stop his mother from coming out the front door when she heard the car and throwing her arms around him in an exuberant greeting.

"We didn't expect you for another forty minutes." She brushed the hair creeping well past the collar of his shirt, but she didn't say anything, which was a significant improvement. "Come in. I'll make you something to eat."

Beck opened his mouth to tell her he wasn't really hungry, then snapped it shut. For one thing, he *was* hungry, starving as he'd only had coffee this morning. And she seemed so happy to be feeding him. It reminded him of being a kid, how she used to wait for him after school and ply him with water and apple slices while she asked him about his day. The memory caused an odd pinching sensation in his chest. He rubbed at it.

"I have some chicken," she told him as she led him toward the house. "I can toss that in a salad, or would you rather go out. There's a great little bistro a few blocks from here."

"The salad will be fine." He unhooked his arm from hers and hitched his bag over his shoulder. The rest of his suitcases were in the trunk, but he'd get them later.

"Your father told me you'd be early, but I didn't believe him." She pushed open the door and called for him. "You were right," she said as his father made his way down from the second floor. "He's early."

"Dad," Beck said when his father reached the landing.

They shook hands, then his father pulled him into an awkward hug. "Thanks for coming," he said quietly, so the words were just between the two of them. "This means a lot to your mother."

A funny heat slid up his neck. Beck brushed off his father's words with a brusque nod. He hadn't seen them since that last dinner in Naramata, but he'd spoken with his mother on the phone once a week. It was the most contact he'd had with her since he was a teenager. "I hear there's salad."

"Chicken feed," Harrison said, but the twinkle in his eye told Beck he was only teasing.

"You want to be healthy, don't you?" Victoria asked, putting her hands on her hips. "We've got a lot of missed years to catch up on and you're stuck with me now."

The interplay between the two was clearly familiar territory. Beck told himself they weren't purposely leaving him out. They'd found a comfortable dynamic and hadn't adjusted to him being here yet. He barely got the chance to finish his internal pep talk when his mother hooked her arm through his again and dragged him forward. "Come on. I want to show off my kitchen."

She'd always liked to cook, and she chattered about the appliances with an expectant expression on her face. Beck nodded, though he had no idea why her selections were special. His expertise didn't extend to stove tops and ovens.

The salad was good. Better than chicken feed, and he even said so out loud, earning a prized smile from his mother and a pleased grin from his father.

It was almost like they were a family.

He spent the afternoon with his parents, surprised at how easy it was. And since Jamie and Emmy were in town for his parents' engagement party tomorrow evening, he was on his way to meet them for dinner at a popular steak house in the city.

Though Beck still thought the idea of an engagement party for a third wedding was silly, his mother insisted. According to her, this time would be the last and she wanted to honor it properly.

Beck hadn't seen Jamie and Emmy since their wedding last month, and as he pulled into the restaurant parking lot he realized that he was looking forward to catching up. Though there wasn't as much to catch up on as other times. He and Jamie had been keeping in contact through regular phone calls and email. Beck patted himself on the back for that as he got out of his car, recalling that he was already the proud owner of the knowledge that Emmy was over her morning sickness. Something he was pretty sure he could have happily lived without ever hearing, but hey, Jamie wanted to share and he wanted to listen.

"Jamie." They shook hands and Jamie tugged him into an embrace complete with a solid back-slap, which classified it as a manly hug.

"Good to see you."

Beck smiled and hugged Emmy more gently. She still didn't look pregnant to him, but he didn't want to hurt her or the baby. She smelled like cotton candy. "It's good to see you, Beck."

They chatted easily over appetizers, Emmy and Jamie sharing the details of their honeymoon in Hawaii, while Beck talked about the hotel. The conversation was pleasant and Beck's shoulders relaxed.

And then his stomach dropped.

It was her hair. That glorious red hair, which preceded her into a room like a procession before a queen. He flexed his fingers and whatever Jamie had been talking about floated away.

Poppy was here. In the restaurant with him. Right now.

He watched her move, a friendly smile on her face, as she made polite conversation with the hostess who seated her at a table on the opposite side of the room. He craned his neck to see who else was at the table, but the chair was vacant.

Was she here alone? He swiveled his head, checking for any lone men in the vicinity, but everyone appeared to be seated or heading to a table other than Poppy's. Beck checked on her again.

She looked good, really good. A dress that showed off her tight little body and a pair of sexy red heels. She'd left her hair down, the way he liked. His body tightened.

"Beck?" He dragged his eyes back to his cousin,

who watched him with a smug grin. "See something that interests you?"

"No," he answered quickly, too quickly. But the last thing he needed was for Jamie to see Poppy here. His cousin had been disappointed when Beck explained things weren't going to work out and had urged him to rethink and consider if this was something he really wanted to do. If Jamie saw her, he'd be over there before Beck called for the bill. "You two doing anything else while you're down?"

He wouldn't think about the fact that Poppy was in the restaurant, only twenty feet away from him. He could get up and walk right over, sit in that empty seat…

Jamie and Emmy exchanged a glance. "We were saying we're heading to Seattle on Sunday. We're going to spend a few days there, do some shopping."

"Great, great." Beck listened, but only with half an ear. Poppy studied the menu. Was she really here alone? Waiting for a friend? On a date? His hand curled into a fist.

"Beck?" Emmy's soft voice brought him back once more. "Are you all right?"

No, he wasn't. But he would keep that feeling to himself. He was just experiencing leftover guilt from the way he'd handled his relationship with Poppy. Maybe *bumbled things with her* was a better way to put it, as Jamie already had—twice.

"Beck?" Jamie's voice this time.

Beck blinked. "Yes, I'm here. You're going to Seattle for some shopping."

They shared another look. "You should tell him," Emmy murmured, putting a hand on her husband's arm and patting.

"He'll figure it out," Jamie said easily.

Figure it out? "Figure what out?"

"Why you're staring at Poppy like you're lost in the desert and she's an oasis."

"I'm not staring at her like..." Beck trailed off. "You knew she was here?"

"I set this up, and I can see I was right to do so."

Beck stared. "Why would you do that?"

"Because." Jamie leaned forward. "You aren't over her, no matter what you keep telling yourself."

"Don't you think that's something for me to decide?" And who was Jamie to say who he was or wasn't over? And even if it were true, he was still in charge of his own life. "I was trying to do the right thing."

"The right thing is to make yourself miserable?" Jamie shook his head. "I don't want to see you closed off for the next ten years, so yes, I set this up. Now, are you going to talk to her or are you going to sit here like a wimp?"

He was not a wimp. Okay, he was sort of a wimp, but every decision had been for her. Jamie should know that. Beck had explained he was unable to give Poppy what she wanted, what she deserved, enough times that it should have made an impact in his cousin's brain by now.

The waiter came by to deliver their meals. Beck was grateful for the interruption. By the time the man left, he felt more in control. Jamie was wrong. He wasn't miserable. Yes, maybe he thought about Poppy a little too often, but he'd get over that. And she'd move on and meet someone to have her babies with.

He glanced over and saw the seat across from her was no longer empty. All those good thoughts and intentions dried up in a powerful punch of fury. *No.*

Who was this dude and what did he think he was doing with Poppy? He was old enough to be her grandfather with his silver hair and avuncular smile. Probably dentures. And why the hell was she smiling back?

He clenched his fork and stabbed the steak. Both Jamie and Emmy paused and then Jamie started to grin. A huge, I-know-better-than-you-and-don't-you-forget-it grin. Beck scowled and turned his attention to the restaurant instead. The walls were dark wood with exposed brick. Chandeliers hung throughout the room and the chairs were covered in dark red velvet.

And Poppy was laughing. What did she have to laugh about? Was Gramps telling her he'd gone to the doctor for the little blue pill?

The thought made Beck's stomach churn. He sawed at his meat and shoved a piece into his mouth, grinding. He didn't even taste the blue cheese topping.

Jamie finally cleared his throat. "Anything you'd like to talk about?"

"No." He stuffed another bite in his mouth, his gaze still on Poppy. *His Poppy.* In her sexy dress, acting all flirty and friendly. The older man leaned across the table to say something and she laughed, exposing the long line of her neck.

The fork began to bend in Beck's grip. She wasn't supposed to smile at other men like that. She wasn't supposed to be out dating other men. He wasn't out dating other people. And he'd had opportunity. Plenty. He took a swig from his wine.

"Beck?" He turned to Emmy, who gnawed at her lip. "Maybe you should go talk to her."

And say what? That he'd made a terrible mistake? It was too late for that, wasn't it?

"No, I guess he wants to try to kill her with that stare," Jamie said.

"I'm not trying to kill anyone," Beck said, though he wouldn't be too distraught if his evil eye sent the old guy scrambling. He should be ashamed of himself, dating a woman a third of his age.

"No," Jamie said agreeably, digging into his baked potato. "And he doesn't want to see her either. Can't you tell by the way he's not paying any attention?"

"I didn't want to see her." Beck used his best business tone. The one that even shut down lawyers in

heir tracks. But Jamie had known him too long. He
lidn't appear intimidated in the slightest.

"Didn't?" he repeated.

"Don't," Beck corrected. He even shook his head
n an attempt to dislodge the furious thoughts of
striding over there and dragging Poppy out of the
restaurant. He sent the newlyweds a tight smile. "I
lon't."

Another look exchanged between Jamie and
Emmy. This secret, unsaid conversation going on
n front of him was starting to get on Beck's nerves.

"What?" he asked. "What are you two thinking
and not saying?"

"You seem a little upset for a guy who's getting
what he wants," Jamie said. He had the audacity to
continue smirking even when Beck glared at him.
"Maybe you're not so sure."

"I'm sure." Beck sawed off another piece of his
poor, beleaguered steak.

"Well, I'm going to say hello." Jamie pushed back
his chair.

"No." Beck fired out the word like a first volley
of gunfire. He placed his knife and fork carefully
on the edge of the plate. He was no longer hungry.
"Don't get involved, Jamie."

"You got me involved when you started up with
her at our wedding." Jamie's golden eyebrows raised
n a challenge. "Or am I wrong? Maybe you were
never interested in her at all?"

"You're not wrong." Beck bit the words out as

he'd just seen the waiter bring over a bottle of win
to Poppy's table.

The silver-haired man swirled a sample in hi
glass and leaned in to sniff the bouquet. Supercil
ious geezer. What did Poppy see in him?

Beck dragged his attention back to the question
ing face of his cousin. "But at least wait until din
ner is over." Until he stopped feeling as if he'd been
punched in the heart. And throat. And groin. He
glared over at Poppy again.

The rest of dinner was strained, with Jamie goad
ing Beck into talking and Beck doing his best to
ignore him. It didn't help that Poppy and Gramp
seemed to be having a most excellent time.

"Ready?" Jamie asked once the dishes wer
cleared and the bill signed. This time he didn'
merely push back his chair but stood up.

Beck swilled the last sip from his wineglass. No
he wasn't ready. He had no clue what he was sup
posed to say or do. Didn't even know if there wa
any point.

He must have accidentally said that last part ou
loud because Emmy turned to him with a concerne
frown. "Why not?"

"It wouldn't work." Beck shrugged and tried to ac
as if he hadn't been grinding his back molars dow:
into tiny stumps.

"Why not?" she asked again, her blue eyes sof
with worry. For him. Another rush of emotion as
sailed him, less irritated than the last. Oh, he wa

still irked, but this was his family, standing by him, pushing him because they thought they were helping.

"He's afraid," Jamie answered for him.

Beck narrowed his eyes. Okay, maybe family wasn't so great after all. "I'm not afraid. I'm doing what's best for her." Wasn't that what he'd decided all those weeks ago when he'd first returned to Seattle?

"And who are you to decide that?" Jamie's eyebrows were up again. Emmy reached over to give his hand a conciliatory pat, but the eyebrows didn't drop an inch.

"I'm doing her a favor, okay? Let it go."

Jamie should understand that doing the right thing killed Beck. Every time he looked at Poppy, he wanted to haul her out of that chair and up against his chest where she belonged.

His gaze was drawn to her again. The curve of her neck, the way her throat moved when she sipped her wine. Beck didn't find it so easy to be noble when she was sitting right in front of him.

"Emmy and I are going over to say hello." Jamie reached down to assist his wife to her feet while pinning Beck with a challenging stare. "You're welcome to stay here or you can put on your big-boy pants and come with us."

Beck would have liked to wrap his big-boy pants around Jamie's neck. What was Jamie playing at? He needed to leave things alone. Beck managed to muck up his own life without help.

But Jamie either didn't hear or chose to ignore his

silent pleas. With an annoyed grunt, Beck shoved
his own chair away from the table and followed hi
cousin across the restaurant.

CHAPTER TWENTY-ONE

THE EDGES OF Poppy's smile froze when she spotted Beck walking toward her. What was he doing here? Why was he coming over to talk to her? Why did he look so good?

Belatedly, she noticed Jamie and Emmy were with him, but her eyes returned to studying the man with them.

His hair was longer and moved when he walked. But his eyes were the same. Those dark, deep eyes that stared right into her and saw everything she wanted to hide.

Poppy balled her hands into fists beneath the table and hoped he wouldn't see the pain she was still toting around. She hadn't heard from him in a month, an entire month. Her eyes narrowed. She'd actually given him the benefit of the doubt and called him. Twice.

She'd even texted and emailed, just in case his voice mail wasn't working or he'd lost the phone entirely. But nothing. Her nails bit into her palms. And now he thought he was going to sidle over here to say hello as if nothing was wrong? That nothing had happened between them, or worse, that it hadn't mattered?

She swallowed the firestorm of words dying to be unleashed and pasted on a smile for Jamie and Emmy. She was happy to see them. They looked great, rested and happy. The tans from their Hawaiian vacation were still in effect, though there was yet to be any sign of Emmy's pregnancy.

Poppy sighed. Emmy was going to be one of those lucky women who only showed in the stomach. No bloating, water retention or blotchy skin. Poppy rose and hugged her anyway. Emmy shouldn't be blamed for good genetics.

She didn't permit herself to check out Beck. Didn't hug him either. In her opinion, he didn't even qualify for a handshake.

"Jamie, Emmy. I'd like to introduce you to Ned Stuart." Ned owned a string of car dealerships that sold high-end luxury vehicles to the city's wealthiest residents and held five appreciation events every year to thank them for their business. This year, he'd hired Poppy to plan them.

It was quite a coup. Not only because they provided guaranteed income to boost her bottom line, but the attendees were other business owners and CEOs. If she impressed them, Poppy knew there was a good chance she'd generate more business. And right now? Since her personal life was in the gutter? She was all about the business.

She introduced Beck to Ned as well, but only because her mother had raised her right.

"Good to meet you." Ned rose, exchanging handshakes all around while Poppy tried not to look at Beck.

His eyes were on her, studying. She exhaled softly. What did he want? Why was he staring at her? What were the chances they'd show up at the same place at the same time?

"I hope we're not barging in," Jamie said. "We wanted to come over and say hello."

"No problem at all." Ned indicated the empty chairs at the four-seat table. "Why don't you join us for dessert. I'm sure we can find another chair."

Panic ricocheted through her brain. Thankfully, Emmy saved her. "That's so kind of you, but we can't." Emmy to the rescue. Poppy knew there was a reason she liked Jamie's wife.

While Jamie and Ned fell into discussing the wine business, with Emmy nodding along to the conversation, Beck slid over to stand beside her. Poppy tried to sit down, but he caught her by the elbow and held her in place. She scowled at him, daring him to say something.

He took up her gauntlet. "How are you?"

Like he cared? She shot him a disgusted look. "I'm fine." She wrenched her elbow free and proceeded to ignore his smoking glances, reminding herself she didn't crave his touch late at night in the privacy of her own bedroom. Nope, not even a little.

She was relieved when they finally left, Ned handing out business cards and telling them to swing by for a test ride and he'd get them a good deal. There, that hadn't been so bad. She'd managed to get through without making an idiot of herself. But she felt edgy and out of sorts, and when Ned brought up the events, she found her concentration shaky.

"Ned, would you excuse me for a moment?" She threaded her way through the busy restaurant to the washroom. She'd splash a little cool water on her face, touch up her lipstick and regain some control. She would not let this rattle her. She'd known Beck would be in Vancouver for his hotel and known there was a slight possibility they would run into one another. She had hoped it wouldn't happen, but such was life.

A wet paper towel to the back of her neck and a fresh coat of pale pink on her lips calmed her a little. She would go out there, she would wow Ned Stuart and then she would go home and work.

Feeling more grounded, she stepped out of the washroom and into a broad chest.

"Poppy." She didn't need to hear his voice to know it was Beck. She recognized the scent of him, leather and soap, and those hard muscles beneath her cheek. She jerked back, banging into the wall.

"What do you want?"

He looked lost, like a little boy, and her heart softened before she reminded herself he had done her wrong and deserved none of her compassion. She was the injured party here.

"Well?" she demanded when he didn't respond. "What do you want?"

"I don't know." He ran a hand through his hair. Her fingers ached to slide through the strands. "I keep asking myself the same thing."

"Then quit wasting my time." She moved to slip around him, but he stepped sideways and blocked her path.

"I think we should talk."

Poppy's throat dried up and she forced a swallow, which did little to help. "I don't think that's necessary."

"I disagree." She tried to move around him again, but ran up against a solid wall of man. "Poppy, come on."

"Come on, what?" She wanted to back away, to retreat to the safety of the shadows and the hall behind her, but that would show him he'd gotten to her, that his nearness still affected her so much she was afraid to look down for fear she'd see her knees shaking. "What is there to talk about?"

He frowned. "You're mad at me. I understand."

He understood? Oh, she was going to kick his understanding right in the behind. "Beck, I don't want to talk. There's nothing to talk about."

"I think there is."

"Why? Why now?" Why not a month ago? Or

a week ago? What made today, this very second, so special?

"I just need to." There was a stubborn jut to his jaw. She didn't care.

She wasn't going to allow him to play with her emotions and toss them aside when he got bored. Not again. "No." She shook her head. "I'm not doing this. I need to get back to my table."

"Yes." He was an immovable object, blocking her flight to freedom. "I only want to talk."

"I have to go, Beck."

"Back to your sugar daddy?" The snide tone in his voice made her head snap up.

"Excuse me?" Anger flared through her. Who did he think he was? "I don't have a sugar daddy and the very mention of that insults me."

"No? Then who is he?"

His jealousy didn't flatter or intrigue her. More like infuriated her. After everything, he had the nerve to act as if *she'd* done something wrong? Maybe his understanding needed more than a kick in the behind. She laughed, sharp and hot. She wouldn't have been surprised to learn steam was coming out of her nostrils. "Are you kidding? Where do you get off?"

His face was tight. "Is it a date?"

"That's none of your business, Beck."

"I think it is." He captured her arm when she tried to push past him. "He's too old for you."

"You don't have a say in my life." She wrenched

her arm out of his grasp and brushed the front of her dress to rid it of the outline of his body pressed against her. "You don't have a say in anything I do."

The jut protruded farther now. He was going to dislocate his jawbone if he kept it up. "Maybe I want one."

"Too late." He just didn't like the idea that she might be moving on. "I don't even know why you're bothering. This is a waste of time."

"Poppy."

She ignored the plaintive note in his voice. It didn't mean anything. If he really cared, he would have talked to her before now. He wouldn't have waited until he saw her out with another man before suddenly discovering how he really felt. She exhaled slowly. She needed to gather her control, to remember this was not a fairy tale with a promised happily ever after.

"Poppy."

She almost broke when he said her name again. It took every ounce of emotional fortitude to bear herself up under his gaze, to lift her chin and roll her shoulders back. But she did. She would not go back to the table with her emotions in overdrive. She took a step back and looked up at him.

"Beck." She would maintain her cool if it killed her. "You don't want me. I get it."

His frown deepened. "I never said that."

She took a cooling breath, trying not to let his heat overwhelm her. "You didn't have to. But it's been a month since the wedding. Plenty of time for us to have this talk." She air quoted the last word, flinched when her arms brushed against him.

"Poppy."

"We don't want the same things, Beck. I'm fine with that." She so wasn't, but would rather die than admit it.

"How do you know what I want?"

She managed to keep her temper in check. "I don't because you never told me, but I can infer." And she'd done a lot of inferring in the month since the wedding. He didn't want the same things she did. A future together. Marriage. Kids. A dog. She forced herself to meet his gaze, to look deep into those dark eyes and see the facts.

"Maybe you should ask me before you go jumping to conclusions."

"I didn't jump to anything, Beck." Her anger started to subside, to drain away in the face of the confrontation. She didn't want to fight with him. She wanted to forget him. "You didn't call, you didn't write. You were very clear. What should I have thought?"

"You should have asked."

Her eyes were starting to get that achy, prickling reaction. "I shouldn't have had to."

"Poppy." Her name was a warning in his mouth.

She swallowed the tears away. "I hope one day you'll find what you're looking for." She almost reached up to smooth a hand along his cheek, but she didn't trust herself quite yet. She was only human, after all. "I need to get back to my dinner, Beck."

"Poppy. I made a mistake. Can't you just—"

She interrupted him. Her control hung by a thread. A thin, stretched-to-the-limits-and-about-to-snap thread. "There's nothing left to say, Beck. Good luck."

He reached out for her but didn't stop her as she walked past. His fingers brushed across her hair, but she didn't stop. She kept walking, toward Ned, toward her future of hard work and professional success.

And even though she'd done the right thing, she felt like crying when she sat down.

CHAPTER TWENTY-TWO

BECK PARKED IN his parents' driveway, still smarting about the run-in with Poppy last night. He had not liked seeing her with that Ned fellow. Not one bit. And he'd liked Jamie's busybody behavior in setting the whole thing up even less.

He snatched the gift for the engagement party off his passenger seat. The pretty paper and oversize bow annoyed him. All clean and sparkly and fresh. The whole engagement party annoyed him.

He let himself into the house without knocking. The entry blazed with light from the overhead chandelier, wall sconces and a small table lamp. They all reflected back out of the side mirror and the silver wallpaper. It was a bit like being inside a disco ball. An elegant disco ball, but a disco ball.

But at least there weren't flower petals or other fiddly floaty things festooned everywhere. In fact, it looked like many other parties his parents had hosted back in the day.

The sounds of voices and music led him to the back patio where a crowd of well-wishers had gathered. He placed his gift on the table set aside for them and grabbed a glass of champagne from a passing waiter.

As usual, his mother had spared no expense. Circular tables were scattered throughout the backyard and surrounded the turquoise pool. Each was laid out identically in white and gold. White tablecloths that snapped in the breeze, white plates with wide gold rims, white napkins with his parents' monograms in gold and tall crystal vases that sat well above the seated eye line and housed bouquets of a white flower that Beck didn't recognize. The whole effect was cool and elegant.

Just like his mother, who swanned toward him wearing a fitted white dress with long sleeves. Chunky gold jewelry glittered at her ears and around her wrist.

"Beck. You made it." She leaned in for a hug and kiss, surrounding him with a cloud of perfume.

"Of course I made it." He tried not to sound sullen, but he felt pretty sullen.

"Ignore him, Aunt Victoria," Jamie said, coming from out of nowhere like a snake making a strike. He kissed Victoria on the cheek. "He's annoyed Poppy won't give him the time of day. You look wonderful, as always."

"Oh, Jamie." His mother's hand fluttered as she straightened his collar, and then she turned to welcome Emmy with an equally warm embrace. "And Emmy. I'm so pleased you were able to come down for the party." She wrapped an arm around each of them and smiled at Beck. "Isn't it wonderful they're here, Beck?"

"Fantastic." They either didn't notice or chose to ignore his gritted teeth. He glared at his cousin and clutched his champagne glass more tightly.

After his mother finished fussing over them, asking how their trip down had been, how Emmy was doing and hoping they'd be able to come over for dinner before they had to return to Naramata, she turned her attention to Jamie's other comment.

Beck realized a moment too late that he should have taken advantage of his mother's distraction and excused himself from the group. He shook his head. What was wrong with him? He used to be so skilled at avoiding family awkwardness before.

"Now, what's this about Poppy?" Victoria clasped her hands together and looked eagerly from Beck to Jamie.

Jamie raised an eyebrow at Beck as if to say, *Are you going to tell her or should I?*

Beck growled deep in his throat. "It's nothing. Jamie's idea of a joke."

Beck had already explained to Jamie that there was nothing to talk about. She'd made it very clear she wanted nothing more to do with him. She hadn't spared him another glance. Not even when he made a big production of walking past her table when he left. Beck didn't know why he cared. But he did.

She should have at least looked at him.

He frowned as he'd been frowning all day whenever she'd popped into his head, which had been a lot. The way the edges of her mouth had tilted down as she told him she didn't want to see him again. Because although she might not have said those words exactly, he knew what she'd meant. Beck might not be a veteran of breakups, preferring to never let relationships get to the point where a breakup was necessary, but he could tell when one had happened to him. And he didn't care for it. Not one bit.

"Your son," Jamie said to Beck's mother, "is too stubborn to admit he has feelings."

Victoria sent Beck a little sideways glance. Beck sensed the questioning pressure behind the look. She wanted to hear everything. His guard came up automatically.

He loosened his hold on the champagne flute before he accidentally snapped the delicate stem, glad when he was able to pawn the glass off on a passing waiter. But his family's attention remained on him, probing and prying. He shoved his hands into his suit pockets. No one would be able to see the fisting motion beneath the material.

"Beck?"

But Beck was looking at the pleased smile Jamie couldn't quite prevent from tugging at the corners of his lips. Golden Boy, his ass.

He wondered if Jamie had seen Poppy today. Had she said anything about their little discussion last night? Said anything about him? Did she really hate him or was it a show? He hated that he wanted the answers. It was terrible that he hoped Poppy had been putting on an act for his benefit.

His mother laid a hand on his arm, distracting him from Jamie's smug expression. "Beck?"

"I'm fine." Her lack of demand was worse than if she'd tried to dive into his personal life like it was an ocean and she was on fire. "Don't listen to your nephew. He's trying to cause trouble over nothing. Nothing." He repeated that last word for Jamie's benefit.

His cousin didn't have the grace to look embarrassed and Beck decided it was best to escape before Jamie said any more. Bad enough he'd figured out how strongly he felt now that it seemed to be too late. He didn't need his cousin rubbing his face in his failure.

"I haven't seen Dad yet. I should find him. Say hello."

The excuse was weak, but the best he could do spur of the moment. He glared at Jamie as he passed. Didn't Jamie know that family was supposed to provide support and not throw each other to the maternal wolves?

Since he didn't want to talk to anyone, he headed back to the house and straight to the large kitchen, which was empty. Even the catering staff had departed for the moment, though trays of food were spread over the counters. But Beck never even got the chance to peek under the domed lids before the door behind him reopened.

"Seriously, Jamie?" He said something rude, expecting to hear the departing footsteps of his cousin.

"I guess that means you don't want to talk?" He turned to find his mother instead, laughter sparkling in her eyes.

He frowned. Great. Not how he wanted to handle this new, burgeoning relationship they were working on. "Obviously, that wasn't directed at you." He ran a finger along the edge of the granite countertop. He rarely spoke without thinking. This was Poppy and Jamie's fault. Getting under his skin and making him question who he was and what he wanted.

"Anything I can do to help?" Concern shone out of his mother's eyes.

"There's nothing to talk about." What red-blooded male wanted to chat with his mother about his love life?

Victoria didn't get the message and seated herself at the long trestle table that ran along one side of the kitchen. "Come on. Maybe I can help." She patted the seat beside her.

"No," Beck said, even as he found himself moving toward the empty seat, "you can't." This wasn't like when he was a little boy and she'd tended to his cuts and scrapes with antiseptic and get-better kisses. This ache went deeper, all the way to the center of his chest, and he didn't like it. "There's no problem to solve. I'll be fine."

He wanted to pummel something, but since there

was no punching bag in the room, he settled for clenching and unclenching his hands.

His mother looked at his motions, then his face. "You sure about that?"

"Sure enough."

Her smile dropped and for the first time in years, Beck saw her age. She wasn't a young woman anymore. She looked good for her age, but she was getting older. He sighed.

"If there was anything to tell, Mom, you'd be the first to know."

"Really?" The pure joy that bloomed on her face was like a spike in his heart. He'd pushed her away. She'd let him, but he was the one who'd initiated the distance between them. And the one who'd kept it alive all these long years.

"I know things haven't been easy between us." He took a deep breath. "And that's my fault."

"No." Her eyes looked wet now. She clutched his hand to her shoulder, her engagement ring cutting into his fingers. "It was my fault. I was the adult. I should have made an effort. You were so angry and it was easier to…" She trailed off. "I'm sorry."

"I'm sorry, too." And he was. It felt surprisingly good to unburden this part of himself to her.

She tugged on his hand until he gave in and sat down. "Now quit trying to be so brave and tell me what's bothering you. I'm an expert in these things."

Beck smiled. "Yes, I would say you are." Or, at

least, more of one than him. "I think I might—" He stopped. How to bring up the subject?

"You're in love with her."

"I—" He stopped again. "Is that what this is?"

"Sweaty palms? Can't stop thinking about her? Irrational anger that she's not with you?"

"Sort of." He dried his hands on his pants.

She studied him. "What are you going to do about it?"

Do about it? He hadn't even known he was in love. "Are you sure it's love? Maybe I just like her a lot."

Victoria laughed. "Oh, I'm sure you like her a lot, too." She laid a hand on his arm. "But yes, I think you're in love." She was quiet for a moment. "A little scary, isn't it?"

"Try terrifying." He thought he might have a heart attack right here in the kitchen. But as his pulse slowed, so did his swirling emotions. He heard the sounds of the party through the door. His mother's party. He shouldn't be monopolizing her when she had guests. "Maybe we could talk about it later?"

"No." Victoria was firm. "This is the first time in years you've actually been willing to have a conversation with me about your personal life. I'm not letting this opportunity slip away." She smiled as she patted his arm. "Let me help you."

"How, Mom? I don't know what to do." He studied her, the pretty smile that was always full of love no matter how many times it had cut her off at the knees. "Any ideas?"

Her smile widened. "Just one."

CHAPTER TWENTY-THREE

POPPY WAS ALMOST certain this was the biggest mistake of her life, but it was too late to back out.

She continued down Granville Street, dodging other businesspeople, bike couriers and residents walking their dogs. She was only a few minutes away from the meeting site. Though her heart knocked hard against her chest, she knew planning Victoria and Harrison Lefebvre's wedding might be the biggest boost her career had ever received. Bigger than Ned's events. Bigger than anything she'd ever planned before. And she'd have been insane to turn the couple down.

Even though it was sure to put her directly in Beck's eye line.

He was their only child and would obviously be a big part of the celebration. But, as she'd reminded herself multiple times already, this was a risk worth taking.

The Lefebvres had lots of friends, wealthy, corporate friends. The kind that owned their own companies and held parties for their staff and clients on a regular basis. The very people Poppy hoped to add to her stable of clientele. The chance to show them her styling and management skills in person proved impossible to resist.

Yes. She'd be foolish to turn the business down because of her personal relationship, or non-relationship, with Beck. He probably hadn't given another thought to their restaurant run-in. No, he'd probably spent the last five days wining and dining the pretty women who populated the city while she stewed alone in her apartment. She still hadn't forgiven Jamie.

He'd confessed immediately that he'd set the whole thing up in order to force Beck's eyes open. Poppy had given him a blistering lecture that she didn't need his help with her love life and if the man in question needed his eyes opened, then he wasn't the right man for her in the first place.

And there was still a chance she wouldn't see much of Beck anyway. He wouldn't care about flowers or room flow or which officiant to hire for the ceremony. If she was fortunate, she might not have to see him until the actual day and then she'd be busy with the details—she wouldn't have time to notice him.

Also, she'd be completely over him by then. Completely.

But even with the rallying cry running through her mind, Poppy was nervous as she crossed the street to the front of the hotel under renovation.

Victoria and Harrison were having the ceremony and reception at the hotel that Beck had finalized purchase on. Victoria had explained the hotel might not be at its best now, but it would be stunning upon completion. They wanted to have the wedding there as a sort of soft opening. To show off to their friends and family as well as create some buzz. She'd warned Poppy that imagination would be required to see past the drop cloths and dust, but imagination had never been Poppy's problem.

While the front didn't appear impressive at the moment, Poppy recognized the potential. She estimated the building to be about ten floors, with large windows and pillars to add architectural detailing. Beneath the years of grime and disuse, the exterior stone was black granite and would shine after a good polish. A pair of stone lions guarded the front doors and reminded her of the ones in front of Chicago's Art Institute. Once she got past the flanked guards, the front doors were stunning even with the cracked panes of glass. The art deco–inspired arches made of metal and glass would be a showstopper when they were repaired and cleaned.

She checked in with the site manager, Lou, had her name checked off the list and was given a yellow hard hat to wear as they navigated through the maze of construction. Lou was a chatty fellow and happy to answer Poppy's questions about what the hotel would look like once completed.

"Marble flooring, limestone and marble walls, lights everywhere so the whole thing glows. Going to be a beaut."

Although they walked across wood subflooring right now and the walls were only partially up, Poppy could imagine the finished product. The lobby was large and circular with steps that led to a plateau where, Lou informed her, a circular desk would sit, so people would be able to check in on all sides. The counters would be covered in cool metal with glass details to offset the warmth of the natural white stones everywhere else. Loads of natural light would spill in from all the oversize windows.

The buzz of saws followed them as they walked, and the scent of sawdust filled the air. Poppy tried not to breathe it in, tried not to think of the last time she'd smelled sawdust with Beck on the brain. She'd been young and foolish then.

"Yo, boss." They stopped outside a closed door. Lou rapped once and stuck his head inside. "Your appointment's here." He smiled at her. "You stop in and see me on your way out if you have any more questions."

"Thank you." Poppy smiled back and stepped through the door. She had a lot of questions whirling through her mind already. The flow of the event and how they should utilize the lobby as more than just a pass-through. Whether the ceremony would be taking place indoors or on the garden patio that the site manager had mentioned. What vision did Victoria have in mind?

Then she saw who sat at the small metal desk

waiting for her, and all her questions dried up and that lovely little bubble popped. Her eyes narrowed.

"What are you doing here, Beck?" And why did he have to look so good?

He smiled. He wore jeans and a black tee that had dust smudges on the arms, which only served to highlight his biceps. "Nice hat."

Poppy immediately yanked off the offending yellow plastic monstrosity, ripping out a couple strands of hair in the process, and dropped the hat onto the desk with a clunk. "Just following safety procedures," she told him.

If *his* head was uncovered, she saw no reason to keep the hard hat on. Really, the only danger of anything hitting either of them was if she decided to throw her briefcase at Beck's head. Which he would totally deserve.

Instead, she kept her fingers curled around its handle and sat in the orange plastic chair on the opposite side of the desk. Beck watched her, smiling the whole time. She didn't like it. What did he have to smile about?

"Where's your mother?" she asked, pulling out the file she'd started after she'd agreed to take on the project. She told herself this was a manageable situation. She didn't need to sit around making nice or engaging in chitchat. Get in, get out and act as if his presence didn't affect her in the least.

"You look good, Red."

She frowned at him. She couldn't help herself.

He knew her hair was auburn and not red. He was doing it to goad her. She was annoyed that it worked. "Thanks. Your mother? Where is she?"

"Something came up."

She stared at his grinning face, her irritation rising. He was so smug, as though he'd just put one over on her. *She didn't think so.* She shoved the file back into her briefcase. "Then we'll have to reschedule."

"No." He rose when she did. "She said we should still have the meeting."

Poppy sniffed, her disbelief likely evident. "You're asking me to trust that your mother wants you to plan her wedding?"

"God, no." She smirked at the pained look on his face. Then he smiled and for a second Poppy forgot she was supposed to be mad at him. "But since I know more about what the hotel will look like once it's finished, she said I should handle this part."

Poppy noted the logic in that, even though she didn't want to. "Still, I think Victoria should be here. I need to know what she wants before I can determine how to use the space."

The tiny office had started to feel claustrophobic. She didn't think she could remain here, with Beck, without doing something to embarrass herself. She flicked open a button on her cream-colored blouse to get a little air, realized her error when Beck's eyes darkened and his eyebrows shot straight up. "Get your mind out of the gutter," she told him, rebuttoning her top. "I'm warm."

"Do I make you all hot and bothered?"

"In your dreams," she scoffed.

"True."

They were getting nowhere and Poppy had no intention of letting him bait her into something she'd regret saying. "I'm here to plan your parents' wedding." She pinned him with what she hoped was a shaming stare. "If you don't want to help, I'm leaving. I have other business to take care of today." She clutched her briefcase in front of her for protection.

"No, wait." He came around the desk, caught her shoulder when she turned to leave. The touch sent a shock of awareness through her. "Don't go."

Poppy closed her eyes and wished for strength. She had to remember she and Beck wanted two entirely different things out of life and pretending they didn't was only going to lead to disappointment. "Why shouldn't I? You clearly don't want to talk about the wedding."

"I do." He grimaced. "Okay, I don't. But I'm willing to. If you'll stay."

She eyed him. "You promise?"

He didn't respond to her question, just slid his hand down to her elbow. She hated the responsive tingle that followed and considered ripping her arm free. But she feared any aggrieved response on her part would only show him how much she continued to be affected by his presence.

"I want to show you the ballroom." He tugged her toward the door. "I think you'll love it."

Poppy found herself propelled forward, all too close to Beck for her liking. Well, no, that wasn't true, which was the problem. She liked being near him too much.

She slipped her arm free as he grabbed the hard hat she'd deposited on his desk. He placed it on her head, carefully brushing her hair from her eyes. "There, now you're safe."

But Poppy didn't think so. His finger traced a path down her cheek. Her breath caught in her throat. No, she wasn't safe. Not safe at all.

She pulled back and glared at him, her only defense. "Do you mind?"

"Do you?" He stepped forward.

"You're crowding me."

"I like to think of it as getting to know you better."

She put her hand on his chest, ignoring the pull of need that told her to leave it there for a fraction longer than required to push him away. "You've had plenty of opportunity to get to know me. The ballroom?" she asked, keeping her voice serene and putting her hand back on the briefcase handle.

"Right this way." He grabbed a white hard hat from a hook on the wall, put it on and led her through the door.

Poppy practiced some deep, calming breaths as they headed back into the construction zone and hoped they'd kick in before Beck glanced at her again.

This was unfair. He was completely comfortable,

flirting and teasing as if their conversation on Friday night had been no big deal. While she kept reliving the scene in her head, replaying every word, each motion, wondering what he might have said if she hadn't stopped him. Which was insane. He wasn't the right man for her and she was moving on. Though she found that much easier to believe when he wasn't flaunting his muscles in that tight work shirt. Really, a man shouldn't be allowed to make a T-shirt look that good.

He showed her the ballroom and described his vision for it. Poppy found herself caught up in the imagery of the fabulous deco-inspired space, all black-and-white tiles and silvery accents. Guests would enter and mingle on the tiled floors, eating and drinking as servers carried platters through the room. They'd hire a small band to set up in the corner, and a bartender—that incredible round desk would be an ideal bar station. There was plenty of space for all the ideas running through her head.

"So what do you think?" Beck asked, breaking into her fantasy.

She smiled before she remembered who she was talking to, but even once she did, the remnant of good tidings remained. "I think it will be amazing."

"Me, too." He smiled back and tapped the clipboard she'd pulled out from her bag during their walk-through to take notes. "Anything else you need to ask about?"

"Actually, yes. Will you have kitchen staff in place

or will I need to hire a catering company?" If she needed to hire out, she'd have to act fast. Though the wedding was still a full three months away, and late October was never popular for parties except of the casual Halloween variety, good caterers got booked up no matter what the time of year.

"The kitchen will be operational. I'm interviewing chefs soon." He studied her. "Want to come and do a tasting with me?"

"No, thank you." He blinked, obviously not used to such quick rejection. A dull satisfaction rolled through her.

But he didn't give up so easily. "How about dinner?"

"No, Beck." She swallowed. "Just no."

Because there was nothing else to say.

She left shortly after, making her way back to her office, and threw herself into her chair as soon as she reached her desk.

She was fine. This was fine. Everything was fine.

Her face grew warm. She fanned it. Probably the heat of the day or the hurried walk she'd just had.

"How did it go?" Wynn strode into her office, no shame that he'd come for the dirt. "Do you have a sense of what Victoria wants? Was *he* there?"

"Victoria didn't make it." She fanned harder.

Wynn frowned and dropped into the chair across from her. "She skipped the meeting?"

"Yes."

She didn't need to explain what that meant. Wynn got it. "So it was just the two of you."

"Yes."

"And?"

"And what?" She wouldn't make it easy for him. If he wanted the dirt, he could dig.

"Any of those old feelings?" She'd told Wynn what had happened on Friday and he'd agreed she'd handled herself well.

Poppy sighed. There was no point in lying. "He flirted with me the whole time, which is why I've decided that I need to go on a date."

"Really?"

"Yes." She'd made her decision on her walk back to the office, bypassing men in suits, in jeans, in sweatpants, in shorts. Any one of them might be a good match for her. But she wasn't going to meet Mr. Right sitting in her office. She needed to get out there.

"Well, you know what they say," Wynn said with a nod. "The best way to get over someone is to get under—"

Poppy held up her hand. "Please, stop. Haven't I been through enough today?"

"—someone else."

Apparently not.

CHAPTER TWENTY-FOUR

BECK THOUGHT THE meeting with Poppy had gone rather well. True, she'd turned him down twice, but he sensed a wavering. She'd done her best to keep her irritation front and center, but he noticed her slips when she didn't focus. Those little hiccups gave him hope. She was angry, but the breach wasn't insurmountable. He just had to convince her to give him a chance.

He'd considered calling her—more than once—but had decided to let her be for the week. His mother had been thrilled when he'd told her of his progress and was certain by the time the wedding rolled around, Poppy would be more guest than organizer. But she'd also told Beck not to push too hard, too fast. He didn't want to scare her off.

For the first time that he remembered, Beck listened to his mother's advice. Instead of calling Poppy to ask if she'd like to get together or to tease her until that fiery temper of hers broke open, he'd spent the last seven days wandering the area, learning which cafés sold the best coffee, which bistros made the best sandwiches and which sushi restaurants stayed open late for those midnight cravings. But he looked forward to seeing her today.

He'd even tidied up his dust storm of an office— shoving scattered papers across his metal desk into a somewhat tidy pile and sweeping the empty coffee cups and napkins into the wastebasket. When he noticed the guest chair was covered in a layer of dirt, he dug one of the napkins back out of the bin, checked to make sure it was clean and then scrubbed the chair down. Work zones were impossible to keep shiny, but he wouldn't want to be anywhere else. He liked being in the midst of the construction, watching the pieces of his vision come together.

He'd also taken the time to groom himself in the reflection of his computer screen. This consisted of running his hands through his hair and making sure there was no drywall dust on his face, but he was pretty pleased with himself. Not that he thought he was a model, but he looked good. He'd dressed for a proper business meeting in a suit, which he'd been told he wore well. He hoped his professionalism might sway Poppy to go out for lunch and discuss the wedding in a more casual setting.

Despite his success when they were teenagers, Beck didn't think sawdust and wood shavings set the tone he wanted. To that end, he'd made a reservation at Coast, a popular and well-loved seafood restaurant, and pulled together a folder of plans for the hotel, including materials and layout, so she'd have something concrete to look at.

And so when Wynn walked through the door instead of Poppy, Beck's stomach plummeted. "What are you doing here?"

"Nice to see you, too," Wynn announced with a sniff. The hard hat placed at what Beck figured was supposed to be a fashionable angle bobbled. "Thanks for cleaning up."

Since Beck had made an effort, he was both annoyed and insulted. He scowled. "Where's Poppy?"

"She couldn't make it." Wynn's smile was tight. "I'm filling in."

Great. That was just great. Beck scowled some more, but it didn't appear to intimidate Wynn in the slightest. "I think she should be here. She needs to see the space in person."

Wynn lifted a pale eyebrow at him. "And I think your mother should be here."

Touché. Beck had the grace to feel embarrassed. "Fine. What was so important she skipped out?" And her reason had better be good or he would pick up the phone and shame her into coming down.

"She's in Naramata." Wynn glanced down at the plastic chair, disgust visible on his face. He pulled out a handkerchief and gave the seat a quick wipe.

"I already cleaned that," Beck told him.

"Not very well." Once Wynn polished it to his satisfaction, he lowered himself into the chair. Somehow Wynn had dressed to match the hard hat in a pale gray suit, with yellow shirt and tie. "Cami had the baby yesterday. Poppy flew out this morning."

"Oh." So much for shaming her. He couldn't even be annoyed, which annoyed him. "Everything go okay?"

Wynn blinked as if he was surprised, which insulted Beck all over again. He wasn't a complete brute. He cared about people.

"I didn't ask for details." Wynn made a face. "Cami will tell me whether I want to hear them or not, but according to Poppy she had a smooth delivery. Another girl. Lily."

"Pretty." He'd have to send something. He needed to win them all over, not just Poppy. He thought at first to ask his assistant to send something, then reconsidered. That would be keeping distance and he was trying not to do that. Even if Cami would likely appreciate the elegant taste of his assistant, she'd also enjoy knowing it was something he'd picked out himself. He hoped Poppy would, too. "So she wasn't avoiding me?"

Wynn pulled a binder out of his briefcase and flipped it open with a little shrug. "I wouldn't say that. More like excellent timing. Now, let's get down to business."

But Beck wasn't done. "So she is avoiding me." He crossed his arms over his chest and waited. Wynn met him stare for stare.

"Is there something you'd like to ask me?" Wynn finally said.

"Is there something you'd like to tell me?" Beck returned.

"No." Wynn glanced down at the binder in his lap. "I see Poppy's mentioned something about having a cocktail party in the lobby between the ceremony and the reception. They are both happening here, correct?"

"Yes." Beck was a little discombobulated by the quick change of subject. "Ceremony in the garden and reception in the ballroom." He shook his head to clear it. "What's going on?"

Wynn paused his intense study of the binder. "Why do you think Poppy was at the same restaurant as you that Friday?" He tilted his head, somehow the hard hat stayed on. "Did you really think that was just coincidence?"

Now Beck was really discombobulated. "I thought Jamie was responsible for that."

"Who do you think told Jamie where she would be? And she was not easy to get there, but I managed. And what did you do? Screwed it all up."

"I didn't—"

"You did. She doesn't want to see you again. Too bad." He eyed Beck speculatively. Beck sensed he was being judged and found lacking. Wynn heaved a disappointed sigh. "I thought you could make her happy."

"I can." Beck's molars were clamped together. "She won't let me."

"Oh?" Wynn looked interested.

"Yes." Beck wasn't sure what Poppy had told

Wynn, but he doubted it was the truth. Not as he saw it. "She won't talk to me."

"Do you blame her?"

"No." Beck unclenched his jaw. He wasn't mad at Wynn, not really. "Look, I was an ass. I know that. I thought things couldn't work out between us." He reminded himself that grinding his teeth would only upset his dentist and explained the different cities again. "I knew she wanted more than that. She *deserves* more than that and I thought it would be better to let her think I didn't care than to drag things out in what would inevitably end in a breakup. But then I couldn't stop thinking about her. And when I saw her at the restaurant with that old guy…"

Wynn looked delighted. "You were jealous."

"It sounds petty when you say it like that." But it was the truth. He'd been jealous. Still was. His hands fisted thinking about her with that old fart. "Anyway, it wasn't only that." No, there was the whole part where he hadn't been able to stop thinking about her and this stupid ache in his chest. "The point being, I tried being the good guy and it didn't fit. I want her back and now I'm going to fight for her."

There was a long moment where Beck wondered if Wynn was going to chew him out for being an idiot or tell him he and Poppy were no longer going to organize his parents' wedding. His mother would be devastated. Hell, he'd be devastated. Then Wynn smiled.

"For the record, she wasn't on a date. That was

a client." Beck's sense of relief was overwhelming. Wynn tapped his pen on the binder pages. "And despite the fact you have mucked up every opportunity you've had with her, I still think you're good for her. So let's call this your lucky day."

Beck raised an eyebrow.

"I'm going to help you."

"He cornered you at the restaurant?"

Poppy rolled her eyes at her sister. "Don't go thinking we shared some romantic moment where he declared I was his one true love and he didn't know how to go on living without me. It wasn't like that at all." Though that would have been nice.

She swayed her newest niece who slept peacefully in her arms all bundled up and smelling soft and sweet. She bent her head and inhaled, making the tufts of hair on Lily's head dance. Although she was only a couple of days old, it was clear Lily was going to have the Sullivans' auburn hair.

Cami grinned from the couch where she snuggled under a blanket with Holly curled into her side. Poppy had arrived this morning and proceeded to send their mother home for a nap. The woman had been at the hospital all day and night waiting for the news and hovering. She meant well, but Poppy sensed Cami was near her breaking point. Plus, Poppy didn't want to face down both of them at the same time.

"Well, how did you tell him you were done? Did you just blurt it out?"

"Is there some way to ease into it?" Poppy asked, still studying Lily. Her baby skin was so pure and unblemished. Nothing bad in life had touched her yet. Poppy's heart hitched. "I told him we didn't want the same things in life and left."

Cami ran a hand over Holly's strawberry-blond curls. "I thought you cared about him."

"I do. *Did,*" Poppy corrected hurriedly.

But she was too slow. Cami was on that slip of the tongue at light speed. "Ah, so you do still care. I knew it."

"Well, I'm sorry if my feelings don't magically disappear. But it doesn't matter. He's not the right guy for me." He never had been. "So I told Wynn I'm ready to start dating."

She'd thought that little snippet of information would pique Cami's interest. Her sister had been hounding her about getting back out there for the last ten months. Ever since Evan had gone on his quest to find himself. Instead, Cami frowned. "You're not ready for that. You need to figure out this thing with Beck."

"Cami." Poppy let the exasperation leak into her voice. "There is no 'thing' with Beck. We're over."

Cami sniffed. "Doesn't sound like it to me." She softened her voice. "Maybe he made a mistake, too. You can't go jumping to conclusions."

"How have I jumped to anything?" Poppy lowered

her voice when Lily twisted and started to snuffle. She returned to the soothing sway, rocking away her own irritation at the same time. "I explained what I wanted and he made it clear he didn't want the same thing."

"Oh, really?" Cami got that superior, know-it-all, older-sister look on her face that Poppy hated. "So you actually sat down with him and told him exactly how you felt?"

Not quite. But since Poppy didn't want to admit that, she said nothing. Though she needn't have bothered....

"Exactly." Cami nodded as though she'd just solved the problem of world peace and how to make high heels comfortable in one brilliant idea. "You didn't tell him. And now here he is, asking you out at the wedding meeting. How do you explain that?"

"I can't." Poppy hadn't been able to pigeonhole that into a tidy package. "He's probably just bored. He's going to be in town overseeing the hotel renovations and he wants someone he can booty call when it's convenient."

"Do you really believe that?" Cami studied her as if Poppy had lost her mind. The look reminded Poppy of the time she'd asked her sister if it was true that using a tampon meant you were no longer a virgin. She'd felt foolish then, too. "Beck is a good-looking guy. A rich, good-looking guy. I'm sure he could find someone to warm his bed if that was all he wanted."

"Ew. Are you saying he could hire someone?"

"Ew." Cami looked as grossed out as Poppy did. "I did not say or mean that. I was simply stating I don't think he'd find it difficult to meet someone in the city. A nonpaid someone." She shifted, drilling Poppy with a stare. "And yet, here he is cornering you at a restaurant and setting up a meeting for the two of you."

"His mother was supposed to be there. Something came up last minute."

Cami raised her eyebrows. "Oh, I know you're not naive enough to believe that."

No, she'd figured that out pretty quickly. No last-minute emergency had come up to keep Victoria away. She'd plotted to throw Poppy and Beck into the same room. And Beck was obviously part of the scheme. She just didn't know why. "No, but we still aren't a good match."

Cami made a rude snorting sound. "Actually, you are."

"Cami, he didn't contact me for a month." Lily shifted in Poppy's arms. She began rocking again. "A week ago you were ready to string him up."

"That was before he tried to make amends. I'm all about forgiveness." She stroked a hand across Holly's forehead. Holly turned toward her mother and curled in closer.

The deep ache went all the way to Poppy's bones. She wanted this. Badly. So badly that she had to sit down in a chair before her knees gave out on her.

But with Beck? She tried to picture him in the cozy little vignette. Hank had been so careful this afternoon, bundling all his women into the house, making sure Cami had everything she needed and politely slipping upstairs when Cami told him they needed some girl time.

But Beck? Big, oversize, demanding Beck? No.

"It's not about forgiveness," Poppy explained. "It's finding someone who I'm compatible with."

"You and Beck are compatible. You get along great."

"Yes, but that doesn't matter if we don't have the same life goals." She lifted Lily up to her shoulder, stroking the baby's tiny back. "I'd be wasting my time. I'm almost thirty. I don't have that much time to waste."

"You aren't even twenty-nine yet," Cami pointed out. "You're hardly in a position to be panicking."

Maybe not, but in five years? Seven years? What then?

"He's stomped on my heart twice, Cami. I don't think I'd survive a third time."

"Aren't his parents about to have their third wedding?"

"Yes, and that's fine for them." But not for her. Twice was two times too many already.

The third time would not be a charm.

CHAPTER TWENTY-FIVE

POPPY STARED AT the new messages waiting for her on the dating site. From such class acts as SexNinja, ChainsnWhips, and LadyKillah. It made the unoriginal 1983Dude seem positively romantic in comparison.

Still, she dutifully read through the messages. Perhaps she could find her diamond in the rough. After all, a person's profile name wasn't necessarily an indication of them as a human being. She'd finally settled on TheCourseWhisperer for herself, which was hardly going to set the world on fire with its originality.

From: SexNinja
Hey sexy,
Do you like sexy times?

Barf. Delete.

From: ChainsnWhips
I'd like to tie you up sometime. Or let you do the same to me. Your choice.

Ugh. Delete faster.

From: LadyKillah
Hello,
I'm looking for a sweet, sensual lady and you seem nice. I liked your profile…LOL…I won't tell you your beautiful…I'm sure you here that all the time…I live with my parents…had to move in about six months ago but Im looking for my own place…LOL.

Poppy didn't know what all the pausing and LOLing was about. She did know she didn't want to find out. Delete.

From: 1983Dude
Hello,
Your profile intrigued me. I also enjoy golfing and wine-tasting. I'd be interested in getting to know more about you. Perhaps one day we can go for a round together?

She reread the message from 1983Dude. He seemed normal enough. Since she didn't have a better offer and no one said this had to be The One, she replied and agreed to meet him for a drink.

Her hopes were high, or at least buoyant, when she walked into the lounge she'd selected for their drink date. As the day wore on, her dating in-box had filled with messages. Many of them similar to the first three who didn't make the cut, but she found a few possibilities in there, too. Who was to say that Liam29Vancouver, ProfessorVance, or Friendly-Warren might not be her ideal mate?

Or *1983Dude*. She thought meeting her future husband on the first go was unlikely but not impossible. And that would be a pretty sweet story to tell. Might even rank up there with her mother and sister and their high school sweethearts.

Although the day had been gorgeous, the sun had already started its descent and the temperature had cooled noticeably. Summer was over. A little tug yanked at her heart. She was always sad to see the end of the season even though she loved autumn—sweaters, crisp breezes and the crackle of leaves changing colors.

She'd chosen a pair of skinny jeans, a floaty cream-colored top with an adorable black sash and a pair of gorgeous black heels. Stylish yet casual. Sexy but not too sexy. Her hair swung around her shoulders in a mass of waves, which was why she'd chosen not to wear earrings, but a chunky bracelet and cocktail ring instead.

The lounge was moderately busy. About half the tables were filled and all the seats along the bar were taken. She found a small table near the front of the lounge, but to the side. Close enough to the door that he'd be able to find her without looking too hard, but not right in the middle of the action where they'd be on display for anyone to watch. She checked the time on her phone and hoped he wouldn't be late.

Poppy didn't realize until she was getting dressed that she only knew her date as 1983Dude. He hadn't posted a picture, but she'd been so irritated with Beck she'd made the date anyway. She hoped he wasn't a troll. Or toothless.

She'd considered not showing up tonight, but the thought didn't last long, even when she questioned the safety of such a meeting. In the end, she'd decided texting Wynn the guy's profile name and telling him where she was going to be would be sufficient. She wasn't meeting 1983Dude in a quiet location and didn't have any plans to share personal information with him. And if he was a creeper, she'd swill her drink at warp speed, pay for herself and bolt out of there. Nothing to be panicked about.

But her stomach was in knots anyway.

She'd just ordered a glass of wine—the need to have something to do with her hands had outweighed her concerns about rudeness—when Beck walked through the door.

Oh, no. Come on. Was the universe out to spite her?

It seemed so as Beck homed in on her and immediately headed over.

"No." Poppy held up her hand in the universal stop sign when he was still ten feet from her. "No. Go away." She didn't want him hovering, messing up her vibe when 1983Dude came in. He might think they were together. "I'm meeting someone."

"I know." He dropped into the empty seat across from her with a smug smile.

Poppy glanced at the door. No sign of the handsome Mr. Right yet. "Beck, please. Just go. You can't be here."

"I'm 1983Dude."

"What?" She stared at him, noticed he wore a yellow striped shirt just like 1983Dude had said he'd be wearing. The nerves in her stomach congealed into a hard ball.

"I want to talk."

"No, Beck." The waitress arrived with her wine, interrupting what she'd been about to say. Poppy clutched the glass as if it was a life preserver. No. This was not happening. She closed her eyes and wished she was somewhere, anywhere else. But when she opened them, the situation hadn't changed.

She pushed the wine away and gathered her purse. "If you won't leave, I will." She was not going to sit here and make nice while he intruded all over her life.

"Poppy, wait." His hand snaked out to wrap around her wrist. "We're out. It's a nice night. Stay. Have a drink with me."

She didn't want to. She couldn't.

"Five minutes and then I'll never bother you again."

It might have been the only thing he could have

said to stop her. She sank back into her seat. "Fine, but only five. I have things to do tonight."

She didn't. She'd cleared her schedule hoping the date would go well. He ordered a beer, flirted with the waitress when she brought it over. Poppy rolled her eyes.

"So this is nice." He leaned back in the large leather club chair, looking right at home. "I'm glad to see you. I missed you at the meeting last week."

"Oh, yeah. I can tell you missed me terribly." Her eyes flicked to the waitress, an adorable blonde who was probably an actress waiting for her big break.

"I did."

Poppy wasn't sure how to respond to that, so she didn't. She swirled her wine instead. Her stomach was too upset to take a sip.

"How's Cami?"

She eyed him, debating between asking why he cared and answering politely. Manners won out in the hopes they might speed this up. "She's great. She appreciated the gifts for the kids."

He'd sent a soft receiving blanket with a small lily embroidered in the corner for baby Lily and a pair of shiny red shoes with little holly berries as buckles for Holly. Cami had gotten all starry-eyed when she'd seen them.

Poppy hated to admit it, but she'd been a little starry-eyed herself. She swirled the wine again and reminded herself his assistant was probably the one with the great taste. She didn't need to be attributing qualities to Beck that he didn't have. It was bad enough her body still responded to him.

"I'm glad she liked them," Beck said.

Poppy put the wine down. "You didn't come here to talk about my sister. What do you want?"

"I want to see you."

"I'm right here." She twisted the heavy bracelet around and around her wrist.

"Poppy."

"Beck."

"I want to see you."

"I heard you the first time." Which was a miracle, considering the thunderous heartbeat in her ears.

"So it's going to be like this, is it?" He picked up her wineglass and took a long, slow sip.

"No, Beck. It's not going to be like anything." She snatched the glass back and curved her arm around it. He should have ordered wine instead of beer if he'd wanted some.

"I was a complete idiot. I should have called you."

"I'm aware of that." She shrugged as though this was no big deal. Nope, she was totally fine. Cool as can be. That wasn't her knee bounding up and down like a mad game of horsey under the table. Absolutely not.

"Poppy." He leaned forward. She recognized the intensity in his eyes, forced herself not to get sucked into the swirl of his emotions. She had enough dealing with her own. "I know I messed up. I've messed up a lot."

She shouldn't sit here and listen to him, shouldn't let herself believe what he said might be true. "I have to go, Beck."

But all those old fantasies floated back to the surface anyway. The one where he crashed her high school prom and whisked her into his arms for the last dance of the night before squiring her away under a blanket of stars to tell her how much he'd missed her. Or the one where he called and cried that he couldn't live without her. Or the one where they stood on the dock with the rain pouring down where she demanded to know why he never wrote and he said he wrote her every day for a year. And then they kissed and he carried her, now soaked to the skin, into the house and made love to her.

That last one was a particularly good fantasy.

"I've missed you," he said.

So was this one.

Her heart began to pound. She swallowed. "Beck."

"Will you give me another chance? I want to try."

Oh, she wanted to let him try, wanted to open her arms wide and let him in and believe everything would be okay. But she'd already done that. Twice. "I don't know, Beck." This wasn't safe or smart. Two things she needed to keep in mind.

"I'm going to be living here until the hotel is finished. I'm asking for the chance."

Her hands were gripping her clutch so tightly she was surprised she hadn't accidentally ripped off the blue beading. "It can't be like it was."

"I know." He reached out. She jerked back before he touched her. "Wynn told me you want to date, so—" he took a deep breath "—I'm open to that."

Her head spun. Wynn knew about this? Wynn was working with Beck? And what did that have to do with her dating? "What?" she finally managed to ask, though it was more like a whisper than a demand for information.

"If you want to date other people, I'm okay with that. Just give me a chance, too."

She shook her head as all those pretty fantasies crumbled under reality. He didn't want her. Not really. He wanted the convenience that being with her offered. And no worries about getting attached again. Oh, no, he'd solved that rather neatly by allowing her to date other people at the same time. As if she needed his permission.

"No, Beck. I want more than that. I deserve more than that. Is *that* what you want?"

He blustered a bit. Not a good sign. "I'm saying I want to try. I can't promise it'll work out. But who can?"

The sliver of remaining hope that hadn't already dried up and blown away disappeared. He hadn't changed, he'd just dressed up the same old, same old in a new package. "That's how we're different, Beck. I won't go forward locked into the idea that we're already doomed to fail."

"I didn't say we were doomed."

She smiled at him sadly. "You did. You just don't

realize it." She stood, grateful her knees supported her. "I have to go. Good luck."

"Poppy."

"Goodbye."

"Wait." He rose, too. "I want this. I want you."

But she didn't believe him. "You'll get over it," she told him and left the table.

"I won't." His voice followed her across the room. Her heart squeezed so tightly she was afraid it might burst. She had to grab onto the door handle when her knees threatened to buckle. Wouldn't that be a fabulous way to end the night? She'd lay herself prone at his feet for him to walk all over her.

Again.

CHAPTER TWENTY-SIX

POPPY GAVE HERSELF one week to grieve the loss of what might have been. Then she decided the only way to move forward was to get out there and date again. Not that Wynn had the right idea—she was not getting under anyone. Not until she'd gotten to know him.

But there would be no more nights of sitting in front of the television or staying late at the office either. If she wanted to put Beck behind her, she had to take the first step. But he and Wynn weren't allowing her to move on.

They were sabotaging her dates.

Between the pair of them, no man went unresearched, no restaurant went unstaked out and no date went uninterrupted. It was a miracle she managed to schedule anything at all.

She'd thought they'd grow tired of their game. But they hadn't. For the past two months, they'd kept up a running attack on her dating life. Poppy wouldn't be surprised if she was on one of those "Avoid this person" websites with stories about the two men who crashed all her dates.

Like tonight when Beck had inserted himself

into the evening and chased off her date before the server had even swung by to ask if they'd like another drink. The poor guy had looked as if he was about to have a coronary when Beck strode over, all six foot two and bulging muscles, and asked if he was going to leave on his own recognizance or if he wanted to be thrown out.

Poppy was growing weary of it. And confused. What was Beck looking to get out of all this? He was heading back to Seattle right after his parents' wedding, and since that was happening tomorrow, she couldn't figure out his angle.

Unless he meant it?

No, she shook her head as she unlocked her apartment and stepped inside. She'd bruised his ego and this was his way of assuaging his hurt feelings. She ignored the little voice that asked if anyone in their right mind would do what he'd done for two months without a break.

She'd barely closed the door behind her when her phone rang. Her feet hurt. She slipped off her shoes before answering. She already knew it would be Wynn making sure she'd arrived home safely. She'd tell him to ask his new BFF Beck about her date instead, seeing as he'd been there for the whole thing.

She didn't know why Wynn had taken Beck's side in all this, but there was no doubt he had. The first time Beck had shown up at her rendezvous point, acting as her date, she'd chalked it up to coincidence. He'd seen her profile picture and acted accordingly.

But when he'd crashed a date with a stranger, not one, but two, three and four times? Dates he could not have known about since she hadn't told anyone except Wynn, the betrayal was undeniable. *The little traitor.*

There was also the fact that when asked, Wynn readily admitted his involvement. His only response to her repeated inquiries about *why* was that he thought he was helping her.

Well, she had a thing or two to say about that. Her phone rang again and she dug it out of her purse and answered it without checking the screen. Wynn needed to understand that as *her* best friend, he should not be assisting her nemesis in his nefarious schemes.

"Seriously, Wynn. I've had enough. You and—"

"It's not Wynn."

She almost dropped the phone. "Beck." She'd recognize his voice anywhere. Had, in fact, listened to it all the way home as he'd insisted on walking her back. Nerves made her mouth suddenly dry. She swallowed and parroted his name again because it was easier than considering why her body had suddenly gotten all warm.

It was silly. He'd only left her building a few minutes ago when she'd told him he was not welcome to come in for a nightcap. Her body had been totally fine then, no sign of need or overwhelming desire to rip off his clothes and have her way with him. Or almost no sign.

"I'm downstairs." She realized her phone hadn't been ringing with an incoming call. It had been the front buzzer she'd programmed to come through her phone. "I want to come up."

"No."

"Yes."

She hung up.

Her phone rang again. And again. She stared at the screen until it stopped and beat back the swell of disappointment when it didn't start back up immediately. She didn't want him to call back.

The phone jingled again, her text tone this time.

I've got all night

She swallowed, fingers flying over the screen.

Good for you. Hope you find the sidewalk comfy.

She'd been finding her decision to excise him from her life increasingly difficult to rationalize the last few weeks. When one of her dates had gotten handsy, Beck had scared him off and taken her somewhere else to eat. When another one had ditched her with the bill, Beck had stepped in to pay. She hadn't let him, but he'd tried.

If the memory of him so casually dropping her hadn't been fresh, Poppy didn't think she would have been able to maintain her stance.

Even so, she found it increasingly difficult not to

notice that he'd changed. Not a huge change, but a change nonetheless.

The phone rang again. She was grateful for the interruption, not wanting to pursue that dangerous idea. The one that swept over her late at night when she wondered if maybe Beck did want something more than just a casual fling. The one where he got down on one knee and she took his name because Lefebvre was a good name and they all lived happily ever after. "Yes?"

"I'm not leaving. Buzz me up."

She thought about it. What could he do from down there? Press the button the rest of the night? Or buzz someone else who would let him in. And he'd be up here anyway, only she'd have no chance to prepare herself.

"You have five minutes," she said and hit the button.

She double-checked to make sure her front door was locked. If he thought he was going to stride in without a fight, he was wrong. She rolled her shoulders back and twisted her neck like a prize-fighter preparing for a championship bout.

At least she was still in her date clothes: a skin-tight black dress, so fitted that it was a good thing she'd only had salad for dinner, and a collarless, cropped leather jacket. She straightened her skirt and wondered if she should slip her black peep toe heels back on. Her feet screamed they were willing to disown her if she tried, and she decided it wouldn't make a difference anyway. Beck still towered over her.

She tossed her phone onto the small console table beside her door. It missed the little bowl she had for it, clanging against the edge and making the keys inside rattle. The vase of flowers beside it shook, too, one petal drifting to the top of the table.

Poppy ignored the mess. Who cared about a fallen flower petal? Her nerves were threatening to leap out of her skin, did when the knock came. She looked through the peephole. Her body jerked when she saw him standing there, waiting. All calm and strong and so much of what she wanted.

Stupid raging hormones.

He knocked again and her stomach dipped. *He was leaving town soon.* She'd been trying not to focus on that, but her breath caught and did its best to choke her as the truth set in.

After his parents' wedding tomorrow night, once the last toast was made, the last glass clinked, the last kiss shared, she'd never see him again. He'd go back to Seattle to his gorgeous hotels, his stylish city life and she could move on.

Her lungs squeezed again and she shut her eyes. But she'd never see him again. Never hear that teasing tone when he tried to rile her up, experience the gentleness of his large hands or see that look in his eyes that made her feel as if there was no one in the room but them.

"Poppy? Come on. I need to see you."

She peeked through the peephole again. She didn't want to want him.

"Poppy, please."

There was a longing note to his voice that matched the expression on his face. She swallowed. She shouldn't do this. She knew better. Nothing had changed and those late-night fantasies were just that: fantasies. Okay, so maybe he wasn't as much of a playboy as she'd thought, but he wasn't looking to become husband material. And that's what she wanted. She watched her hands flip the dead bolt and turn the knob. She was two parts numb, three parts on edge.

"Hi." He smiled, stepped inside and closed the door behind him.

"Hi." She would explain this was not a good idea. That it was best they shake hands and go on with their lives as though everything during Jamie's wedding had never happened.

She didn't get a single word out before he yanked her to him and kissed her. Their mouths slammed together, hot and hungry. His hands slid beneath her jacket, stroking the soft material of her dress. A low growl of approval rumbled from him. She shivered in anticipation.

"Beck."

"What?" His mouth had worked its way down her neck, nibbling and biting and leaving a trail of the most delicious tingles in its wake. Really, it was a good thing she left the shoes off. She was pretty unsteady as it was.

"We shouldn't."

"We should." He resumed kissing her.

She tried to open her mouth to tell him he was wrong. Cooler heads must prevail. She hadn't let him up here for this. But she couldn't.

Her body responded, clinging and binding herself to him. The months apart had been long, made worse since he'd been so close for the last two of them. Being with him but never acting on those needs that accosted her every morning had been torturous.

This was their last night.

Maybe their last chance. She shrugged the thought away. No, this wasn't about chances, this was about closure. This could be her closure. One fantastic goodbye before he left, and then she would take the necessary steps to move forward in her life.

"This doesn't change anything." She felt compelled to tell him, to inform him she wouldn't be chasing after him or expecting a relationship.

"Yes, it does."

She was afraid to believe. She opened her mouth to explain it was okay, she accepted what he had to offer. But all the words and thoughts got twisted up when he stripped off her jacket, pulled down the neck of her dress and ran a finger along the curve of her bra.

Her skin pebbled when he yanked the lace out of the way and replaced it with his mouth. His beard abraded the soft skin, but she didn't care. The wet warmth of his mouth was enough to make her forgive just about anything. She ran her fingers through his thick hair, enjoying the extra length that allowed her to twist and tug.

"Bedroom," she told him when he scowled, annoyed at the interruption of his exploration. "I'm not a teenager anymore."

He chuckled and let her drag him down the hall. He kissed her onto the bed and lowered himself, covering her with his bulk.

Every part of her was in contact with him. Chests pressed together, legs tangled up, arms wrapped around, fingers reaching and touching, mouths fused.

"God, I've missed you."

Poppy pulled her head back. "It hasn't been that long."

"Trust me, it's seemed like a very long time." He bent his head and nipped at her neck. "And there are a million things I want to do to you with my mouth, but none of them involve talking."

"Dirty." She sighed and moaned as his tongue licked at a particularly sensitive spot. "Oh, that's nice. I like that a lot."

Her fingers scrabbled over his back, tugging at his shirt until it was free of his jeans, pulling it up over his head and flinging it to the far corner of her bedroom so her hands were blissfully free to run up and down his bare skin.

It was so smooth, as if he treated it with lotion and scrubs on a regular basis, but Beck would never be caught dead doing something so girlie. She stroked up and down, letting her hands dip lower each time until they were fully buried beneath his jeans.

Beck was busy rolling the arms of the sexy little dress off her shoulders and down her body, and dispensing with the bra with a practiced flick. The room was dim, but she saw his face by the lights sneaking in around the blinds. The hunger and possessiveness there shocked her. She brushed it away. It didn't mean anything. He was a guy about to get into her pants—or in her case, dress—there was nothing more to it.

She inhaled sharply when he reverently stroked her bared stomach and bent his head to taste. The contrast of his bristly beard and soft tongue made a wildness build inside her.

She might not be blessed in the curves department, but she'd never know it from the way Beck carefully and thoroughly investigated every inch of her body. She gasped when his fingers closed over her breast, arched her back when he rolled the nipple between his thumb and finger.

Her dress was still around her waist and he'd only lost his shirt, but Poppy wasn't sure how much more she could stand. Beck, though, seemed to have other ideas.

"No," he said when she tried to hurry him along

by moving her hand to the front of his jeans to un-button them. "I'm not rushing this."

"Beck." It was half whine, half demand.

He shushed her with a hard kiss on her mouth and two soft ones on either side of her neck. "Just let me love you."

Her heart shook before she reminded herself he hadn't said he loved her. It was a euphemism for the physical. And the physical was very nice, the way his fingers were slowly wiggling her dress over her hips and down her legs was very nice indeed.

She attempted to help with the disrobing, lifting her hips and drawing her knees up, but Beck stilled her with a soft hand. "No, let me." She lay back while he murmured words of endearment and kissed each new band of skin as he exposed it.

"Now." She moaned when she couldn't take any more. "I want you now."

He smiled between little bites on her neck. His teeth nipped into her skin and made her shudder. She moaned again when his hand finally made its way below the waistband and under the elastic of her underwear. High-cut, lacy, black underwear. Thank-fully, she hadn't pulled a Bridget Jones and worn a pair of gigantic granny panties in nude.

She reached for the condoms in her nightstand while he ripped off his pants and boxers. She'd stopped at the drugstore a few weeks ago, telling herself it was being smart in case one of her dates actually went somewhere, but she knew now it had been for this moment. For Beck. She helped him roll it on. She didn't care anymore what the future held. She just wanted this and him. Whatever he gave her would be enough.

He kissed her again, pressing her back into the pillows. She pressed her palms into his back and let them slide across his shoulders, his muscles shifted as he levered himself up. She wanted him deep inside her and sighed when he fit himself to her, fit their bodies together, and did just that.

His gaze was hot and the friction between their bodies grew as he stroked in and out. She wanted to touch and kiss him everywhere, but she settled for bringing her knees up to take him in even further and gripping his shoulders.

She told herself it was enough. It had to be.

CHAPTER TWENTY-SEVEN

BECK AWOKE SMUG and satisfied. The feel and taste of Poppy lingered on him exactly how he wanted it. Last night had been incredible. She'd been willing and open. He was certain she understood him now. He reached out a hand, expecting her to still be at his side, but found an empty expanse of sheet instead. The spot was cool, as if she hadn't been there for a while.

"Red?" he called out. The apartment was silent. His only response was the low hum of traffic on the street below and a horn. Her clothes had disappeared. His were neatly folded on top of the dresser. Along with the quiet, they told him what he already sensed. She was up and gone, leaving behind only the scent of lavender on the pillow and coffee in the air. Coffee. He sniffed and called out again. "Poppy? You here?"

No answer. But when he glanced at the time on his phone and saw it was already past nine, he wasn't surprised. She hadn't run out on him, she was working. She had a lot to do for the wedding today. For that matter, so did he.

He climbed out of bed, hoping the coffee wasn't

a teaser, a lingering trace from a pot Poppy had made for herself earlier, because he could use a cup or twelve.

When he padded into the kitchen, he found a fresh pot and a cup sitting next to it. He grinned as he filled it up. What a woman.

After grabbing a quick shower and getting dressed, Beck noticed that there was a set of keys on the kitchen counter and a note that said to lock the door and return the keys to either her or Wynn. As if he was ever giving these keys back. He tossed them in the air, caught them, then let himself out and dialed Poppy's number.

"Yes?" It was a harried tone, telling Beck although he hadn't been rushing around, she had.

"Morning, Red."

"What do you want, Beck?" He didn't get offended. She was probably juggling caterers and florists and making sure the space for the band was acceptable. He'd double-checked everything at the hotel yesterday, but Poppy would still want to go over it herself.

"Thanks for the coffee." He'd finished his first cup while still in the shower. "Your place is all locked up."

"Great, just find Wynn and give the keys to him. Anything else?"

"Isn't a man supposed to call the next morning?"

"Beck," she started and then sighed. Some of his good mood ebbed.

The sounds of activity carried through the phone. Beck was aware her responsibilities for the day were massive, but that didn't explain her terseness. "Everything okay?"

"Fine." But she didn't sound fine, and Beck knew when the word was used in that abrupt tone it meant nothing was fine at all.

"You sure? Is there something I can do to help?"

"Nothing."

She sighed loudly. One of those sighs that announced she was tired of standing around talking about nothing.

The rest of Beck's good mood disappeared. "Is there a problem? I know you had a good time last night. Three good times in fact."

The keys pressed against his thigh as he walked, but he didn't move them. They were his badge of honor, a promise he'd made even if she didn't want to hear it. Those keys were staying right where they were and if she thought he was giving them back, she was in for a long wait.

"I'm busy. I told you."

"So let me help you."

A small pause. "Why would I do that?"

"Because we're a team." Why did she think? Did she believe he went around foisting himself on any unsuspecting woman? "Now, let me help you, damn it."

"Beck, last night was good."

"I think three times deserves a great," he insisted,

knowing it probably sounded like he was digging for a compliment. He didn't care. It had been great and she was going to admit it.

"Fine. Last night was great, but it didn't change anything."

A chill settled over his skin despite the bright sunlight. It was one of those dazzling October days that tricked a person into thinking summer wasn't really gone but had only been in hiding for a few weeks. "What does that mean?"

"Just what I said." He didn't know if it was better or worse that her voice was so flat. No inflection, no hint of where her head was. "As far as I'm concerned, things are the same as they've always been."

Beck thought of her beneath him, that sweet cry of release as he buried himself inside her. The way her arms and legs had wrapped around, pulling him tighter as though she couldn't ever get enough of him. The breathless sigh when he curled his body around hers and kissed the side of her neck. No, things were not the same. Not even close.

She was talking again. "I thought we were on the same page about this. I had a good time."

"Great time," Beck barked.

"I had a great time," she revised. "But after today you're still going back to Seattle and I'm staying here. And I'm okay with that. You don't have to worry about me chasing you down and insisting on a relationship. You can go back home without any guilt."

It wasn't guilt twisting through his blood right now. Not guilt that had his hands tightening over those keys so the edges bit into the soft tissue of his palm. "Wrong."

"Beck, be reasonable."

He didn't want to be reasonable. The thoughts spinning through his head, which went something along the lines of dragging her back to her apartment—the wedding could go on without them—and keeping her there until she confessed she felt the same as him, weren't reasonable.

"You know it wouldn't work. We'd end up hating each other. Can't we enjoy what we had and part as friends?"

"No."

"I'm sorry." Her voice was quiet. "I hope this won't affect today."

Oh, it sure would. Just not the way she expected. "I'll see you later, Poppy." He hung up before she said anything else.

She might think she'd had the last word, that he was going to roll over and allow her to have her way, but she was sorrowfully wrong.

IT HAD ALMOST killed Poppy to keep up the facade on the phone with Beck, but she'd managed. And as much as it hurt and was going to continue hurting, she couldn't regret last night. No, last night would live on in infamy and keep her warm on those long, lonely nights until she got over him.

He didn't mean it when he said things had changed. He never meant it. And she didn't want to play, didn't want to get sucked back into the game, because if she did, she might not get over it this time.

When he'd arrived at the hotel, she'd ducked behind a pillar. Pathetic and cowardly, she knew. But he wore a tux. He was almost impossible to resist in a tux, and her resolve was already so low.

He'd been mad about this morning and she understood why. It was a conversation they should have had in person, but she hadn't been able to do it. She'd looked down at him, sleeping in her bed, all large and manly and so hers, and she'd known if she didn't leave immediately, she'd let him do whatever he wanted. And her heart couldn't bear it.

At least she'd left a note and answered his call. If she copied his M.O., she'd have left town, never contacting him again.

Still, it was hard to hold the moral high ground when she cowered like a mouse. She straightened the folds of her dress, finished checking on the flowers and returned to the suite where Victoria was getting ready.

Beck's mother looked beautiful. She'd selected a simple white sheath with exquisite lace overlay that covered her shoulders but left her arms bare. A wide silver belt showed off Victoria's trim waist. "You look lovely," she told the woman, who was pink with excitement.

Victoria smiled. "So do you. My son is going to trip over himself when he sees you in that dress."

Poppy smiled. She did look good. Her dress was a neutral golden beige reminiscent of a Grecian toga. She'd pulled her hair back into a sleek knot and hair sprayed it into a helmet that wouldn't move in a hurricane, and wore only a pair of drop earrings to accessorize. But the simplicity allowed her to blend into the background, too. It wasn't her moment and she had no intention of outshining the bride.

Not that she could have even if she'd tried.

Victoria was glorious and not only because of the beautiful gown and shoes, or the jewelry or flowers, either. No, it was the joyous love that seemed to surround her. She was a woman who loved and was loved. No dress or diamond on the planet could compete with that.

Poppy kept her sigh internal. Maybe one day that glowing bride would be her. But for today, she needed to focus on making Victoria's day as perfect as possible.

"Have you seen my errant son, by the way?" Victoria asked as she slipped a knot of diamonds into her earlobe.

"I think he just arrived." She was not about to confess to hiding and watching him like some sort of creepy stalker. "Did you need to speak with him?" She'd text Wynn and ask him to get Beck. It wasn't avoiding exactly, it was sharing the responsibilities. Victoria needed her in here.

"Oh, no." Victoria inserted the other earring. "I wondered if you'd had a chance to talk to him."

About what? The fact she'd sneaked out of her own apartment this morning like a thief? "Afraid not. Is there anything else I can do for you in here?"

Victoria indicated she had things under control, so Poppy left the suite, careful to check the hall for any sighting of Beck, and headed to the kitchen. She spoke with the serving staff, explaining how she wanted the first rounds of appetizers to come out in the lobby to encourage guests to mill about among the gorgeous tiling and soaring ceiling, and then double-checked that the band had enough space for their instruments.

It was almost six and she'd been here since eight, making sure everything was perfect. The guests were starting to arrive. She was tired, running on adrenaline and fear, but she put on a smile despite it all.

They'd set up white tents and heaters on the garden patio so guests would be comfortable in the cool October evening. As the blooming season was often painfully short in the Northwest, the landscapers had selected evergreens to fill the space, and Poppy had wrapped white lights around the trees and shrubbery. All white and black and green. The effect was stark and ethereal.

As it was her third wedding to Harrison, Victoria had declined the usual wedding trappings. There was no bunting along the aisle or bows on the chairs.

Instead, she'd requested simple black chairs, and the only flowers were the two five-foot white manzanita trees planted in black pots bookending the altar.

With a check of her watch and a look at the filled rows of seats, Poppy realized it was finally time to start the ceremony. A trio of two violinists and a cellist began playing at Poppy's signal. A moment later, Beck and his mother stepped onto the end of the black-and-white damask runner.

Poppy had to blink back a tear when she saw them together. The protective way he escorted her down the aisle and dropped a kiss on her cheek before shaking his dad's hand and taking his spot to the side. She swore the entire female audience and some of the men had sighed.

It was ridiculous. This wasn't her first time at a wedding or even a remarriage. But maybe because the participants were more than just clients, it was different. Her eyes landed on Beck, saw him watching her instead of his parents. She made a gesture for him to pay attention, but he kept watching her. He wasn't happy.

Her pulse raced. He was just upset with her for not bending to his wishes. Nothing more. He certainly wasn't about to tell her that he'd reconsidered his life choices and realized he *did* want the same things as her.

Fire licked up the length of her body as he continued to stare, and she had to remind herself last night was last night and today was something else entirely. And he had no right to glare at her. Quietly, without catching the notice of any other guests, she slipped out of the ceremony. When the guests came out, she wanted it to be seamless. The champagne and wine should be poured, ready to serve. The bartenders should be prepared for anyone who wanted something else. The servers should have the hors d'oeuvres plated, to offer guests in the lobby.

The wine was ready, but the champagne was still on ice when Poppy went back to check. By the time it was uncorked and poured, the fizzy bubbles filling the expensive coupes—she hadn't been able to resist a champagne tower—the guests were beginning to filter out. She caught sight of Wynn competently maneuvering people through the French doors and into the lobby where a second band, a five-piece swing band, played cheerful tunes about dancing cheek to cheek and being in heaven.

Servers worked the room offering nibbles and napkins while Poppy checked in on the ballroom. Someone had bumped the table that held the escort cards and scattered them into an ugly mess. She tidied them up, riffling through to make sure they were still in alphabetical order.

Everything else was pristine. The tables were draped in black linen, with simple centerpieces of more dark manzanita branches and white orchids. Bamboo-back chairs with white seats circled the large tables. Scentless white candles had been placed in frosted vases and lit to create a stunning effect, while large chandeliers hung overhead, each crystal gleaming.

Beck had done a fantastic job with the renovations. Even though she'd been able to see a lot of it as it was unveiled, the overall effect was breathtaking. The floor was a glorious dark wood, and the walls were painted a delicate, pale gold, offset with strips of wide white wood to create a paneled effect. It was a wonderful place to get married. Poppy's heart squeezed at the thought.

Satisfied that nothing else required her attention, she slipped back into the cocktail reception. Her phone hadn't buzzed, but there was always something that needed a second pair of eyes or a confident hand. That was her job. To make sure from the outside it appeared to be a smooth, effortless event. No one was aware that tucked into a side closet she had an emergency kit of the usual suspects, like bandages, cotton balls, emery boards, a needle and thread, mouthwash and antacids, as well as the more unusual, such as extra wedding bands, backs to earrings, a blue handkerchief and a pair of sneakers in the bride's size.

She circulated, thinking everything was going off without a hitch, when she saw Beck. Her breath caught as he spotted her. He started toward her, intent clear in every movement. She didn't want to find out what that meant for her.

She turned quickly and headed down the hall toward the bathroom. It was ridiculous, she lectured herself as she pushed open the door to the washroom and locked it behind her. No group washroom at this boutique hotel. They had single units decked out for royalty with gilt walls and oversize mirrors. All the better to see the panicked look on her face.

She knew nothing would come of her and Beck. Had known that for weeks, which was why she'd made certain not to get involved with him again. Except she had last night.

Poppy closed her eyes and sank onto the cushioned settee across from a floor-to-ceiling mirror. She didn't want to look at herself anymore. Didn't want to see the naked need shining in her eyes.

Why had she let him come up last night? Why had she let him into her apartment? And why had she taken him to bed?

Because she was in love with him.

Her heart and breath hitched in unison. It was crazy and foolish and would not come to a good end. She knew all that. But she couldn't help it. Her attempts to put up a barrier had been pitiable at best. She hadn't even been able to last three months.

Poppy stayed there for a few minutes, grateful that no one else seemed to need her. Then ran a paper towel under cool water and dabbed the back of her neck. She might have fallen apart inside, but she was determined no one would notice.

She'd go back out, smile, make sure everything was perfect for the wedding and then she'd tell Beck goodbye without even a quiver.

Tomorrow would be soon enough to shatter into a thousand pieces.

CHAPTER TWENTY-EIGHT

SHE WAS AVOIDING HIM.

It was obvious to anyone with two brain cells to rub together. But she couldn't stay away from him forever.

He watched Poppy skirt around a group of gentlemen laughing uproariously over something before turning down the hallway. He didn't chase her. He didn't have to. He knew the hotel, having practically lived here every moment he wasn't crashing one of her dates. There was no other exit from that particular hallway unless she went through the fire exit.

Not only would the alarm signal him, and everyone else, but Poppy would never consider it. A fire alarm would ruin the wedding and she wouldn't risk her reputation just to stay away from him.

He was counting on it.

What he wasn't counting on was the fact that as the only child of the bride and groom, people would want a little time with him. They wanted to know more about the hotel, how long it took to renovate, if he had plans for other hotels in the area, if they could book the space for upcoming holiday functions and how happy he was that his parents had gotten back together.

Though he kept his eye on the hallway and even saw Poppy when she emerged a few minutes later, he wasn't able to extract himself from the clutches of a chubby businessman and his hungry wife. He'd longed to growl an excuse or walk away from them midsentence, but it would get back to his mother and she'd never let him hear the end of it. And he liked this new, less inflammatory relationship they had going on. He wasn't about to do something to mess it up.

So he listened while the man talked about the new car he'd recently bought and how fast he'd pushed it on the Sea to Sky Highway, while his wife looked longingly at the small bites of food as they passed. But his mind was on Poppy.

Beck kept an eye on her as she worked the room, that sexy gold dress fluttering around her legs, every so often giving him a peek at her thigh when the slit fell open. He wanted to peel the dress off her, yank those pins holding her hair back in that tidy bun and tumble her into bed with him.

He watched her when the doors to the ballroom opened and everyone filed in for dinner. Studied her through his speech about how love was worth taking a chance on, even second and third chances, which got a laugh from the audience and a single tear from his mother. Stared at her while she got the music started and his parents onto the floor for their first dance.

But he didn't get the chance to talk to her for another hour and a half, by which time he was seriously considering interrupting the whole wedding. The only thing that stopped him was that Poppy would never forgive him for ruining her event.

"Beck, really." She tried to edge around him when he caught her by the wall near the cake table. "I don't have time right now."

"So make some." He put his hand against the wall in case she had any ideas about dodging him and exiting the room. Half the guests were working off their dinners on the dance floor while the others sat around the tables catching up with old and new friends. "You've gone out of your way not to see me today."

"No, I…" She trailed off when she looked at him. Her chin rose to an irritable jut. "So what if I did?"

She was clearly looking for a fight of some kind. He wouldn't give it to her. "I didn't like it." He kept his voice easy, low-key, very isn't-this-a-lovely-evening.

"Too bad." Her chin rose another inch.

"Lucky for you I'm a good-natured kind of guy."

She snorted. "You? I'm sorry, have you confused yourself with someone else?"

Beck ignored the dig. "Which is why I'm going to forgive you and ask you to dance." He ran his hand down her bare arm and linked their fingers together.

She stared at their joined hands. Beck prepared to tighten his hold in case she attempted to jerk free. He wasn't letting her get away, not now. Not ever. But she didn't pull, just let her fingers go limp. "I'm working, Beck."

"You can take five minutes." He threaded his fingers through hers, remembering how demanding they'd been last night. She might be playing hard to get now, but she wanted him. He knew she did.

"No." She met his gaze head-on. "I'm not going to let you do this."

"Do what?" He was only asking for a dance, five minutes of her time. She should give him that.

"This." She waved her free hand between them. "I'm not like you." He saw a flash of hurt in her eyes before she masked it with cool competence. "Last night was—"

"If you say it was a mistake, I'll be forced to throw you over my shoulder and carry you out of here." He flexed his hand to indicate this wasn't a joke. "Don't push me."

"Why not?" Her eyes flashed again, with anger this time. "All you've done since you walked into my life is push and push and push. When you're not pulling away and pretending I don't exist, of course." She sounded disgusted. He didn't know if it was with him or herself.

"I was an ass," he said. "I know that. But, Poppy, please…"

"Beck." The anger melted away, but it was replaced with something Beck didn't like. He didn't like it at all. Resignation.

"One dance," he said before she finished her thought. "Just one."

She sighed. "Fine. One dance."

He led her to the floor, clearing a small space near the edge and taking her into his arms. She felt so right there. She had to feel it, too.

She put her arms around his neck but kept her fingers linked together, so as not to touch him any more than necessary. He reached up and unlinked them, pressing one into the back of his neck. He liked it when she touched him there, when she let her fingers run through his hair.

She didn't oblige. "Beck."

"That was quite the little stunt you pulled, running off this morning."

"It wasn't a stunt." She looked at him. "I was busy. I had things to do."

"You should have woken me up." He turned her so they were moving away from the crowd of bodies on the dance floor. "But it gave me time to do some thinking. I don't think you believe me when I say I've changed."

"Have you?" She arched an eyebrow at him.

"I think so. I'm trying. Or have my attempts to date you gone unnoticed?"

A smile peeked out of her eyes before she blinked it away. "Is that what you were doing?"

"Trying to." They danced for a moment. He smiled

when her hands started to relax. They weren't in playing-with-the-hair territory yet, but it was a start. "I'm not perfect. I've made a lot of mistakes in my relationships." She swayed against him but didn't say anything. "But I'm working on it."

"With your parents."

"With everyone. You were right when you told me that I had to forgive my parents if I wanted our relationship to improve. And I did."

Her face softened. He wanted to kiss the smile on her lips but refrained. He wasn't finished yet.

"So I'm asking you to forgive me, to give me another chance."

"Beck…" The smile was gone now.

He wasn't giving up. "I need you. Whatever it takes." These last months of living without her had been torture. "It killed me to see you out with other guys."

Apparently, that was the wrong thing to say, because her arms dropped. "You told me that's what you wanted."

"I was trying not to scare you. I thought if I blurted out everything, I'd chase you away."

"Oh, I think you did a pretty good job anyway."

"No." He threaded their hands together when she tried to step back. "Hear me out."

"There's nothing to say, Beck."

"There is." He heard the rasp of desperation in his voice. "I'm going to screw up. I'm screwing up right now. But you have to tell me when I do and I'll fix it. I need you."

"No, Beck." Her mouth turned down sadly. "I'm a convenience to you. I don't know why you're doing this. You got what you wanted and you're leaving town tomorrow. Can't you just let me go?"

"No," he said simply. "I can't. And I'm not leaving town tomorrow."

"Then the day after or next week." She struggled to pull free. He held on. "The point is, you're leaving."

"I'm not. I bought a place here. I'm staying."

She blinked. "But what about your company?"

"We're expanding." He rubbed a thumb across the back of her hand. "My dad has this idea about building in Naramata, but even if that doesn't happen I'm staying. I can't leave you." Couldn't lose her.

Her eyes turned down at the corners. He hated that it was his fault, that he'd put the sadness there and lost her trust.

He lifted a hand to her face, stroked her soft cheek. "I don't know if I can ever make it all up to you, but I've got a lifetime to try." He heard her breath hitch, felt the little sob as it ran through her, and he tightened his hold on her. "Please, let me try."

"And what happens when you change your mind? Or when things get too hard?"

"They won't. I won't." He'd spent a lot of time the last couple months thinking about this, knowing if he wasn't entirely committed, he had to back off because he loved her. But that was just it. He loved her.

"How can you be so sure?"

He took a breath. "Because I'm in love with you."

She stilled, her eyes wide. He hoped that wasn't horror. Oh, Christ. If that was horror...

"You're what?" She tried to step away from him, but their hands were still linked.

"I'm in love with you," he repeated. It was scary saying it out loud, but scarier to think of it trapped in his chest and never coming out at all. "I've been in love with you for a while."

Her mouth moved but no sound came out. He hoped that was a good thing.

It was time. He reached into his tuxedo jacket and pulled out a small blue box.

POPPY COULDN'T MOVE, couldn't speak. She could barely feel or think. What was he doing? Scratch that. She knew exactly what he was doing.

She just couldn't believe it. Her insides were about to bounce out of her skin. She blinked as Beck let go of her and lowered himself to one knee. "Poppy Sullivan, will you marry me?"

He flipped the box open, displaying the most perfect ring Poppy had ever seen. She reached out to touch it reverently. It was her ring. The one she'd picked out for herself that Wynn always teased her about. And it was twinkling back at her.

She looked at Beck, who still knelt before her, a hopeful, nervous expression on his face.

But he didn't want a family or a picket fence or a permanent relationship. Hadn't he made that clear with every word and action? Hadn't she spent the entire day reminding herself of just that?

Except, if she really thought about the past couple months it was her who'd denied the connection between them. Granted, she'd been perfectly within her rights to do so. She'd only been trying to protect herself. But Beck hadn't given up, simply kept hammering away at every wall she erected.

She blinked at him again.

"Come on, Red." His smile wavered. "Say yes."

It was the nickname that did it. That awful, horrible nickname that he refused to stop using. She knew then he was serious. No man attempting to win a woman over with sweet whispers and thoughtful gestures would ever be so crass as to call her Red when her hair was so clearly *not* red.

She started to cry. Ugly, choking tears. She loved him. Always had. She'd just stopped believing he might ever love her back. But he'd changed. She saw now that the only person she'd been punishing all those long, lonely nights for the past three months was herself. Maybe it had taken Beck longer than she'd given him to figure out what he wanted, but he'd figured it out. And she had, too.

"Yes," she managed to say, her hand shaking so

hard she was amazed Beck managed to slip the ring on her finger. "Yes."

She didn't even hear the muted clapping that started, led by Beck's parents, and quickly traveled the entire room. She was too busy staring at her fiancé. How had she ever thought she'd get over him?

Not that she was going to tell him. She had *some* pride.

"You scared me," he murmured as he scooped her up into a hard embrace. She shivered in the steel grip of his arms. Poppy didn't think she'd ever been held so tightly. "Don't do that again."

"Don't call me Red," she told him, still sniffling. "My hair is auburn."

His laugh rumbled through her. "Whatever you say, love. I'll call you whatever you want as long as you promise to be mine forever."

She sniffled again. "Forever is a pretty long time." She held her hand out, admiring the ring. "How did you know? Did Wynn tell you?"

"I just knew."

"So Wynn told you," she confirmed, reading between the lines.

"He suggested the store," Beck admitted. "But I picked it out."

As if he could be any more perfect. She smiled and wrapped her arms around his neck, letting her fingers play with the soft curls at the edge of his collar.

He sighed and pulled her closer. "You know, you still haven't told me you love me."

"I agreed to marry you," she pointed out, hiding her smile. He already knew. He wouldn't tease her if he wasn't certain.

He inclined his head at the truth of that statement. "Still, a guy likes to hear that his fiancée thinks he's a good catch."

"You're a good catch."

He laughed as the song came to an end and bent his head to whisper in her ear. Her skin pebbled in anticipation. "You'll pay for that later."

"I hope so." There were many inventive ways she'd be happy to pay him back over and over. She cupped his face in her hands, running her thumbs along his jawline. Hers. He was all hers. Forever. "I love you, Beck."

LATER THAT NIGHT, when they were lying in her bed together, legs tangled, hearts pounding from the payment he'd just extorted from her, Poppy lifted her head from his chest and studied him. "What would you have done if I'd said no?"

He opened one eye to look at her. "I was pretty sure you wouldn't. But," he continued before she asked how he'd been so certain, "I still had your keys, which, by the way, you are not getting back."

"Oh, I'm not?" She raised an eyebrow at him.

"No." He closed his eye and settled more fully into the pillows. "They're mine now. Just like you are."

She probably shouldn't be getting all warm and melty at his conceited statement. She wasn't a possession and she was in charge of who had keys to her apartment. She told him so, but he only laughed.

"I'm still not giving them back." His arms tightened around her. "And I'm not giving you up either. Deal with it."

She started to say something but couldn't think of anything witty, so she laid her head on his chest. Listening to the thump of his heart and letting his warmth soak into her was much better anyway.

"So when do you think we should get married?"

"Tomorrow."

She lifted her head to look at him. "Very funny."

"I'm not kidding. Although maybe tomorrow is a bit soon. How about next week? You, me, a tropical beach somewhere."

"Beck, be serious." She played with the ends of his hair. "What about the summer? August is always beautiful."

"I am not waiting until August." He captured her hand, brought it to his lips. "Next week," he murmured.

"No," she murmured back. "August."

"You say no now." He let go of her hand and pulled her down for a long kiss. "But I think I can convince you."

She kissed him back. "I'm willing to let you try."

EPILOGUE

THE WEDDING TOOK place six months later.

Poppy had done her best to push for a summer ceremony when the weather would be hot and all the flowers and trees in bloom, but Beck had negated her concerns by reminding her that in the tropics the weather was warm and flowers bloomed year-round. They'd settled for the end of April at his parents' house in Naramata, and unlike some compromises, in this instance everyone was happy. Beck didn't have to wait too long and Poppy got her white Gatsby party.

"Oh, Poppy."

Poppy turned to find her mother, hand covering her mouth, tears in her eyes. "Don't start," she warned, dabbing a tissue beneath her lashes just in case. "It took me forever to get my makeup right and if you get me going, my face will be ruined."

And she refused to walk down the aisle looking like a raccoon. Not even one wearing the most amazing wedding dress ever.

Her mother simply sniffed and came to stand behind her in front of the mirror. "You look beautiful."

Poppy smiled. She felt beautiful. Her square-necked dress had spaghetti straps, a fitted bodice covered in lace, and it belled out at midthigh to spill to the floor in tiers of chiffon. Her hair was pulled into an elegant bun and her only jewelry was a pair of drop chandelier earrings. Missy would be proud.

"Are you nervous?" her mom asked.

Poppy pressed a hand to her stomach, careful not to wrinkle the delicate fabric. "Just about being tripped when I walk down the aisle."

"I did not trip Cami," her mother said.

"You stepped on the hem of her dress." While Poppy and the other wedding guests stood by wide-eyed.

"She walked in front of me."

"She was the bride."

"Never mind." Her mother smoothed the sides of Poppy's hair. "I promise not to trip you."

"Who's tripping?" Cami asked, entering the room with both her daughters. Holly immediately sprinted forward, screeching about her shoes and demanding to see Auntie Pop-pop's, while Lily watched from beneath a furrowed brow, an elastic bow wrapped around her wispy-haired head.

"Mom," Poppy said. "She says tripping the bride is a family tradition."

"I did not say that and I didn't trip—"

"The fact that I didn't fall doesn't mean you didn't trip me," Cami informed her, jiggling the baby.

Poppy held her foot out so Holly could see her very tall, very sparkly silver heels. "Pretty," Holly oohed.

"And high," Poppy said with a nod to her mother. "So no tripping even if I do walk in front of you."

Her mother took the baby from Cami and cooed at her. "You don't listen to them, Lily. Your grandma would never trip anyone." She shot Poppy and Cami a quick glance. "Even if they deserved it."

Cami laughed and produced a bottle of champagne from her diaper bag. Poppy texted Wynn to come join them for a drink, and the sun, which had been peeking out from the clouds all morning, broke through.

Poppy smiled. Her guests would not be doused by rain or buffeted by wind, which wasn't always a guarantee in April.

The ceremony would take place in the side yard with the lush forest as their backdrop. Ball lanterns hung from the nearest trees and rows of golden chairs were laid out for seating. Ropes of pearl necklaces lay draped across the chair backs, as did feather boas in pristine white.

As much as she loved how the side yard was decorated, Poppy didn't think it compared to the back. Not that she was trying to brag, but she'd outdone herself there.

Instead of traditional round tables set up on the expansive patio and still-winterized and covered pool, Poppy had mixed dining seating with loungers. The comfy chairs and long L-shaped couches were a peach shade so delicate it appeared white at first glance and matched the seats of the dining chairs, while the tablecloths were a darker hue and threaded with a diamond pattern in gold. The centerpieces were squat glass vases, so guests could converse easily during the meal, and filled with peach roses, white sweet peas, green buds and ivory feathers.

Spiral chandeliers hung from the patio's awning and lent a glittery ambience. Heat lamps both standing and rolling ensured no one would be too cold. A jazz band was set up in the corner by the bar, where guests could order anything and everything, including a popular summer beverage made from an English liqueur and lemonade, bourbon poured from vintage, square-topped bottles and, of course, champagne from a tower.

It wouldn't be a real Gatsby party without one.

Beck had even surprised her by renting period cars. She'd been shocked when the gray convertible had rolled up to her parents' home to take them over to the compound. Her dad had called it a Silver Ghost with something close to awe in his tone. Poppy figured it was a guy thing. She didn't get it, but the car's beauty was undeniable.

Cami and Wynn texted that one had been sent for them, too, and more sat parked out front to complete the entire scene. As if she didn't already love Beck enough.

"Put the wrap on," Wynn said, sipping his champagne and pointing to the faux-fur shrug Poppy was still internally debating. She loved the wrap but feared it would hide the lace detailing of the gown's bodice. "And the headpiece. We need to see the whole effect."

Poppy took one more mouthful of bubbly, set the glass down and faced the mirror to affix the headpiece made up of netting and feathers and pale blue crystals. The jewels sparkled against her bright hair. She admired herself for a moment then slipped into the shrug and rose, doing a slow rotation for her audience.

Wynn stepped back with a critical eye before nodding. "You gorgeous thing. You look like a czarina."

Cami cleared her throat. "I know everyone wants to look like a princess on their wedding day, but czarina might be taking the styling too far."

"Your dress had a train," Poppy pointed out.

"Yes, which is why Mom tripped me."

"I didn't." Her mother defended herself, still rocking the baby. "You didn't hit the ground."

"Moot point."

"You know what would have been perfect? Not that I don't love your headpiece," Wynn mused. "A matching fur hat. Like the ones the Russian army wears." A brief pause. "Too much?"

They all stared at him.

"Okay, fine. Too much."

"How are you feeling?" Beck's mother popped into the room he'd commandeered to get ready.

Beck finished straightening his bow tie before glancing at her. He still thought he and Poppy should have taken off for a warm beach somewhere and returned as Mr. and Mrs., but she'd been unwilling to negotiate on the subject. "I'm fine. Ready."

Victoria brushed the shoulders of his jacket. "Your hair's a little long."

He shrugged. "No one's going to be looking at my hair, Mom."

Their relationship still wasn't perfect. Beck had a tendency to pull back when she got too invested in his life, and Victoria still had what Beck liked to refer to as a "problem with oversharing," but the majority of their old hurts were mended.

"True." She fiddled with his hair anyway. "They'll be watching Poppy. She's gorgeous." And Victoria would know as she'd just returned from checking in on her "almost-daughter-in-law."

Beck smiled. "She always is." And in a few short minutes, she'd be his forever. He fingered the wedding bands in his front pocket.

They'd decided against having attendants, opting for a smaller celebration with only their closest friends and family. Although Beck hadn't wanted to put anyone else through the chore of trying to organize a bachelor party, nothing had been able to stop Jamie from kidnapping him from the office one Friday afternoon to fly to Vegas for a weekend with his closest buddies. Everyone had a great time and only minimal tequila was consumed. Even with Wynn in attendance.

"I'm so happy for you, sweetheart."

"I know, Mom." She told him often. He'd come to enjoy hearing it, too, which was a big step. "Poppy's been good for all of us."

After their engagement, she'd begun insisting on regular family dinners and threatening Beck with a family vacation if he tried to cancel last minute. It had smoothed over some of the awkwardness that still existed between him and his parents. Beck had even begun looking forward to the visits, though he didn't admit it.

His mother fussed a little more, tidying his hair again, giving his suit another brushing with the lint roller, making sure the rings were in his pocket, and didn't stop until his father finally arrived to save him.

"Everyone's here and seated. You ready?" Harrison reached out for his wife's hand.

Beck studied the pair of them, a solid family unit, fingers linked together as they waited for him. He pictured himself and Poppy in the same position years down the road. "Definitely."

There were only about seventy people in attendance at the wedding, but it was everyone who mattered. Their family and closest friends, including the newest addition, Jamie's baby girl, Amy. Fatherhood suited his cousin and Beck smiled when Jamie had the baby give him a thumbs-up as he walked to the end of the aisle where the officiant waited.

Beck knew Poppy was good at what she did. He'd been impressed at the ease with which she'd solved

Emmy's dress fiasco, and his parents' wedding at the hotel had drawn endless amounts of compliments and questions about who had been responsible for the event. But what she'd accomplished here blew him away. Not because there wasn't a single scrap of satin or any scattered pink rose petals that would "clash with her auburn coloring," but because it was so her.

Everything was elegant, simple and warm. It was almost enough to make him agree that a tropical elopement would have been a mistake. Not that he was one to get all teary-eyed and emotional about weddings.

Low music played over the murmurs of the guests. Beck folded his hands in front of him and tried not to bob. He wasn't nervous. Not exactly. He just wanted to get this part over with and get on to the good stuff. But his palms got a little sweaty when the music changed and the crowd let out an excited "ooh."

He turned to find Poppy, flanked by her parents, standing at the end of the aisle. His heart pounded as she made her way toward him. Her mother whispered something in her ear when they reached the end and Poppy laughed, the bright sound rolling through him and erasing the tightness in his lungs. She was gorgeous. More than gorgeous.

Beck tried not to swallow his tongue as he went through the motions of shaking her father's hand and hugging her mother, but his eyes didn't leave his soon-to-be wife. He caught her hand and held it tight even though they hadn't reached that part of the ceremony yet. He didn't care.

She stared up at him. "Are you okay?"

Okay? He was more than okay. He nodded and squeezed her hand. "Promise me one thing, Red."

"To never answer when you call me Red? Done."

He smiled. "That as much as I love you and despite how beautiful everything is, this is the last wedding I'll ever have to participate in."

She smiled back. "I do."

* * * * *

LARGER-PRINT BOOKS!

HARLEQUIN *Presents*

PASSION GUARANTEED SEDUCTION

GET 2 FREE LARGER-PRINT NOVELS PLUS 2 FREE GIFTS!

YES! Please send me 2 FREE LARGER-PRINT Harlequin Presents® novels and my 2 FREE gifts (gifts are worth about $10). After receiving them, if I don't wish to receive any more books, I can return the shipping statement marked "cancel." If I don't cancel, I will receive 6 brand-new novels every month and be billed just $5.05 per book in the U.S. or $5.49 per book in Canada. That's a saving of at least 16% off the cover price! It's quite a bargain! Shipping and handling is just 50¢ per book in the U.S. and 75¢ per book in Canada.* I understand that accepting the 2 free books and gifts places me under no obligation to buy anything. I can always return a shipment and cancel at any time. Even if I never buy another book, the two free books and gifts are mine to keep forever.

176/376 HDN F43N

Name _____ (PLEASE PRINT)

Address _____ Apt. #

City _____ State/Prov. _____ Zip/Postal Code

Signature (if under 18, a parent or guardian must sign)

Mail to the Harlequin® Reader Service:
IN U.S.A.: P.O. Box 1867, Buffalo, NY 14240-1867
IN CANADA: P.O. Box 609, Fort Erie, Ontario L2A 5X3

**Are you a subscriber to Harlequin Presents books and want to receive the larger-print edition?
Call 1-800-873-8635 today or visit us at www.ReaderService.com.**

* Terms and prices subject to change without notice. Prices do not include applicable taxes. Sales tax applicable in N.Y. Canadian residents will be charged applicable taxes. Offer not valid in Quebec. This offer is limited to one order per household. Not valid for current subscribers to Harlequin Presents Larger-Print books. All orders subject to credit approval. Credit or debit balances in a customer's account(s) may be offset by any other outstanding balance owed by or to the customer. Please allow 4 to 6 weeks for delivery. Offer available while quantities last.

HPLP13R

ReaderService.com

Manage your account online!

- Review your order history
- Manage your payments
- Update your address

*We've designed
the Harlequin® Reader Service
website just for you.*

Enjoy all the features!

- Reader excerpts from any series
- Respond to mailings and
  special monthly offers
- Discover new series available to you
- Browse the Bonus Bucks catalog
- Share your feedback

Visit us at:
ReaderService.com